The Eighth Sin

Krystyna Fulford

The Eighth Sin

Vanguard Press

VANGUARD PAPERBACK

© Copyright 2024
Krystyna Fulford

The right of Krystyna Fulford to be identified as author of
this work has been asserted by her in accordance with the
Copyright, Designs and Patents Act 1988.

All Rights Reserved

No reproduction, copy or transmission of this publication
may be made without written permission.
No paragraph of this publication may be reproduced,
copied or transmitted save with the written permission of the publisher, or in
accordance with the provisions
of the Copyright Act 1956 (as amended).

Any person who commits any unauthorised act in relation to this publication
may be liable to criminal prosecution and civil claims for damages.

A CIP catalogue record for this title is available from the British Library.

ISBN 978-1-83794-275-6

This is a work of fiction. Names, characters, businesses, places, events and
incidents are either the products of the author's imagination or used in a
fictitious manner. Any resemblance to actual persons, living or dead, or actual
events is purely coincidental.

Vanguard Press is an imprint of
Pegasus Elliot Mackenzie Publishers Ltd.
www.pegasuspublishers.com

First Published in 2024

Vanguard Press
Sheraton House Castle Park
Cambri England

Printed & Bound in Great Britain

Dedication

To Iain, who kept me sane through the whole adventure

Prologue

Heavy rain hammered down on a well-trodden road, the tiny bullets hammering against the unyielding grey stone. The silvery droplets raced over the smooth surface, soaking into the muddy curb. A dim slither of light reflected in the turbulent puddles as the waning crescent moon turned its back on the world below.

A lone figure wandered the deserted road. The wild winds snatched at her heavy black cloak callously, desperately trying to pull her away from her goal. Her determined footsteps were lost in the tempest as she trudged along the water-logged cobblestones, any sound muffled by the tumultuous storm.

The orange glow of light came upon the road abruptly, the frosty night seemingly having no power in the shadow of the hearty tavern, stubbornly repelling the darkness.

She raised a black gloved hand towards the thick oak door before her, her other hand clutching at her waterlogged hood.

This is a mistake, she thought. *He will never forgive you.*

She clenched her fists, her long crimson nails burrowing into the tender flesh of her palm beneath the fine black silk gloves.

She took a deep breath, the frozen air filling her lungs with resolve.

The rough door seemed to be repelled by the closeness of her raised hand, the well-used iron hinges screaming as it was pushed open.

Warmth bathed her face, hidden beneath the hood. It embraced her tenderly as she crossed over the threshold to the busy tavern, a bastion of neutrality in the raging war. The raucous merriment of men surrounded her, their laughter bouncing over the bustling room.

Her wary gaze searched the jovial faces silently, her hidden eyes squinting in the light. Although the large room was only dimly lit with half-burned sconces and candlesticks, it was vastly different to the darkness that she had wandered about for so long.

As though he sensed her presence, a pair of golden eyes watched the newcomer steadily through the shadow of her heavy hood.

He sat in a darkened corner, four men drinking quietly around him. Although they each wore plain clothes, the weariness that lined their faces and the rigidity of their muscular bodies made it clear that they were seasoned soldiers.

The locals avoided them, knowing that it was better to stay away from those involved in this seemingly eternal war. That was the true joy of this busy tavern; the patrons could relax in this neutral zone, before the inevitable walk into demon or human territory where the war continued to rage on after countless years.

She stepped quietly towards him, careful to avoid the animated gestures of drunken townsfolk that she walked past, weaving between their crowded tables towards the far corner of the room.

He stood, his companions finally turning to her presence. Their brows furrowed, their hands reaching for the weapons hidden at their sides in an instant.

"Be at peace, friends," the man whispered, authority dripping from his deep voice. "Yours is not a face I would have expected to see here. To what do I owe this pleasure?"

She darted her eyes over his companions, her head held high. Although they could not see her expression, they must have felt her burning gaze, for their scowls grew deeper. One even took a step towards her, his hand tightly gripped on the experienced dagger at his side.

The golden haired man smiled, placing himself between the newcomer and his agitated companion. His large hand firmly grasped the other man's shoulder, his grip tightening.

"Leave us."

A gentle smile spread over his thin lips, but one that did not quite reach his cold gold eyes.

"My lord?"

He sat back down, folding his golden hands neatly on the table in front of him. "I am in no danger here."

Begrudgingly, they turned to leave, the golden haired man never taking his eyes away from the woman in front of him.

"It has been a long time," he said softly, gesturing for her to sit.

"Let's skip the pleasantries. You know precisely why I'm here."

She stood rigidly in front of him, her hand gripping the empty chair before her.

He snorted, the corner of his mouth turning upwards slightly. "Perhaps I want to hear you say it."

"Have the years really made you so vindictive?"

"I don't think you are in a position to ask such a question," he replied, his voice cold.

She turned her face away, gritting her teeth as humiliation brushed over her pale cheeks.

"I wish to seek peace," she whispered. "I refuse to watch him destroy himself any longer."

His golden eyes searched her face, turned away from him below the shadows. The years had clearly taken their toll, for her dark crimson eyes that had once been full of life and wonder, always seeking adventure, were now shrouded in darkness, devoid of life.

Her polished alabaster skin no longer glowed, her high cheekbones further exacerbated by the hollow shadow of exhaustion.

"If you choose to follow this path, there is no going back."

She firmly met his gaze, the determination glowing like a faint ember beneath the fear.

"I know what I must do."

280 Years Later…

Chapter 1

A crisp late winter wind danced over the blackened stone walls of the ancient fortress that was Dunsberg Castle.

Golden lichen comforted the cracked grey stone as the raging rain bit into the sixty foot high outer walls, the four corner towers of the square keep barely holding steady against the elements. The aged timbers of the battlements desperately tried to free themselves from the stone as they waited to be relieved by new recruits that the inhabitants could ill afford.

The inner keep itself was only marginally in better condition, with a handful of stones regularly being replaced. It was but a shell of its former glory, with a number of the rooms having been closed off, the windows blocked up to save on the number of staff needed to maintain the imposing castle. Two sections of the castle had long been dismantled; the stone reused to restore the living quarters of the stoic lord who called this land his home. Rudimentary wooden shelters had been erected in their place, housing the resident knights within.

The ancient cobblestones grunted beneath the weight of ten of warhorses, the cracks widening below their diligent steps. Their heavy footfalls sang loudly, the rhythmic thuds of two dozen soldiers marching in unison joining the chorus of their iron feet as they marched proudly through the gateway of Dunsberg Castle.

The few servants that remained in the once infamous stronghold watched them approach silently from the decaying wooden battlements, the morning mist clinging stubbornly to their grey woollen uniforms. Their frozen bones creaked as they bowed their heads to the passing royal standard; the crest of a golden cockatrice standing rampant on a crimson field watching them carefully beside the church's blazing golden sun on a white field.

At the head of this throng of men rode a slender man, his blonde hair falling loose about his square jaw. His golden eyes bounced over the walls surrounding him, taking note of the dutiful citizens as he rode past. He wore a finely crafted golden suit of armour, roses intricately decorating the large sword that adorned the centre of his broad chest plate. He clutched the oiled black reins of his muscular white mount carefully, the warm smile on his smooth lips hardly touching his eyes.

"Be on your guard, Your Highness. I doubt that Lord Hugo will take kindly to our presence here."

The golden prince smiled softly. "Do you think me a fool, uncle?"

The old knight clenched his square jaw tightly, his face shrouded in shadow by his well-worn black iron helmet. His hand unconsciously reached forward, stroking the neck of his black mare, white foam of sweat covering her shining fur. A tingling sensation spread over the back of his broad neck as they emerged through the grand arch into the large courtyard, and his hand instinctively reached for the broadsword at his side.

"Is something amiss?" The prince's smile didn't falter for a second as he met the oncoming gaze of his host, waiting atop the grey stone steps ahead of them.

The old knight's silver eyes bounced over the castle walls quickly, landing on an open window in a derelict tower, the grey stone spire leaning dangerously to the side. His keen eyes narrowed, trying to make out the features of the ethereal figure watching them from above before it suddenly disappeared.

"Nothing," Daryl replied, his eyes lingering on the now empty window.

"I expect you to be on your best behaviour, Daryl," Arvyn continued, his uncle's cold eyes meeting his through the shadow. "This is the last noble house where I may find information on the holy artefacts that Mother wanted; I would hate for there to be a mistake now."

"It would have been a better use of my skills for me to be defending the eastern border from the imperial army," the black knight said gruffly.

"Trust me," the prince said, turning his notorious charming smile on his trusty companion. "Should this visit go smoothly, I will insist on my father providing more men on the border for you."

Daryl said nothing, watching his twenty-two-year-old nephew silently. He rolled his silver eyes under the shelter of his well-worn helmet as they drew to a stop at the base of the castle steps.

The golden prince silently turned his gaze to the four figures at the top of the steps, the smile never once leaving his lips as he dismounted.

Marquis Hugo was a tall, broad man, made even squarer by the vast black fur cloak that hung limply from his broad shoulders, held in place by an overly large golden brooch depicting a blazing sun. In his youth, he had been an impressive jouster, winning many victories in the annual Summer Tournament in the Capital. Arvyn remembered watching him from the stands as a boy, dreaming that one day he could be just as skilled in the arena. But, an unsuccessful bout against the king had left the burly man with a limp. In his shame, he retreated to Dunsberg Castle, where he had not left for almost twelve years.

The move had not been kind to his wife, ten years his junior. Her long chestnut hair had begun to thin and was now streaked with flecks of grey. Her skin had taken on a sickly pallor, her blue eyes losing their shine. Unlike her husband, the dense cloak around her shoulders seemed to swamp her once elegant figure as her frail body swayed in the gentle breeze. Her hands clutched at the rose quartz prayer beads draped over her hands, the blazing sun in the centre gilded in silver.

"Welcome to Dunsberg Castle, Your Highness," the marquis said loudly from atop the steps, bowing as low as his rotund physique would allow. "I trust that God granted you an agreeable journey?"

"Most agreeable, Marquis Hugo," the golden haired prince smiled, striding up the steps with ease. "Although,

I must say that the weather in the north is not quite as pleasant as the Capital; perhaps I should have brought a warmer cloak. You are looking well, Marchioness Hadley."

"Thank you, Your Highness. I apologise that my ill health keeps us from court. But, it is God's Will." The small woman smiled meekly, subconsciously holding her white lace handkerchief to the corner of her thin lips. "Allow me to introduce my eldest daughter, Takisha, and my youngest, Raelyn."

The eldest, a girl of no more than sixteen by the prince's reckoning, looked up at him shyly from underneath a layer of thick black eyelashes, a secret smile spread over her pink lips. Her soft hands gently lifted her red velvet skirt as she curtsied, her head held high. Arvyn could not help but notice that her long billowing sleeves were embroidered with the holy blazing sun.

Her younger sister, a spitting image of her, hurriedly did the same, although her movements were not so refined.

"A pleasure," Arvyn said, returning the eldest daughter's smile. "Allow me to introduce my dear uncle, Duke Wynford. He has been assisting me in my inspection of the northern defences in the king's stead."

The girl turned her warm amber eyes towards the knight beside him, her bottom lip quivering slightly as she gazed upon the legendary Black Knight for the first time.

Just like the prince that he guarded, he was a tall man, standing a good few feet above her. A dense rose bush crawled over his black chestplate, the sharply polished thorns glistening in the dim afternoon light as he stood proudly. Takisha was sure she could see the faint stain of blood on the delicate rose petals, surrounded by scrapes and scratches that could never be erased from the metal. Although his face was hidden, she could feel his calculating, murderous silver eyes from within the shadows.

In his youth, the knight had been infamous on the battlefield, defending the kingdom from invasions and revolts. But, when his sister mysteriously succumbed to an illness shortly after the Third Prince turned four, he returned from the front lines to take up the mantle of Arvyn's bodyguard.

The teenager struggled to hide her discomfort as a shiver fought its way down her spine.

Marchioness Hadley looped her arm through her daughter's, her body swaying in the gentle wind.

"Takisha will show you to your room, Your Highness," Marchioness Hadley said loudly, gently squeezing her eldest daughter's arm. "You must be tired after such a long journey."

"A rest would be greatly appreciated, thank you my lady," Arvyn smiled politely. "And then, perhaps, a tour of your delightful castle would be in order, if you would allow it. I have read much about Dunsberg; I am excited to see its rich history for myself."

* * *

A lone figure watched the strangers climb the crumbling grey stone steps, her pale face emotionless as they drew near to the rotund keeper of Dunsberg Castle. Her thin fingers clutched at the dark windowsill before her, tiny stakes of the ancient wood embedding into her thin skin.

She gently raised her palm to the cold glass pane, pushing it slightly ajar.

Crisp winter air raced into the room, jumping into every crevice it could find. It rattled around her, scraping over the exposed translucent skin of her pale shoulders as she dropped the heavy burgundy blanket to the floor.

"Get away from the window!"

The old woman's shriek washed over her unmoving form as she leant further into the bitter breeze.

She let her gaze linger on the great host below as her skeletal body was pulled hurriedly deeper into the room by the old woman's calloused hands, another maid quickly pulling the dirty window shut before the thick burgundy curtains blocked the sunlight from the dingy once more.

A soft smile danced on the woman's thin lips, the movement making them crack even more.

"Honestly, Lady Cliona" the old maid muttered, her wrinkled hands gripping tightly on the pale lady's shoulders as she pushed her into the chair before the vanity mirror. "The Master would have my head if you fell. Why must you punish this old woman so?"

"I don't understand why the Master is so insistent on caring for her," the second maid said quietly, brushing the woman's fragile white hair gently.

The old buxom maid sighed, wringing a dirty rag in a bucket as she continued to scrub the fresh red stains from the rough floorboards.

"I would hardly call this caring for her, Marianne," the old woman hissed through gritted teeth. "What other noble lady do you know who is confined to a crumbling tower, given nothing but rotting bread and only visited by the Master when he wants to vent his own frustrations?"

"It does sound like the start of a fairy tale," the teenage maid replied, pushing her spectacles up her nose.

The young woman giggled, her dark crimson eyes twinkling as she turned to Marianne. She grabbed the maid's hands, smiling.

"Dance with me, Ria!" Cliona laughed, her frail body spinning over the uneven wooden floor.

The maid glanced at her older colleague desperately but was only greeted with a solemn nod as the frail lady pulled her to the middle of the room, her mellifluous laughter echoing over the tiny room.

"At least she can still smile," Belinda sighed, scowling at her work.

She had cared for the young lady for the past nine years, and not once in that time had the young woman ever been granted permission to leave her room. Every day the resident priest would come and read scriptures to her before whipping her to cleanse away her sins, at the request of Marquis Hugo. At least once a week, he would even join him. Those days were the hardest to stay silent for the old woman, as she watched the girl get double the lashings.

And yet, Cliona was always smiling as she sang and danced around her room.

Belinda clenched her hands tightly as she pushed herself up.

If only this truly were a fairy tale, she sighed. *I just pray that the Lady's insanity continues to protect her.*

Chapter 2

Cold black eyes darted over the silent scene below, feathers quietly rustling as the crows settled on the old oak beam that stretched across the ceiling. They were joined by the glassy eyes of Marquis Hugo's many hunting trophies of stags and bears guarding the wall behind his chair at the head of the ancient oak table.

The peeling whitewashed walls themselves were bare but for these shadows of Marquis Hugo's youth, and a single faded tapestry that hung over the recently lit fireplace. The edges were frayed; the once vibrant threads now dull in the dim evening candlelight. It depicted a proud grove of dark brown trees sporting faded pink blossoms. A gentle brook passed through the scene, silver threads once glistening on the water's surface. A single ghostly figure sat on the water's edge, their features eroded with time.

A log shifted on the fire, echoing over the stone walls.

Daryl lay down his silver knife, silently sipping the wine from his large goblet.

"I must say, Marquis Hugo," the prince said warmly, "I was surprised to see such an ornate suit of armour in your library. From my father's stories, I would not have expected you to have such a keen eye for ornaments."

"On the contrary, Your Highness, that suit has been in this castle far longer than I have; I can take no credit for such a handsome piece."

"It is blessed by God himself," Marchioness Hadley smiled. "It belonged to the First Marquis Samiel Dunsberg, and is said to have been used in the battle against the demons."

The marquis lay his thick hand over his wife's gently. "My family and I pride ourselves in our connection to Marquis Samiel, Your Highness."

"He was a great hero in the founding of our nation; I would expect nothing less, my lord. Mighty families such as ours should always revel in their history."

"Agreed, Your Highness. It is an honour that you have such an interest in our family history."

"Of course. I have a keen interest in the tales of our nation's past. And what inquisitive mind would not revel in the objects that hold so much history?"

The marquis smiled, his steady gaze cold as he watched the prince.

"Alas, Your Highness, I doubt that we would have much to pique your curiosity any further on the matter. After all, many of our own family treasures have been gifted to the royal treasury over the years as a sign of our loyalty to the crown."

"You have nothing to fear, my dear marquis. The purpose of my visit is not so sly as to search for more tribute from our loyal lords. I apologise if my own scholarly interests made you think otherwise. I was merely curious." The marquis nodded, his eyes still hooded as he continued to eat.

It was a well-known fact amongst the nobility that the late queen's love of beauty and antiques had led to the king forcibly demanding gifts from the oldest aristocratic families, their most precious heirlooms locked in to the royal vaults within the capital. Even the reclusive Marquis Hugo had heard rumours of the Third Prince scouring the country for yet more rare treasures.

The prince smiled, his eyes meeting his uncle's as they both took a sip from their goblets.

"I heard that you're a fan of music, Your Highness?" Takisha smiled from across the table to the prince, her lips darkened with makeup.

"I am," Arvyn replied, his golden eyes meeting hers across the table. "In fact, a song or two whilst we eat would not go amiss, Marquis Hugo. Perhaps you have a musician who knows local folktales that would intrigue me?"

Hugo snapped his robust fingers, drawing a sullen servant out from the shadows. The man's eyes went wide as his lord whispered a command in his ear, his knuckles going white over the finely polished tray in his hands as he scurried quickly out of the room.

"Do you play any instruments, Duke Wynford?"

The dark haired knight looked down at the younger daughter sat beside him, her amber eyes still focused on her half empty plate, ignoring the glare from her mother and older sister when she deigned to open her mouth.

"My duties on the battlefield and guarding His Highness have meant that I do not have time for such frivolities."

She nodded to herself quietly.

"There is no harm in enjoying the finer things." The prince laughed. "I rather enjoy it when my sister plays the lute in the evening."

"Perhaps then, Your Highness," Takisha cooed, "I could sing something for you after dinner?"

"What a marvellous idea, Takisha," Lady Hadley smiled. "God has certainly blessed her with a beautiful voice. It would be a shame not to share such a gift, Your Highness."

He smiled, reaching for his silver goblet.

"Do you play as well, Lady Raelyn?"

The younger girl's amber eyes doubled in size as she nervously nibbled on her bottom lip.

"Unfortunately God only blessed one of our children with musical talent, Your Highness. Raelyn is much more suited to listening to our dear Takisha."

The prince inclined his head, his attention distracted by a tall figure appearing in the doorway to the derelict great hall.

"Ah," Marquis Hugo grunted, leaning back into his chair. "Your Highness, may I introduce a distant relative of mine who is also staying with us. Aside from Takisha, Cliona has the best voice in Castle Dunsberg."

The frail young woman curtsied low, supported by an older maid beside her. Her long white hair rippled with the movement, dancing over her low-cut white dress, the skirts trailing behind her as she walked slowly into the room.

"Play some folk songs for our honoured guests," the Marquis grunted, snapping his fingers.

The young woman nodded, allowing her companion to help her sit on the step before the fire. She raised a shaking pale hand to her mouth, covering a cough as the maid draped a thick burgundy blanket over her shoulders. The woman laid a small ivory lyre on her lap, a pair of finely detailed white swans adorning the smooth instrument.

Her fingers moved delicately over the silver strings.

The prince watched, entranced as her mysterious words washed over him, her honeyed voice rising and falling in perfect time to the gentle music. He prided himself on knowing eight languages, and yet her lyrics were foreign to him, dancing around the room gracefully.

Arvyn laid his cutlery down having finished the meagre quail, quite bland in his opinion. He took the final sips of his white wine when his eyes met those of the musician. Even from this distance, his breath caught in his throat, her unusual crimson eyes seeming to shimmer.

She smiled softly as she shifted her position slightly, her almost translucent hair glittering in the candlelight as she moved.

Her fingers delicately plucked at the silver strings once more. She took a deep breath, her fingers playing slower than before as her gentle voice filled the air with a new song.

For ancient powers that you seek,
Sev'n challenges you must beat.
In The Forest of Winterfold,
Lay the long forgotten souls.

Boughs of oak, chestnut and yew,
Protect them from the hearts untrue
Resting in a peaceful bower,
Stands the long forgotten tower.

Only with the swords of yore,
Can we peace restore.
Rise up and defend this land.
Rise and fight, great Demon Clan

Chapter 3

"He's definitely hiding something," Arvyn said quietly, flipping the page of the ancient tome laid out on the library desk in front of him. "The question is what?"

Daryl leant against the decaying timber pillar in the centre of the room, watching a nightjar silently preen itself in the boughs of the castle's dying apple tree outside the open window.

"You can't possibly believe that that lout is hiding a demonic relic, Your Highness?"

"All of my research suggests that it's here in the north, and this is the last castle we have to check. Besides, Dunsberg Castle is notorious for not involving itself with the king's wars unless they hear a voice from God. How could a lowly lord get away with such insubordination if it wasn't here?"

"And, so what if it is? I doubt that His Majesty would be able to force the marquis to part with an heirloom; the lords would never stand for it again."

The prince's expression flickered for an instance.

"I will stop this damned Glerian Empire from encroaching on my father's kingdom once and for all." He smiled, his golden eyes shining. "With the best bodyguard by my side, of course."

The aged knight stood, stretching his lengthy arms high above his head. Arvyn raised his hand up to the sky, watching the stars shine between his fingers.

"The answer is here in this castle somewhere, uncle; I know it."

They sat quietly, watching the little nightjar fly away into the night sky. A bitter breeze whistled around them through the window, causing the golden prince to pull his heavy cloak closer around his shoulders.

A gentle lyre lullaby danced on the breeze, filling the prince with a strange sense of serenity. He stood, smoothing his clothing as his feet followed the tender sound towards the meagre garden below the crumbling north tower.

Aside from the sturdy culinary herbs that lined the left wall, very little grew in this small square of the castle. A single white lavender bush stubbornly flowered beside them, its meek scent unable to fill the alcove. Ivy and moss ran rampant over the crumbling grey walls, watching the intruders silently. It had taken hold in every crevice of the high walled garden, providing some sense of life in this little corner.

Every space except one.

In any other castle, this large door would hardly seem noteworthy, and yet the care taken to preserve this single section of the derelict castle could not go unnoticed. The dark oak was finely cared for; carefully polished black iron hinges curled into spirals over the smooth timber, rows of black iron studs lining the surface. Although the ivy had dominion over every surface in this garden, it dared not approach the dark wood.

In front of the open door sat the pale musician from earlier that evening, her lyre resting peacefully in her lap as her fingers caressed its strings. Her silvery hair glowed in the orange light of a lit torch on the wall behind her, her smooth skin almost translucent.

The men said nothing as they watched her, her eyes closed as she played, a gentle hum sneaking out of her pale lips.

"It is a cold night," she whispered after a while, her fingers still dancing over the pale strings. "Are you searching for paradise too?"

The prince's golden brow creased.

"I'm not sure what you mean," he replied softly.

She smiled coyly, her eyes meeting his steadily.

"You are searching for an ancient relic, are you not?"

"How did you," Arvyn started, clearing his throat as he regained his composure. "As a scholar, I am certainly interested in the history and lore of my kingdom."

She smirked, letting out a gentle chuckle as her fingers slowed to a stop. Her thin body seemed ready to break at any moment as she stood, her long white skirts billowing around her legs in the gentle breeze.

"You have the Mark of Oleksander," she whispered, her eyes momentarily clouding over. "Do you wish to see Dunsberg's biggest secret?"

She gestured for the strangers to follow as she stepped over the ancient threshold of her crumbling tower, removing the lit torch from the wall.

"Your Highness, this could be a trap," Daryl hissed, grabbing the prince's arm.

"Don't worry. I'll keep my wits about me. Besides, I have you with me."

The entryway was narrow, not wide enough for the prince and his trusted guardian to stand side by side. The floor was layered with the same dull cobblestones as its exterior, the whitewashed walls devoid of any detail. A spiral staircase lay before them, leading up into the tower and deeper underground.

She glided down the well-worn steps, her long white skirts gently embracing the ancient stone.

"How much do you know of the Gods of Nour, Your Highness?"

The prince blinked in the darkness.

"They were the deities that our ancestors worshipped before the Demon War five hundred years ago. The stories say that they were selfish and cruel monsters who ravaged humanity," the prince replied, following her closely. "Realistically, they were probably just nefarious criminals worshipped as gods."

She stopped, glancing over her shoulder at the young stranger.

"Long ago, this land was divided into many different kingdoms, all vying for power. They fought for centuries, the borders constantly shifting. Seeing this weakness, eight demons came to seize control of these lands."

Having reached the bottom, the ground began to even out, leading into a large room, already adorned with lit sconces.

Dozens of cold stone faces watched from small alcoves cut into the walls around them, their hands clasped tightly over swords or axes for all eternity. From their broad features, it was clear that they were the past lords of Dunsberg Castle, the second oldest family in the entire kingdom.

"In the great Battle of the Demons, King Oleksander the First cut them down, his sword of pure light shattering the darkness that had spread over the land. But, the eight Gods of Nour could not be killed, for they were too powerful. So, he trapped their souls in the land of the dead. Only his descendent may break the seal and release them, granting him the Sword of Nour. But, the cost of their release will be great."

She turned her deep crimson eyes on him, the light dancing on her pupils as she smiled.

"Or so the tales say, Your Highness." She shrugged nonchalantly.

"I will pay any price I must to defend this kingdom," Arvyn said, his jaw clenched as his hand subconsciously rested on the hilt of his untested sword.

Daryl stood behind him, silently placing his hand on the prince's shoulder.

She smirked.

"There is an altar, hidden in the Temple of Nour. You must return the seven artefacts; beloved trinkets that, once returned to the temple in which these gods are entombed, will summon them back to this realm. They were hidden over the kingdom hundreds of years ago, before Oleksander erased their existence from all records."

"And how are you so knowledgeable?"

Daryl's eyes narrowed at her.

"At the end of the Demon War, the Dunsberg family was charged with guarding the location of the Temple of Nour for all eternity." She smiled softly, tilting her head. "This story has been passed down diligently for generation upon generation of the Dunsberg family."

Cliona stepped gracefully to the centre of the room, where a black marble tablet stood vigil. Her hand gently caressed the ancient silver runes chiselled into the smooth stone. Eight small gemstones were embedded into a perfect circle on the marble. In the centre was a large silver rune that seemed to glow in the dim light of the crypt.

"So you know the locations of these items?" The prince interjected.

"The legend says that King Oleksander banished the followers of each god to their own otherworldly domains. It is said that only Oleksander's heir can be granted a guide to these domains and reclaim the items."

The two men looked at each other, the knight's hand resting on the hilt of his sword.

Cliona sighed, her fingers gently running over the black monolith beside her.

"Dunsberg Castle was built around this monument almost three hundred years ago, to keep its secrets safe. According to the legends, when all artefacts are collected and ready to be returned to the Temple of Nour, these gems will glow, and a gateway to the Demon Realm will open."

"Why would anyone want to release the demons?" Daryl asked firmly, his steely eyes cold in the darkness.

"A mythical weapon would not be worth the cost of releasing such monsters."

Cliona gritted her teeth as she turned away from them.

"Only by collecting all seven of the artefacts and returning them to the Temple of Nour can a descendant of the First King claim the Sword of Nour. The blade itself is said to control the Demon Lords, if scriptures are to be believed. By controlling the Demon Lords, one could control the entire Demon Army and vanquish any foe."

Arvyn turned to his uncle. "Uncle, this is a chance to protect our country from the Glerian Empire. Surely you must see that as a blessing?"

The old knight clenched his jaw.

"Your Highness, please reconsider this."

She smiled sadly, turning her face to the prince.

Ever since he was young, he had had a fascination with old myths and tales. Perhaps it was because they were the happiest, clearest memories that he had of his mother before she died. Or, perhaps he was simply drawn to fantastical tales of magic.

He turned to his uncle, hoping his smile was less nervous than he felt. "It couldn't hurt to try it, Daryl. Besides, we did come looking for proof of a mythical weapon hidden in the north and we've finally found it!"

"Your Highness," the bodyguard sighed, his eyes pleading as he squeezed his nephew's shoulders tightly.

Arvyn pushed his uncle away, looking at Cliona.

"All right. What must I do?"

Cliona smiled, walking to one of the nearby statues, the face completely eroded with age. She pressed her hand over the figure's chest, muttering something in a strange ancient language that Arvyn was unfamiliar with. As she stepped back, the prince noticed a flint dagger with a black iron hilt resting on a golden cloth in her hands.

She stopped in front of the golden prince, placing the dagger in his expectant hands.

"You must willingly feed your blood to the stone," she whispered, ignoring the tense duke unsheathing his sword. "If it is satisfied that you are, indeed, a true heir of Oleksander the First then it shall bestow upon you a gift to guide you."

Arvyn looked down at the dagger.

As a prince, he had participated in dozens of hunts and tournaments in the last twelve years. He may never be as skilled with a sword as his eldest brother Oleksander, but he had certainly never shied away from them either. And yet, he had not once actually harmed another person, let alone allowed himself to be injured.

Daryl lay his hand on the prince's shoulder.

"This does not sound like a wise decision, Your Highness. I strongly recommend that we leave this place at once."

"Ultimately, the choice is yours," Cliona said softly, turning her back to the prince.

The prince swallowed, aware of the dozens of stone eyes watching, waiting for his decision.

Finally, he stepped to the monument.

Taking the blade in his hand, he closed his eyes as he sliced through his open palm, grinding his teeth against the sharp pain. Wincing, he lifted his palm to the monolith, the dark marble cool beneath his jagged flesh.

As soon as he made contact with the stone, his head began to pound. His breathing and heart sounded loud in his ears as his hand grew warm. The silver runes around the edge of the stone turned crimson as it greedily drank his blood. He clutched at his chest as pain coursed through his entire body, his skin burning.

Daryl made to move towards his charge, only to be blocked by an expressionless Cliona.

"Causing harm to the Royal Family is treason!" The duke spat, raising his broadsword towards her.

"If you interrupt the ritual then he will surely die."

"How dare you!"

Just as he raised his sword, the prince fell to his knees, coughing.

Cliona silently held her breath, as the duke ran to him, the worry clear on his normally stern face.

The prince sat on his heels, his breath coming quickly as his uncle wrapped his large arms around his shoulders. As he looked down, his vision hazy, he saw a pristine book resting on the floor at his feet, a subtle silver glow dissipating around it. The black letters on the red velvet cover seemed to transform as he gazed at it, turning from runes to the alphabet he was used to.

The Incomplete Histories of the Conquerors of the Twelve Realms.

Arvyn clutched the book tightly to his chest as the duke helped him to his feet, consciousness trying to escape him.

In his bewildered state, he was certain that he caught a glimpse of tears rolling down the polished cheek of the old statues as his uncle pulled him from the room.

The runes had begun to glow in the dimly lit crypt, pulsating in time with the prince's steady heartbeat.

Cliona smiled.

Chapter 4

The grey cobblestone courtyard glistened as the tiny raindrops bounced along them, puddles beginning to form in the mossy cracks of the old stones.

Daryl stood tall, his black cloak rippling in the bitter early morning wind. His hand rested on the hilt of his broadsword as he watched over the grooms and squires hurrying to ready the prince's convoy.

He clenched his jaw, listening to Marquis Hugo's eldest daughter laugh coyly with the prince behind them, sheltered by the gnarled oak doorway.

"You must convince your father to visit the capital for the Spring Hunt, my lady. I believe that you would thoroughly enjoy yourself, and High Society would surely be better for your presence."

"I will look forward to it, Your Highness," Takisha looked up at him through her thick eyelashes, a smile dancing on her lips.

Marquis Hugo forced a smile beside them, his scowl evident as he tried not to watch his daughter.

"Your Highness." Daryl nodded towards the narrow pillared corridor that led to the crooked tower.

Cliona danced around happily, her cheerful face a stark contrast to the ghostly woman he met in the gardens last night. She raised her pale face to the sky, relishing the cold winter rains washing over her sun-starved cheeks. If her bare feet felt the chill of the bitter rain then she did not show it as they elegantly moved over the battered cobblestones of the courtyard.

Her elderly maid stood just behind her, attempting to pull a cloak over Cliona's slender shoulders, a scowl engraved on her aged forehead as the girl deftly dodged the woman.

The prince kissed Takisha's hand.

"I shall bid you all farewell. I am grateful for your hospitality, albeit only for a short while, and I do hope that we will meet again soon."

He strode quickly down the steps towards Cliona, his expression serious as his uncle fell into step beside him.

"My lady," Arvyn said firmly, as he stopped before her.

She turned to face him, droplets dripping down her slender nose as her smile hardened.

"My lady," the old maid hissed, finally succeeding in throwing the cloak over her charge's shoulders before dropping into a low curtsy. "You must bow to His Highness, my lady."

The prince held his hand to the old woman.

"That's not necessary," Arvyn said, his voice firm. "Leave us."

The maid curtsied again, her eyes trained on the cracked ground below her feet. "Forgive me, Your Highness, but my lady is not in her right mind."

Cliona laughed, softly through a smile that didn't reach her eyes, entwining her arms with the gnarled woman's as she looked at the prince.

The duke scowled at the maid. "His Highness gave you an order."

The old woman bit her lip, her head still bent low.

"Don't worry, Linda," Cliona smiled, tilting her head to look at the woman's downcast face. "I will dance on the moonlit hill and be right back!"

The wrinkled woman sighed, taking the girl's hands in hers briefly before retreating down the corridor.

The prince turned to Cliona, his golden gaze stern as he stepped close to her and lowered his voice.

"I have thought about what happened last night. We will return to the capital and prepare for an expedition to locate these artefacts."

She nodded. "I wish you luck on your endeavours."

"You shall be joining us, as an expert on the subject, of course."

The girl leant on the pillar, her hand resting over her lungs as she breathed in the cold air. She glanced towards the top of the steps, meeting the cold gaze of the marquis.

"He would never allow it," she whispered.

The prince smirked, turning on his heel. "He would hardly have a choice."

"I must say that I had expected at least a little resistance on your part," the duke said when his nephew was out of shot.

She snorted quietly. "I will hardly miss the sermons," she snorted, her eyes narrowing on Marquis Hugo as his gaze burned into her.

Arvyn turned to face the marquis, slowly limping his way towards the huddled figures. The prince smiled, his noble I once again expertly painted over his golden face.

The old man clutched his cane tightly, not even trying to hide his scowl as he bowed briefly.

"Your Highness, I fear that this girl will cause you nothing but trouble; she is not of sound mind."

Cliona lay her hand gently on the prince's forearm as she covered her mouth with her other hand, pretending to stifle a soft giggle.

"Don't worry, my dear lord," she smiled, her crimson eyes glinting with more vigour than they had in a long time, "I promise that we shall dance on the moonlit hill together soon."

The large man glowered at her, his hand latching onto her shoulder as he tried to pull her away from the prince.

"You will return to your room," he barked, his voice dripping with venom. "We shall discuss your punishment after I have apologised to His Highness."

"Allow me to apologise, Marquis Hugo," Arvyn said calmly, his golden eyes firmly meeting the older man's, "but I'm afraid that I shall be kidnapping your dear relative. I was rather taken by her last night in our brief encounter."

"She has never left Dunsberg Castle, Your Highness," Hugo said through gritted teeth, "and she has never learnt any sort of etiquette. I fear that she will only offend you."

Arvyn smiled. "I appreciate the concern, my lord, but my decision has been made. Have no fear; I shall see to it that your dear lady is well educated and cared for."

"You are most kind, Your Highness," the marquis hissed as he ground his teeth, inclining his head.

Cliona smiled at him as he turned to storm back to his wife and daughters, his cane angrily banging against the cracked stones with every laboured step.

Daryl turned to his nephew, his own brow furrowed. "It is not wise to make the marquis angry, Your Highness. Especially for a woman you don't even know."

Arvyn flashed his golden eyes to the duke, snorting.

"Since when did a prince have to bow to a lord?"

"Your Highness," the duke replied firmly, laying his hand on his shoulder. "Prince Oleksander needs the support of every noble when the Glerian Empire arrives."

The prince's face darkened.

"The support of petty nobles who only care for their own face and money will be of no use when I bring my brother the strongest weapon."

"And if there is no such thing? It is a myth, Your Highness; a bedtime story that your grandfather used to read to soothe your mother to sleep."

Arvyn clenched his fists as his eyes angrily met his uncle's.

"Did you not see what happened last night? A book appeared out of thin air! How can you say there is no chance that it exists?"

"Your Highness, I have been a soldier for over twenty years. I have seen too many of my comrades die bloody deaths to believe in such fantasies. My faith is in the men that I serve with, and our own skills, not some legendary weapon or mystical being."

"Would you not do anything you could to prevent more deaths? You visited the Glerian Empire as an envoy with Oleksander four years ago; you of all people know how strong they are."

"Yes, and I also know that praying for assistance from some illusionary force is futile and just gets more people killed." After a long moment the duke sighed, running his palm through his greying hair. "As your guard I will support you. But as your aide and uncle, I strongly advise you to be rational."

"I am being rational, uncle. Gathering all our soldiers will not be enough to defend our border; we need another solution!"

"Your Highness, chasing folk stories and wives tales is hardly rational. His Majesty will never allow you to search for it. You are fortunate that Prince Oleksander convinced him to let you travel north alone as it is. I suggest that you do not throw his generosity back at him."

The pair stared at each other, their muscles tense.

Cliona sighed quietly beside them, casting her eyes again to the marquis, speaking frantically to his frail wife beside him.

"I suggest that you make your decision," she said. "The dear lord might not allow you to leave if you delay much longer."

"Escort Cliona to the supply cart. I will hear no more of this, uncle," Arvyn hissed.

The prince plastered his charming smile onto his face once more as he turned his back to his uncle, inclining his head to the furious marquis in the distance before striding to his ready mount.

Daryl sighed, clenching his jaw as he offered her his hand. "Should anything happen to His Highness on this foolish quest of yours then know that your life will be forfeit."

She smiled, her dark red eyes glinting.

"You may ride with the squires," Daryl said gruffly to their new companion, pointing to a simple transport cart. "I assume a woman of your disposition would not be suited to a long ride on horseback."

"I hope to be well enough to do so soon, sir knight."

He nodded, his square jaw clenched as he returned to the prince's side.

A few of the youngest squires had already settled into the cart, sharing out the thick blankets that made the hard wooden seats a little more comfortable for the long journey.

"I'm Nierne," a blonde squire said, offering her his hand from inside the cart when Cliona stepped behind it.

She smiled softly, taking a seat in the simple cart beside the teenager. She rested her precious instrument gently over her lap before her fingers tuned the strings.

"Here, take this. Your cloak is not very thick, and it gets a bit cold heading down the mountain," another squire said, offering her one of the few dry blankets.

Satisfied, the prince swung his leg over his white mount's back, landing gracefully in the black saddle. One of the castle's grooms quickly arranged his long grey cloak over the gelding's hind as the prince inclined his head once more to Marquis Hugo.

With a wave of his arm the convoy began to trickle out of the castle gates, a genuine smile shining on the young prince's face.

Cliona sat quietly in the cart, a faint smile spreading over her lips as she raised her face to the cold rain, Dunsberg Castle gradually fading from view as they followed the road southward towards the Orville Forest.

* * *

It was not until early evening that the vast forest rose into view before them. The sky had begun to clear, the rain no longer accompanying the thunderous hooves of the convoy. But, as the rain faded, so too did the winter sun.

Arvyn raised his fist to call the convoy to a stop, urging his horse off the main road and up a small hill. The animal breathed heavily at the effort, the sticky mud pulling at his hooves.

But, the view of the magnificent sea of green was worth it.

The Orville Forest was both revered and despised by the people of Vyst. It stretched almost the entire width of the landlocked country, separating the people in the very north from the rest of the land. Although it hindered travel across the country, the forest had never been touched by the people. Some said that vicious tribes of dwarves, goblins and orcs still lived deep within the forest, whilst others preached that God would smite any who dared defile the sacred forest. Either way, no king had yet succeeded in cultivating the sea of trees, and the wildlife had been left to spread over the countryside, supposedly swallowing whole villages over time.

He breathed in the crisp evening air, lifting his hand to reach the low branch of an ancient oak standing proudly atop the hill, its branches still desperately trying to hold onto the golden leaves as it kept watch over the valley below.

"Shall we divert to rest at Stalybridge, Your Highness?"

The prince looked at his uncle as he pulled his horse alongside him, stroking his mount's mane gently. He glanced down at his entourage waiting on the road below him, the squires having hurriedly draped extra blankets over the sodden horses.

"No," Arvyn replied. "I wish to reach the capital as soon as possible. We'll camp on the road tonight."

The old duke sighed as his nephew nudged his horse back down the hill once more. He rolled his neck, his seasoned bones creaking beneath his heavy armour.

It would be twelve more days of riding until they reached the familiar streets of the capital city, and the knight was well and truly looking forward to his bed. Unlike his royal nephew, he had had his fill of camping in his armour, his sword always in hand. But, he knew that this was still just an adventure to the twenty-two year old. After all, it was his first official duty without either of his brothers to accompany him.

He wearily trailed after his nephew, already shouting orders to set up camp for the night.

The squires and knights quickly set about unsaddling the horses and erecting a small number of rudimentary canvas tents that royal convoys were required to carry for emergencies.

A handful of the royal knights grumbled as they worked, unwilling to sacrifice the homely comforts that they were used to. But a simple look from the old duke silenced them, leaving only the gentle song of evening birds and the happy nattering of the squires to fill the air.

Cliona bit her bottom lip and tried to steady her breathing, fighting to control her trembling hands as she laid her freshly polished silver lyre against the tree stump that she perched on. Her eyes wandered along the treeline beside them, hoping that the gentle songs of woodland birds would drown out the jovial camaraderie of the squires and guards as they settled around the fires of their make-shift camp for the night.

How long has it been since I was outside like this? She thought, removing her thin black slippers slowly, digging her toes into the damp ground beneath her feet. She closed her eyes, raising her face to meet the delicate warmth of the setting winter sun.

She inhaled the scent of the wet forest slowly, counting silently as she willed her mind to calm.

A shadow crossed over her, blocking the little sunlight from her pale face.

As she lowered her face once again, her eyes met those of the prince, his hand extended as he offered her a full goblet of his personal red wine.

She shook her head slowly.

"Suit yourself," he replied, sitting beside her on the felled log with the two goblets. "You will catch a chill like this."

She chuckled softly, revealing a neat row of pearly teeth. "You need not worry about me. The fresh air will do wonders for my constitution."

Arvyn's brow creased as he watched her raise her hands to the air, a gentle smile spread over her pale face.

"Why were you confined to that tower?"

A shadow crossed over her face as she pushed a tendril of pale hair behind her ear.

"It's been so long that I doubt anyone at the castle would remember." She turned to face him. "Why did you bring me along?"

He took a drink from his cup, his eyes wearily watching the guards that his father assigned him as he retrieved the leather-bound tome from the bag at his side.

"Something tells me that you have yet to tell me everything. Besides, this book is of no use; it is just patterns scribbled on the first five pages."

Cliona smiled, holding her hand out to him expectantly.

The prince watched her as she slowly opened the book. Her long fingers moved carefully over the strange symbols that littered the page in deep black ink. Her pale brow creased slightly as her crimson eyes focused.

"To think that a descendant of the mighty Oleksander could not read the ancient demon script."

Arvyn narrowed his eyes on her.

"The demon-tongue has been a forbidden language for centuries. Even the High Priest cannot speak or read the cursed language."

"Well, luckily for you, I am well versed in this 'dead' language," she smiled, handing the book back to him.

Arvyn leant back, his head tilted towards the sun setting over the horizon.

"The north is a very sheltered place and not very good with keeping up with current affairs, yet even so I would have assumed that everyone knew. How old are you? You cannot be more than twenty."

"I'm not sure," she said quietly, looking at her hands. "I have been living in seclusion in that tower for a long time."

"You must know very little of the world then," he mused, taking a drink from his heavy goblet. "My ancestor, King Oleksander II, was a very religious man. He banned the study of the demons over two hundred years ago. Those who continued to research the topic were executed as heretics. Which begs the question, how does a girl living under the roof of one of the most religious lords in the whole of Vyst know so much about demons?"

She smiled.

"As I said before, the Dunsberg family takes great pride in their history."

The prince sighed, standing slowly.

"Have it your way, for now. So long as you help me locate the weapon that can help save my kingdom then I will not pry too deeply. But," he said, his expression clouding over as he casually rested his hand on the hilt of his inexperienced sword, "should you betray me then your death will not be swift."

She inclined her head as he walked away, his hand running through his thick golden hair.

A tired sigh left her lips as she steadily plucked at her cheerful lyre, filling the air with gentle song as she was once again left to her thoughts.

She closed her eyes tightly, trying to ignore the cackling fire before her.

Chapter 5

Even the warm blanket of the evergreen trees around them did little to shelter their already aching bodies from the bitter gale as the prince and his entourage rode slowly down the well-trodden dirt road cutting through the ancient forest.

Arvyn pulled his thick travelling cloak closer around his shoulders, the fabric doing little to protect him against the cruel bite of the northern winter winds.

"We should find a place to rest soon, Your Highness," Daryl said quietly, pulling his horse alongside his nephew's. He offered a small silver flask towards Arvyn, the metal wrapped tightly in tanned leather embroidered with the Wynford family crest.

"I believe that a warm bath and hearty meal is in order for everyone when we next reach a town, Daryl," he smiled, his teeth threatening to chatter as he took the flask from his uncle.

The old knight's brown creased as his gaze wandered over his nephew's pale face. The prince's hands shook ever so slightly as he raised the silver spout to his lips, welcoming the small comfort offered by the lukewarm mulled wine.

They had made good time so far, thanks to the prince's decision to send the supply carts and servants along the long road that travelled around the Orville Forest instead. He had claimed that he would not want to risk the wagons getting stuck should the path narrow further down the road, but in reality Daryl knew that his impatient nephew merely wanted to fasten their pace; the lumbering carts were slowing him down. So now, only a dozen of the prince's entourage remained, including Daryl's best knights, two squires and Cliona.

Arvyn had never before left the luxuries of royal life behind. Even along their tour, they had spent a single night camping along the roadside as they travelled under the guise of inspecting the northern lords and their defences. But now that their official duties were done, the fastest route back to the capital still remained the uninhabited path through the Orville Forest, and the sweet comforts of shelter seemed like a long and faded memory. And that meant at least another five nights of camping along the roadside.

Sensing his uncle's worry, the prince smiled at Daryl, holding his head high as he nudged his horse into a trot.

The duke sighed, returning the flask back into his saddlebag.

"Doesn't it seem too quiet, Your Grace?"

The duke looked over to his young squire, Nierne, as he appeared alongside him.

Daryl squinted into the dense undergrowth, the sounds of rustling leaves echoing over the otherwise empty treeline.

"I agree," he replied quietly, tightening his grip on his black leather reins as his eyes scanned the forest around them. "I think it best that we get through this cursed place as fast as possible."

Seemingly sensing his disquiet, the duke's mare began flickering her long black ears, her nostrils flaring. She bounced beneath him as the seasoned soldier tried to steady her, his own senses on high alert as the other horses behind her began to snort.

"Easy, Dahlia," the duke said softly, his eyes racing over the trees.

Arvyn turned back towards his uncle, his brow creasing.

"Is something wrong?" The prince shouted.

Daryl's eyes went wide as he caught a glimpse of a light flashing in the bushes ahead of them.

"Your Highness!"

Arvyn stopped his mare as he turned to face his uncle, pausing just as an arrow shot swiftly through the air towards him, just narrowly missing his face as it met the tree behind him.

"It's an ambush!" The duke turned to his nephew, drawing his sword as their escort readied for combat. "Get behind me, Your Highness."

The prince nodded, going to manoeuvre his mount quickly.

As he did so, his horse reared up, an arrow suddenly protruding from his grey hind.

He surged forward into the trees, the prince holding onto his reins tightly as they raced away from the others. He was vaguely aware of two horses close behind him, but he was too focused on staying in the saddle to look around.

After a few minutes of galloping through the dense undergrowth away from the road, the mount slowed down, his nostrils flaring as his ears flickered.

Arvyn stroked his neck softly, his hand reaching for the arrow in his muscular rump, the shaft broken as they had ridden through the trees.

"Allow me, Your Highness," Nierne said, quickly dismounting his chestnut gelding, Cliona still sat in the saddle of her own sherry bay mount quietly as she grabbed their reins.

The prince's horse flinched as the blonde squire pulled the arrow from his flesh, quickly placing a cloth over the open wound to stem any bleeding.

"We're lucky, your Highness," Nierne said as he put pressure on the expensive horse's injury. "It looks like it just missed the vital points; he should recover. Although, he'll have a limp for a few days at least."

The prince nodded, turning in his saddle to look back down the path they came, the forest deadly quiet around them.

"Um, Your Highness," the squire said, his arms poised to remount as he stood frozen, his mossy eyes fixed on something in the distance. "What is that?"

Arvyn followed the teenager's eyes, noticing a large oak tree a few paces off the dirt track ahead of them, its boughs still bright green despite the harsh winter.

Just above the base of the tree was a large natural hollow, vibrant moss lining the smooth walls of the cavity. Three large flowers grew close to the right wall, their rich yellow and orange petals a stark contrast from the dull brown bark framing them.

But strangest of all was the large humanoid skull placed in the centre of the hollow, carefully resting on a black velvet cushion. The lower mandible was missing, but it was otherwise in pristine condition. It held a pair of elongated canines, more at home on the skull of a tiger from the east than a person. Protruding from its head were two dark horns curving behind the skull, a variety of red, orange and yellow flowers entwined to make a crown around them. Resting in both of the dark eye orbits were two lit white candles, the flames flickering in the wind despite the shelter from the tree.

In front of the tree was a grey boulder, rubbed flat over constant use. The sides were covered in a thick carpet of moss, the top stained with dried blood.

"What the hell is this?" Arvyn whispered, his golden brow furrowing.

The squire tightened his grip on his reins, one hand holding his sword ready as he manoeuvred his mount close to the prince's.

A pain shot through Arvyn's hand, still bandaged after his encounter with Cliona's crude obsidian knife. He clenched his jaw, biting his lip against the pain.

"Your Highness," Nierne said, "I think its best that we return to the rest of the group with haste."

"Agreed," Arvyn replied, clutching tightly onto his reins.

A deep laugh echoed around them, sending a nearby murder of crows to flock to the skies above.

The small mound of discarded clothes huddled beside the strange shrine stood, turning into a hooded figure, a pair of twisted wooden horns sprouting from their head through their black cloak.

"You shouldn't be here," the figure hissed, turning their face to the two men.

Cliona slowly dismounted, stepping towards the figure carefully, her head held high.

"Get away, Cliona," Arvyn said firmly, gripping the hilt of his sword tightly.

Cliona ignored him, her steps unfaltering as she stopped within reach of the horned figure. She took a deep breath, biting her lip as she drew out the last dregs of her remaining magical aura to freeze the prince and squire.

"Your guise is insulting," she said as she met the figure's steel eyes.

"You speak the demon tongue," the stranger said, their eyes widening as they flickered away from the statuesque men to travel over Cliona's slender form.

Her thin white dress clung tightly to her skeletal body, her collarbones very visible thanks to her low cut neckline. The long billowing white sleeves seemed to swamp her curveless figure, her pale white hair limp about her shoulders. And yet the fire in her crimson eyes could not be ignored as she stared at them, her head held high.

"No matter; those too weak are not worthy to gaze upon the sacred altar."

The figure raised their hand towards her steadily, their lips parting to begin a chant.

The figure froze, their hands clutching at their neck as their sounds were trapped within their throat.

Cliona's eyes shifted, gold and black flecks swirling around the irises like a whirlpool. Her presence seemed to grow, a faint smoke emanating from her weak form.

The hooded figure looked to the prince and squire, neither of whom seemed to notice any change in the woman before them. They met Cliona's gaze again, inclining their horned head ever so slightly in retreat as they turned their back to the group.

Cliona's knees buckled as she held her hand to her head, blinking quickly as she tried to regain her composure, her aura receding once again.

Nierne ran to her side, Arvyn still ready for an attack from the stranger.

"Leave, before I change my mind," the figure hissed in the common language again, turning their eyes to gaze on the demonic effigy perched above them.

Nierne quickly lifted Cliona from the ground, shocked at how heavy she was for such a malnourished physique. He bit his tongue as he passed her to the mounted prince, whose gaze was firmly fixed on the horned figure before them.

Arvyn nodded to the squire as he collected his reins, quickly nudging his horse back the way they came, not daring to cast a glance back to the demonic shrine.

When they were gone from view, two more horned figures appeared from the shadows of the trees, similar black cloaks shrouding their features.

"Why did you let them leave?"

"They will return with more soldiers," the second hissed, their hands clenched at their side.

"We must protect the forest."

The first held up their blackened hand, immediately silencing their two companions.

Their black painted lips parted as they smiled, revealing two neat rows of teeth sharpened into points and stained grey. Their grey eyes twinkled as they watched the prince disappear completely from view, their head cocked to the side.

They turned back to the shrine, their eyes focused on the two candles lighting the eye sockets of the demon skull resting in the centre of the hollowed out tree. They lifted their gangly arms to the sky as they began to hum, the long sleeves of their robe dropping to reveal countless scars along their forearms, painted so that their blackened hands faded to grey and white up their arms.

Their companions glanced at each other as they, too, lifted their arms skyward and began to hum, their voices joined by dozens more hidden amongst the trees.

"We must prepare," the first figure laughed, raising their gangly arms up to the sky. "Prepare for the coming of our saviour!"

Chapter 6

Tall white-washed brick houses watched over the hundreds of cheerful faces gathered to greet the golden prince and his entourage parading down the bustling streets of the capital. Crimson banners, each with a hand-stitched yellow cockatrice, and white flags with a blazing crimson sun hung from open windows, swaying in the gentle breeze. Men and women threw white and yellow petals onto the clean swept street, joy evident on their faces. Children laughed and waved at the prince and his men.

The prince waved proudly to his citizens, his horse trotting gracefully behind his standard bearer, the duke riding a short distance behind him.

"The people really like him, don't they," Cliona said quietly, pulling her hood tightly over her silver hair.

"In the capital, of course!" Nierne replied, a broad smile shining below his dark eyes. "His Highness has helped improve the economy of the city greatly. Everyone here has more money to spend, and they're happy for it. He may not be next in line for the throne, but he is certainly well loved."

"I see," she whispered.

Her fingers clutched at her burgundy cloak. Although it was warmer here in the capital than in the northern

Dunsberg Castle, the coarse wool of her cloak had become a comfort blanket that she couldn't bear to part with.

The cart rolled along quietly behind the prince as their destination came slowly into view over the tall buildings.

Built atop a tall hill in the otherwise flat landscape, the royal castle of Goldacre was an imposing sight. It was said that the colossal structure had been built in a single day by an army of giants to ward off the demon armies. The city had sprouted around the keep over the centuries, with the oldest and wealthiest families living nearest to the granite square keep.

The crowd began to thin as the convoy neared the ten foot tall wall separating the city from the sprawling royal gardens. Where once there would have been a drawbridge over the man-made moat encircling the great building, now stood an ornately walled white granite bridge, white swans swimming in the lily-covered water. The black iron gates, adorned with golden roses, were held open by a troop of royal guards. Their golden armour glinted in the late afternoon sun, their crimson cloaks draped over their shoulders.

They stood to attention as their prince passed through, their ceremonial gold tipped spears pointing upward.

As they crossed into the royal gardens, the cobblestone road that they had been travelling abruptly turned into a path of fine white sand, imported from the western coast. Large red and yellow rose bushes lined the well-maintained path, their fragrant aroma filling the air. Hidden by six-foot tall hornbeam hedges lay the acre of beautiful gardens and ponds that the castle was renowned for, reserved only for the royal family and their important guests.

The pale grey granite walls come closer into view, the tall crenulations now adorned with white and black marble demonic gargoyles, ruby eyes watching all that approached. It was a smaller castle than Dunsberg in height, but it sprawled over much more land than the musician's previous home, able to house the royal family and the households of twenty of their favourite courtiers.

The cart rolled to a stop behind the prince as he dismounted his gelding, tossing the reins to a waiting groom wearing the royal crimson livery.

A short series of polished white marble steps led up to the castle's outer archway, a crowned cockatrice carved expertly into the granite above the doorway. Blazing sun banners hung either side of the entrance beside two statuesque royal guards.

A petite girl in a white and crimson gown appeared at the top of the steps, her blonde head held high. Her demeanour softened when her eyes met those of the prince, a delicate smile spreading over her rosy cheeks.

He ran up the steps, two at a time, embracing the girl warmly.

"Welcome home, brother!"

"Have you been behaving yourself, Leonie? How have your lessons been going?"

"Tedious as always; you know that I would much rather read in the library than listen to Duchess Silvia's etiquette lectures." The fifteen year old princess gazed warmly up at her brother, her genuine smile reaching her golden eyes. "So, how was your inspection of the north?"

"Rather ordinary, for the most part. And it was dreadfully cold; you would have frozen to death, little sister."

"I'm hardier than I look," the girl pouted.

Her delicate eyebrows knitted together as she noticed their uncle helping a stranger from the cart.

"Arvyn! Your journey clearly wasn't as terrible as you make it out to be. Who is that young lady with Uncle Daryl?"

Arvyn offered his sister his arm.

"She is a distant relative of Marquis Hugo from Dunsberg Castle. She knows many folk tales and so I've brought her here to help my research."

Leonie's golden eyes darkened slightly as she cast a worried glance at her brother, lowering her voice.

"Are you sure that's wise?"

"I have a lead," he said quietly, his eyes glancing around them as they descended the steps.

"The temple will only let the king indulge you for so long. They're already making preparations to have you branded as a heretic if you continue to try to undermine them. Besides, His Majesty is starting to lose his patience in your hobby, you know that."

"I appreciate the warning, little sister, but I have no intention of giving up yet."

"Just be careful," she whispered, squeezing his arm.

The royal siblings plastered smiles on their faces once again as they stopped in front of the duke.

"I'm glad to see that you have returned in one piece, Duke Wynford," the princess smiled.

"Your Highness," Daryl said, gently kissing her proffered hand. "Not for a lack of trying on Prince Arvyn's part, Your Highness."

The golden haired girl tutted, extracting her arm from the prince's smoothly. She carefully yet swiftly lifted her cream skirts, embroidered delicately with pale pink roses, tiny seed pearls glinting as she moved towards Cliona.

"Brother, how long must I wait until a proper introduction is made?"

The prince raised his hands in the air. "Leonie, this is Cliona. Cliona, may I introduce the Second Princess of Vyst and my younger sister; Princess Eleanora."

"It is a pleasure, Your Highness," Cliona said, quietly curtsying beside the duke.

"Come," the blonde girl smiled, looping her arm through Cliona's. "My brother should make his report to His Majesty, so I will take care of you until he is finished."

Cliona glanced at the prince, but he was already discussing something with his uncle. Hesitantly, she followed the princess through the archway.

Chapter 7

Music danced over the smooth white limestone walls of the royal ballroom as delicately carved cherubs watched the festivities from above. The black marble floor was carpeted in a flurry of satin skirts, moving in time with the jaunty melody of the battling violins that was cheered on quietly by a cello, viola and a harpsichord.

Cliona stood awkwardly at the side of the bustling great hall, her hands shaking around the crystal glass of red wine she was given by Princess Eleanora. She shifted her weight uncomfortably from one leg to the other underneath the multiple layers of white underskirts and dark green and cream brocade that the princess had insisted she wear. Her breathing was laboured thanks to the whale-bone cage of the simple black bodice that the princess's maids had forced upon her.

"I see that my sweet sister enjoyed commandeering you, then."

She nodded slowly, her pale cheeks blushing as the prince slid in beside her, Daryl forever one step behind him.

"She has always loved dressing up her servants since she was small. It is one of her favourite hobbies."

"I don't think that's an appropriate response, Your Highness. The girl is clearly uncomfortable in this setting."

She looked over to the duke, dressed in his silver courtly finery and not his armour for the first time since she met him. His discomfort about not wearing his trusty black armour was evident in his stiff shoulders, his silver eyes constantly darting around the room as he fiddled subconsciously with his black cotton gloves.

"I agree." Arvyn smiled, lifting the dark red curtain over a nearby door and gesturing for the two of them to exit onto the balcony with him.

The cold air was a blessing as it raced through the girl's fragile lungs.

"Now that the king is preoccupied, it would be a good time to take a visit to the treasury and search for this object you mentioned, without attracting any unwanted attention. Besides, I think the treasury is as good a place as any to hide from all these sycophants anyway," the prince muttered, leaning over the white marble banister that overlooked the southern garden, blooming with roses.

He carefully lifted himself over, his strong arms supporting his weight as he dangled over the fifteen foot drop. He stretched his long legs towards a decorative ledge carved above the window below him.

"Your Highness, it would have been easier to go through Her Majesty's parlour."

"My brothers' wives are using the parlour as a respite room when they need a break from the festivities. Besides, this is much more exciting."

The prince swung his body, propelling himself onto the wall below the balcony. From there, he simply climbed down the wooden rose trellis. He managed to clamber his way almost to the bottom, when he pricked his hand on one of the thorns.

His body rocked backwards as he lost his grip, travelling the final few feet in the air and landing inelegantly on his rear.

"Damn it," he muttered, noticing a bloody smear on his thigh.

Cliona pulled the black ribbon loose from her silvery hair, leaning over the railing. Her hands deftly lifted and knotted the mossy dress around her high hips before she moved to straddle the railing. A cough racked through her lungs briefly, the cold breeze ripping through her loose long hair.

"I don't think this is wise," Daryl muttered, his back against the railing beside her, listening carefully as a pair of young ladies stopped the other side of the curtain covering the doorway.

She laid her hand on her chest, steadying her breathing.

The duke sighed, pushing himself quickly over the railings, clambering down the trellis with much greater ease than the prince.

"Jump and I'll catch you."

"Well, this gentlemanly behaviour is rather out of character, dear uncle," the prince mocked, brushing down his white trousers.

"It would be difficult to explain why a young lady is trying to jump over the balcony. I would much prefer not to draw unwanted attention."

Cliona took a deep breath and jumped down, landing gracefully in the duke's arms.

The prince stifled a laugh as the duke lowered her to the ground, gritting his teeth and avoiding her gaze.

A young woman's giggle greeted them, the gentle sway of her skirts rippling over the cold stone floor as she walked to the edge of the white marble balcony railing with her chattering companions. Arvyn moved into the shadows, indicating to Cliona and Daryl to do the same. They clung to the wall, the sharp rosebush thorns embracing them as they hid from the small gaggle of young women that appeared above them.

"Go," the duke mouthed to the prince, carefully sidestepping along the wall to stay within the shadows.

The prince nodded silently, allowing his uncle to lead the way.

Silently, they slipped into the castle kitchen through the servant door, being instantly surrounded by the sounds of bustling scullery maids and cooks.

"You, refill that tray of devilled eggs. You, get those glasses shined quickly. If I can't see your reflection there'll be the devil to pay."

A busy scullery maid, around sixteen, gasped when she saw the prince, dipping into a curtsey as she held a dirty pan in her hand. The prince raised his finger quietly to his lips, a gentle smile dancing there just for her. She nodded, blushing as she pushed a dark brown strand of hair behind her round ear.

The trio snuck silently along the empty corridors of the palace, dodging the few guards patrolling the castle thanks to the expertise granted to the prince by his years of playing hide and seek with his tutors. The jovial music began to dim as they began the long descent into the depths of the old castle, the duke's mercury eyes constantly scanning his surroundings.

As they neared the castle vault, they came across four guards, their golden armour shining in the dim torch light. They stood before a large double door made of sturdy black wood, small runes, painted red and silver, etched into the door.

Seeing the figures, the guards lowered their ornate golden spears.

"Good evening, gentlemen," the prince said warmly as he walked towards them, his characteristic broad smile clear on his golden face. "Would you be so kind as to lower your weapons so as to not frighten my companion? She has a rather delicate disposition."

"His Majesty has forbidden anyone from entering the royal treasury, unless bearing his royal seal. Even you, Your Highness."

The prince scowled.

"Arvyn!"

The prince turned at the familiar sound of his name, as his sister trotted quickly down the steps, expertly avoiding tripping over her trailing crimson brocade skirt not dissimilar to the one she leant Cliona.

"Father said he forgot to give you this," she said, offering him the king's golden signet ring, the crowned cockatrice standing proudly above a castle.

He smiled, taking the heirloom gratefully.

The guards looked to one another before one nodded, unlocking the black iron latch. Two others pushed the heavy door inwards, their back muscles screaming under the heavy weight of the timber. One of the guards handed the duke a freshly lit torch silently.

A pungent wall of69hes slammed into their faces as the prince and his three companions entered the royal vault that had seen no visitors in almost five years. Gold and silver coins glinted in the torch light as the duke lowered the flame to a wrought iron sconce on the wall. The metallic coating of the coins and treasures filled the still air, filling the room with a heady metallic scent that wasn't altogether unpleasant.

The prince bent down, running his fingers over a pile of cold golden coins.

"I forgot just how much His Majesty had been hoarding."

"We're not here to gloat, Your Highness," the duke said, casting his silver gaze over the room.

"And why are you here? It's not like you to run out of a ball, Arvyn."

The prince exhaled, running his hand through his golden hair. "We're looking for a painting that His Majesty moved to the vault after our grandmother died, at the behest of the temple. The one that was hanging in her bedchamber."

His sister narrowed her amber eyes at him, resting her hands on her narrow waist. She pursed her lips into a straight line. "I think I know the one you're talking about. But, there are a lot of paintings in here, so it may be hard to find."

"I remember it being brought down still in its cherry wood frame, so look for wood."

Chapter 8

The prince stretched out his back after two hours of searching, a yawn threatening on his golden face. He looked over to Cliona, stood in front of a large oil painting in a polished cherry wood frame.

The precise brushstrokes of the gentle azure waves rippled over the old canvas, reflecting the clear pale blue sky. Tall chalky cliffs, littered with golden bird's-foot-trefoil and lilac rock sea-spurrey, overlooked a gorgeous white sandy beach. A beautiful woman sat atop one such rock, her bare skin a similar shade to the rose-quartz rock that she perched delicately on. A simple black lyre rested in her naked lap, hiding her modesty from prying eyes as her slender fingers gently plucked at the white strings. Her wavy auburn hair draped over her smooth shoulders, a circlet of white pearls her only decoration. She gazed out beyond the painting, her sea-green eyes overflowing with yearning.

"It is a beautiful painting," Leonie said, her fingers gently brushing over the old canvas. "I can see why it was one of Grandmother's favourites."

"There is an inscription here," the prince said, pointing to ancient golden runes carved into the base of the red wooden frame. "Can you read them?"

"Are you daft, brother? No one has been able to read demon-script for over a hundred years, let alone understand it. It's forbidden!"

Cliona stepped forward, brushing her fingers over the delicate lettering, her sonorous voice speaking a language that her companions did not recognise.

The golden runes began to glow with her words, a fine silver mist leaching from within the frame, swirling around their feet.

The princess' eyes widened as she clutched onto her older brother's arm, his golden eyes narrowed nervously on the painting as the red-haired woman seemed to tilt her face towards him, a charming smile painted on her ruby lips. Daryl reached for the hilt of his sword, only to find it missing due to his courtly attire.

The mist enveloped them, the salty taste of seawater surrounding them.

Leonie dug her long fingernails into her brother's arm. "What in God's name is happening?"

"The painting held ancient magic," Cliona said quietly, closing her eyes to listen to seagulls greeting them from a distance.

Arvyn smiled, extracting his sister's well-trimmed claws from his sleeve before stepping into the crisp water. Waves gently brushed against his feet as they rose slowly over the white sandy shoreline, soaking through his ornamental shoes. His sister followed closely, her attempts of lifting her long red skirts in vain as the waves wrapped around her legs.

The duke stepped backwards out of the water, his broad arms firmly folded over his chest as he scoured the landscape silently.

"Listen," the princess said softly, closing her eyes.

A soft melody hummed along the wind, wrapping itself delicately around them. The serene voice was joined by the gentle drone of an aulos as it enveloped them, beckoning them into the sea.

"It's beautiful," the prince breathed, his body giving in to the pull drawing him towards the source of the alluring song.

"Arvyn, wait," Leonie said, her hand stretching out to reach him.

She gasped, her hand covering her pink lips as she looked at her brother's face. Crimson symbols were carving themselves into his smooth skin, stretching over his high cheekbones and down beyond his clothing, his golden eyes turning a blood red.

"Uncle Daryl," she pleaded, turning to see that her late mother's only sibling was similarly afflicted.

Cliona closed her crimson eyes, embracing the cold salty breeze surrounding them as it bit into her thin white skin. She slowly lifted her face towards the sky, allowing the gentle rhythm of the waves to wash over her as she stepped deeper into the waves towards the fretting princess.

"We are in the domain of the Demon Lord Zuma," she whispered, her fingers dancing over the surface of the water. "The domain of the sirens."

Leonie looked to her brother, tears shining over her eyes, digging her fingernails into the soft flesh of her palm as she watched him trudge deeper into the water.

"The only way to find the item that your brother came here for is to locate the sirens that reside here. And the best way to do that is to follow the siren song."

"I can't," the princess cried. "I can't swim; I'll drown."

The musician rested her hand gently on the girl's shoulder, a soft smile playing on her thin lips.

"Just watch."

The princess did as she was bid, watching as her brother travelled further away from the sandy beach. But, rather than the gentle waves engulfing his body, they slowly parted with each of his steps, never reaching higher than the bottom of his gold rose-embroidered red waistcoat. Just like the duke, his measured steps were leading him towards a large cluster of rocks just a little way off shore, riotous gannets circling on ebony tipped wings above.

"Magical teleporting paintings aren't real. Sirens aren't real. God is just punishing me for drinking and stealing His Majesty's ring. That's all this is."

Leonie slowly followed her brother and the duke, tears quietly falling down her smooth rosy cheeks as her trembling arms wrapped desperately around her chest. She tried frantically to clutch onto any shred of her composure as the waves wrapped around her flowing dress. Being petite in stature, the water reached just below her narrow shoulders, her gold slippered feet just able to walk along the unstable sand.

"May I tell you an old tale, princess?" Cliona asked quietly, sidestepping a patch of floating seaweed.

Leonie inclined her head, being sure to stay no further than two steps behind the stranger.

"Many centuries ago, there was a benevolent king. He cared for his people greatly and wanted their lives to be blessed with prosperity and happiness. But, over time, he did what everyone must eventually do; he began to grow old. Although he had four very capable heirsto care for his people after him, he was still afraid.

"So, the king decided to test his children. 'Whosoever shall find the secret to eternal life', he told them, 'shall have the honour of continuing my legacy'. And so, they each set about to search for that which their father most desired.

"The first explored the world searching for artefacts. The second tried to create a potion. The third tried to utilise the magic of runes in his quest. But, none succeeded.

"As the king lay on his deathbed, surrounded by his advisors and family, he asked his fourth child for the answer. 'My king,' he replied, 'all things must someday return to the earth, so that the next generation may thrive. But, your name shall live on in history, for I shall unify the realms in your name.'

"With that, the dying king smiled and took his last breath, and his son set about conquering the realms in memory of the beloved king so that his legacy could live on."

"I have never heard that story before," the princess said softly, rubbing away the goosebumps on her thin arms.

Cliona gently brushed her hand over the water's surface, biting the inside of her cheek.

"It is an ancient tale that I doubt many still remember," Cliona replied.

She slowed her steps as Arvyn and Daryl abruptly halted before them, their rune-painted faces turned upward to the rocks before them.

Leonie clutched the golden religious pendant around her neck, her amber eyes wide.

Perched on the rocks before them rested a beautiful figure, a warm smile sleeping on their pale pink face. They held their head high as they watched the two men approach, their fingers twisting in their long navy hair, covering their naked chest. A sheer navy cloth rested over their legs, tucked delicately against the grey rock.

"I thought I sensed intruders," the figure purred, raising their sea foam eyes to meet Cliona's. "It has been a long time since we had any visitors."

Leonie stepped closer behind the other woman, her small hand instinctively reaching for her arm.

The figure laughed, the rich lilting sound stretching over the ocean as the waves began to grow restless.

"Llyr, release them."

The figure turned, their round eyes widening at the sight of two female sirens stepping gracefully towards them, each carrying a long double pronged spear and round seashell-encrusted shields. Their pale faces were obscured by their elegant silver helmets, the spiral design matching their light-weight silver chestplates.

In front of them walked a muscular man, his arms outstretched calmly. His bare chest was littered in long curved scars, the pale pink skin blending into crimson as it reached his hips. Unlike the three other sirens, he wore an ornate black leather belt that held dozens of transparent layers of white cloth in place over his well-toned legs.

"Lord Earwyn," the seated figure stuttered, slinking from their perch into the cool water. "These humans have trespassed into our domain, sir. I was bringing them to you for judgement."

The man folded his arms over his chest, his cornflower gaze dancing over the four figures in the water.

"Return to the settlement. I will see to your punishment for casting magic illegally later."

The figure lowered their head, swimming away behind the rocks, one of the guards close behind.

The male siren sighed, raising his hand to the sky. As he chanted an ancient spell, the silver band on his hand glowed with aquamarine runes, causing the waves to grow taller, washing over the duke and the prince.

"Arvyn!"

Cliona held onto Leonie's arm gently, shaking her head.

The siren smiled, slowly lowering his arm.

Leonie gasped, watching the runes etched into her brother's skin slowly drip away with the water. The sea itself parted to reveal the fine sand below their feet. As the magic washed away, Arvyn and Daryl grew slightly weak in their legs, falling to their knees on the sand.

"I apologise for my subordinate's indiscretion. It has been many moons since anyone has journeyed here, and I believe that my people have forgotten how to act around humans." He smiled, holding his muscular arms out welcomingly. "I am Lord Earwyn, Guardian of the Sirens."

Daryl blinked a few times, cradling his head with one hand. The prince, however, retched over the sand, the sea dodging out the way as his sister gently rubbed his back.

"Perhaps introductions are best kept for when you are more composed. I am told that the after effect of our magic is much more potent for magicless races such as humans."

Leonie lifted her brother to his feet, aware of the waves slowly starting to close around them. Cliona offered her hand to the duke, but he pushed himself up alone, his legs wobbling beneath him as the waves rushed to catch him.

They followed Earwyn and his guard as they began walking gracefully over the rocks towards their settlement, the waves returning to relaxed normality as they left.

They stepped slowly over the undulating speckled grey and white diorite, careful to avoid the loose green and yellow seaweed threatening to entangle their ankles. Steep steps were carved into the rock, an archway of driftwood carved with bright blue runes keeping the hands of the sea at bay. A pale green glass tunnel stretched before them, the path lined with tall pillar candles resting in great scallop shells that filled the air with a relaxing salty scent.

"I don't believe that we have been properly introduced," the prince said, striding alongside the tall siren. "I am Prince Arvyn, the Third Prince of the kingdom of Vyst. This is my younger sister Princess Eleanora, my maternal uncle Duke Wynford, and my scholar, Cliona."

The siren glanced over at the so-called scholar, her crimson eyes downcast.

"I am Lord Earwyn, the protector of the siren people. This is my guard, Lorelai."

She bowed her head briefly, her rhythmic steps unfaltering down the sandy path.

"Come; tonight is the last day of autumn, and we have a grand feast prepared. You must join us."

The prince inclined his head, following the muscular siren and his guard up a long series of smooth sandstone steps towards a grand palace.

Great sandstone columns stood before them, the bottom and top carved with seashell motives, glittering silver fish scales decorating the middle. The columns guarded a large driftwood arch, pearls and pale pink queen scallop shells embedded into the timber. Heavy speckled diorite doors stood open beneath the archway, six burly guards standing to attention beside them as the siren lord and his guests returned to the palace. Their feet echoed over the beautiful pink, white and purple mosaic floor, the serene trill of an aulos leading them into a great columned hall.

Eight columns reached high into a vaulted ceiling, painted to resemble a midnight sky, small pearls shining down on them like stars. The columns themselves were painted white, images of dark green seaweed etched into the stone, reaching above the seashell encrusted pillar base. The mosaic tiled floor reflected the light of a silver chandelier hanging low from the ceiling. Lit scallop shaped sconces were carved into the whitewashed sandstone walls, helping to bathe the room in a warm glow. Detailed scenes of sirens singing and dancing on the rocks stretched across the room, the figures interspersed with smiling humans.

A diorite dais, three steps high, looked over the room, large teal curtains tied back with silver cord to reveal a platform. A single throne carved out of pale driftwood, watched over the room, a plush pale pink pillow sleeping on the empty seat.

Noticing the prince's eye, the male siren smiled sadly.

"That is the throne to our great Princess Zuma."

"Will she be joining us?" Leonie asked innocently.

"Unfortunately not," he sighed, directing them towards the large driftwood table in the centre of the room. "Her Highness has been indisposed for a long time now."

"She is one of the imprisoned gods, isn't she?"

The siren nodded, taking the seat to the right of the empty chair at the head of the table, gesturing to his guests to sit too.

"Yes, I believe that that was a title given to my mistress by humans a long time ago."

Servants brought out dozens of ornate seafood dishes, the aromatic smell filling the room as the sirens tucked into the bountiful feast laid before them.

"What can you tell us about Princess Zuma? Why was she and the other gods entombed?"

One of the nearby sirens slammed her drink onto the table, shock evident on her finely chiselled face.

"How dare you," she hissed, her marine eyes filled with malice.

The siren lord held up his hand to her. "Steady, Lwella. It has been close to three hundred years since we lost Zuma to the Temple of Nour. Humans cannot be expected to know about it, at least not in depth."

"My apologies, my lord," she hissed through gritted teeth in her native tongue, dabbing gently at the spilt dark blue wine splashed over her thin white dress.

"As you can see, my people and I are not entirely happy with the situation." His gaze wandered briefly over to Cliona. "The pain still runs deep."

He rested his elbows on the table, interlocking his fingers as his gaze went back to the prince.

"My mistress and her comrades have gone by many names in the past; gods, heroes, traitors and villains to name a few. But to my people she will forever be Princess Zuma."

"And, I must be direct, who are your people?"

"We are the sirens of the realm of Kovira, Your Highness. Our lands may have been conquered by the demon race many centuries ago, but we still pride ourselves in our differences. Especially as it was the Demon Army that wrongfully imprisoned our dear princess."

"I do apologise, Lord Earwyn. I did not intend to offend. What you call history is little more than forgotten legends for us."

"I suppose that it has been a significant length of time."

"There are very few stories remaining, my lord, and those that do are not particularly flattering of creatures such as you."

Earwyn nodded sadly.

"We were working in unison against the demon realm with creatures from other conquered realms; the merfolk, snake-kin, fairy folk, elves, beastkin and the undead. Even a handful of demon kind were sympathetic to our cause and fought alongside us. Our goal was to reclaim our homelands from the ever expanding Demon Empire, nothing more. Due to an unforeseen turn of events, the demons were able to push our forces to the brink of collapse."

"We were betrayed," Lorelai said bitterly, gripping her fork tightly in her pale blue hand.

Arvyn looked to Earwyn, his cornflower eyes closed.

"We had been backed into a corner by our enemy, and there was very little chance of success." His eyes steadily met the prince's. "To rebel against the Demon King is to sign your own death warrant. All laws of war are tossed aside when the Demon Emperor feels he has been slighted. One of the demons who had supported us betrayed us, presumably in the hope of redeeming their name. Our leaders were attacked, tortured and imprisoned in the Temple of Nour. We had no choice but to retreat into the domain that Princess Zuma had created for our protection. Shortly after we arrived here, the enchantment cast on the entrance to our domain, the painting that you travelled through, was altered by a demon, blocking us off from the outside world."

"Only when Princess Zuma is released will we be free once more," Lorelai said proudly, a subtle smile on her round lips.

"I believe that that is why you have journeyed here, is it not? Only humans with an intense desire for power are able to travel here."

The prince inclined his head, pulling out a small leather-bound notebook that he had been carrying in his breast pocket. He quickly flicked through the pages filled with notes on mythical creatures and legends, the corners bent slightly from use. He landed on a page showing a hastily sketched image of the monument below Dunsberg Castle.

"As I'm aware, seven items need to be gathered, one for each of these leaders that you speak of, in order to break the seal on the Temple of Nour. Aside from that, the locations and any details of these objects are currently unknown to me; the tales from your era have long been wiped from human knowledge, so any details you can give us will be truly appreciated."

"Why should we help humans?" Lwella snapped. "They never helped us in the past."

The prince stood slowly, his golden gaze coldly fixed on her. "I do not appreciate being held accountable for the deeds of my forefathers, madam."

Earwyn held up his hand quietly, indicating for his guest to return to his seat.

"Unbeknownst to the Demon Army at the time, each of the leaders left a single magical item, either hidden in their domain or in the possession of their most trusted advisor. These advisors were tasked with protecting the objects from any with malicious intent. When all of these items are placed correctly in the Temple of Nour, the seal will break and they will be released. I do not know where or what each item is, as that knowledge would be too risky for a single person to possess should the Demon Army discover it. However, I do know that one item is hidden within a small cottage hidden in the Orville Forest."

Arvyn nodded slowly.

The gathered sirens and humans spent the rest of the evening joyously, the dark duke piquing the interest of a number of the sirens around him despite his lack of conversation. Arvyn spoke quietly with Earwyn's stoic guard, her emerald eyes lighting up as he told stories of his exploits in the jousting tournaments and hunts. His sister sat beside him, quietly eating her meal, aware of a pair of sea foam eyes watching her cautiously from the other end of the table.

"Princess Eleanora," a tall siren said as he appeared quietly beside her when the feast had been cleared away, pushing his thin spectacles up his long nose. "The sunset from this palace is most beautiful at this time of year. Would you like to see it?"

She blinked.

"She'd love to," her brother replied for her, gently nudging her forward.

As she allowed the siren to lead her towards the balcony, a small gaggle of other sirens ushered the duke to the balcony too, their flirtatious giggles filling the columned hall.

The prince offered his arm to the female guard who had escorted them to the city. Her pale pink face, having revealed little emotion since their meeting, blushed slightly as she followed him, still carrying her two-bladed spear.

Cliona followed alone, quietly leaning against the smooth sandstone wall behind her, a sad smile dancing on her thin lips as she watched them all from a distance.

Joy engulfed the balcony as the group gathered against the spiral sandstone railing, watching the peach sun set against the distant horizon, casting a pale pink shadow over the crystal blue water. Soft smudges of aquamarine, periwinkle, rose and cornflower stretched over the serene sky.

"I did not expect that I would see you here again, Lady Cliona."

Earwyn appeared beside her, carrying two goblets made of hardened white coral. She smiled, quietly taking the sweet wine he offered.

"I wasn't sure if you remembered."

A cocky smile played on the side of his lips as he glanced at her, swirling the navy liquid slowly in his hand.

"I suspected that it was you, my lady, when I sensed intruders traversing our barrier; you have a rather unique aura, after all."

Cliona sipped her wine, her eyes watching the sunset over the water.

"Do you plan to kill me then?"

"That is not my intention," he said, offering her his muscular arm.

She took it, handing her goblet to a servant as they returned to the room, quietly taking a seat at the empty driftwood table.

"I may not agree with the methods, but I know that, if she had not been entombed, then Princess Zuma would no doubt have been executed long ago." He rested his elbows on the table, his cornflower eyes watching her sharply. "Tell me truthfully. Do you intend on releasing my mistress?"

Her gaze shifted to Prince Arvyn, his back facing her. She held her head high, her dark red eyes swirling in the candlelight as she turned to look directly at the siren in front of her.

"I plan to reclaim what is ours by right, Earwyn. I am tired of slinking in the shadows."

He nodded, sitting back in his seat.

"Then, provided that you return Princess Zuma to her rightful place, the sirens will fight with you once more. You shall have the full aid of our sorcerers, when war inevitably comes."

She inclined her head, clenching her fist over her heart in an ancient salute that she had not done in nearly three hundred years.

"I am truly grateful, General Earwyn."

He chuckled, closing his eyes as some of his guests began to filter back into the hall. "General. How much I miss that title."

The pair sat, quietly drinking their wine whilst lost in their own thoughts, listening to the cheerful chatter of the humans and sirens outside.

"Lord Earwyn," the prince said when he finally returned, bowing slightly before him. "I offer my sincerest thanks for your hospitality this evening. I am truly grateful for your help on this quest."

"The pleasure is mine. I have had rather a nice evening reminiscing about my old life with your dear friend Cliona here." The prince glanced at the girl, her eyes gently closed. "Besides, provided that Princess Zuma is released, then I am more than willing to be of use."

"I am most grateful," the prince replied, sipping once more from the unusual beverage before him. "To that end, any information that you could provide on that subject would be most appreciated. For instance, where the artefact belonging to Princess Zuma is hidden."

Earwyn's brow creased briefly, a smile still on his handsome face as he pushed himself from his seat.

"There is no need to rush, descendant of Oleksander. Perhaps I may interest you in a visit to Her Highness's portrait gallery first?"

Arvyn scowled at the siren, his own fists clenched at his sides.

Just as the prince went to speak, his sister laid her hand gently on his arm, a serene smile decorating her comely face.

"Arvyn, Mother would have loved to see this place."

The prince sighed. "All right. But be quick."

Earwyn smiled, offering his arm to the young princess as he led her into a large room filled with elaborate oil paintings.

Arvyn ground his teeth as he followed after the siren, his fingers twitching impatiently.

Each painting was expertly crafted, the cool paints seeming to shimmer in the light of the magical candles lining the wall.

As they walked around the room, listening to the soft music playing through the open doors, Leonie's eye was caught by a painting much smaller than the rest, the paint glimmering as though it had still not dried. Unlike the ethereal sealife depicted in the other art, this showed a carefully painted yew tree, bent over a small grey tombstone. A woman, naked but for a thin white cloak draped over her slender shoulders, knelt before the well cared for stone, her hands cupping her face.

Seeing her stop before the small painting, Earwyn smiled, leaning close beside her, his voice low.

"You have a keen eye."

"It is beautiful," Leonie replied, raising her hand to her religious pendant. "But, she seems lonely."

"The creatures you now call demons are all separate races, all from different realms that the demon race has conquered and assimilated into their empire. Our home world was called Kovira and was home to four different races, or tribes if you will, each one created by the Mother to keep the world in balance. First, came the sirens, children of the water. Next were the faintiers, children of the fiery mountains. Then were the ash'tai, children of the sky lands. Finally were the dryads, children of the forests. We lived in harmony, the four queens ruling our people together. But, when the Demon Army came, we were laughably ill prepared."

Leonie glanced at his face, a dark shadow shrouding his cornflower eyes.

"First fell the faintiers, their people almost entirely annihilated but for those visiting the other tribes. Having never known war, they were decimated in a single night. Next came the ash'tai, their measly defences pitiful against the might of the empire. Then came the dryads, many of whom sacrificed their own lives so that their younger brothers and sisters could retreat into the ancient grove of the Mother and enter hibernation to wait out the invaders. And finally they came for the sirens. Those of us who were not slaughtered were taken as tribute for the Emperor."

He turned a sad smile to the young princess.

"They say that the Mother wept tears of toxic blood when her four chosen daughters were slaughtered in her shrines, cursing our homelands to be polluted until the Demon Emperor is held accountable for his sins."

Leonie looked sadly at the painting again, her hand reaching out to the woman mourning.

As she did so, the painted woman stood, her flowing black hair fluttering in a gentle breeze as she disappeared into the tree line.

Leonie looked over at Earwyn, his eyes watching her carefully.

"If the Mother has called to you, descendant of Oleksander, then you must follow."

"Leonie," Arvyn said firmly, laying his hand on her shoulder as he glared at the siren. "It's dangerous. Let me."

She shook her head, pushing away her older brother's hand. "Let me help, Arvyn. Like he says, I am as qualified as you for this task."

Arvyn clenched his fist, saying nothing as she turned to Earwyn.

"What do I need to do?"

Earwyn smiled.

"Within this painting are the four sacred shards of the Mother which gave life to the sirens and our kin. Return them to the gravestone and you will be rewarded with Princess Zuma's treasure."

Leonie glanced at her brother, his unease clear on his golden face as she nodded.

"I won't be long," she replied, lifting her long skirts carefully as she stepped into the picture frame.

A cold mist enveloped her as her feet met the muddy ground. The air was deathly still, the leaves of the yew tree hanging limply from the twisted branches. As she looked around, she wrapped her arms tightly around her shoulders, goosebumps spreading over her delicate skin.

She walked quickly to the tombstone, her hand reaching out to the grey stone, running her fingers over the moss covered tablet. As she pulled at the damp green surface, she uncovered a small eight pointed star. The four small tips held tiny silver teardrops, each one twinkling like starlight. But, the larger four circular indents were empty, knife marks scarring the surface within.

Leonie looked around carefully, noticing an unlit campfire behind the gravestone. She squatted in front of it, holding her skirts close to her legs as her neatly trimmed fingers rooted through the black ash. She brushed against a warm circle, her fingers pulling it from the soot and carefully brushing at the smooth surface. As she rotated it in her hand, she realised that it was a small ruby.

She went back to the tombstone, gently pushing the gemstone into one of the empty indents.

Sure enough, as she did so the stone began to glow, and the air itself seemed to grow warmer, her arms no longer trembling from the cold.

She stood, looking around once more.

A small brook trickled over the cracked ground to the left of the gravestone, the water so gentle that it hardly made a sound. As she squatted along its bank, she noticed a pale blue pebble glinting under the surface.

She smiled, taking the pale sapphire to the tombstone.

But this time, when she tried to press the gemstone into the stone, she was not greeted with a soothing glow.

Instead, thunder echoed over her head, heavy rain suddenly pouring over her.

She gritted her teeth, removing the gemstone.

"There must be an order," she muttered, carefully putting the sapphire into her pouch.

Her eyes landed on the old yew tree. Aside from the darkness threatening to engulf this small area, the tree was all she could see. So, she carefully knelt at the base, her hands fumbling around the cracked roots and fallen leaves. After a while, her fingers brushed against another smooth circle, revealing a small piece of jade.

She placed it in her pouch with the other gem, standing slowly.

It was then that she noticed a small hollow in the tree above her head. She leant against the old tree, the rough bark scratching against her smooth skin as she reached blindly into the hollow. As her hand rummaged through the darkness, she felt her fingers graze over a soft nest of feathers and twigs. Reaching further in, her balance unsteady, she brushed over four spheres, each one slightly rougher than the gems she had already discovered. Finally, she felt the familiar smooth surface of a gemstone, pulling out a dark blue piece of sodolite before heading back to the stone tablet.

She tucked her skirts carefully around her legs as she sat in front of the stone, laying the three precious gems in front of her.

"Let's think," she said quietly. "These must represent the four races that he mentioned. The green jade is probably the dryads of the forest, and the red ruby is definitely the faintiers of the fiery mountains. But, which is the sirens and which is the sky people?"

She looked down at the gems, her hand hovering over them each in turn.

"Maybe, it's the order that they were created, but then the ruby shouldn't have been first; the sirens were. So, maybe the order that they were defeated? Then, next should be the sky people, so let's try the blue stone I found in the tree," she said quietly, selecting the sodolite.

As she pushed the dark gemstone into the stone, it began to glow, a gentle breeze dancing through the stagnant air.

She smiled, reaching for the jade next.

As she pushed the green gem into the stone, the scent of roses and wet grass surrounded her, the ground becoming soft as grass sprouted from the cracked earth.

Finally, she pushed in the pale sapphire, being greeted by the sound of the brook flowing with purpose once again.

She smiled, proud of herself.

As she stood, the darkness dispersed and she found herself once again stood beside her brother and Earwyn in the portrait gallery.

"Did you see?" Leonie asked Arvyn, clasping his hands happily.

He shook his head, squeezing her hands tightly. "I'm glad you're all right."

A broad smile spread across Earwyn's square face as he let out a long, relieved sigh. "As a symbol of my thanks, allow me to offer you Princess Zuma's, precious treasure, my lady."

He raised his hand, chanting in an ancient language that even the oldest sirens could not understand, for it was the tongue of an ancient dark magic, forbidden long before their births. A small pink whirlpool formed around his hand, emitting a bright light that caused those gathered to blink. As the light faded, the magical water began to dissipate, leaving behind a large pelican's foot shell in his hand.

"As the keeper of Princess Zuma's trusted treasure, I grant it to you, Princess Eleanora, descendant of Oleksander."

He smiled, turning the white and coral shell over in his hand.

"The Siren Princess is a great sorceress, renowned for her charm and poise. She imbued this shell with a special enchantment that allowed the user to speak to another person thousands of miles away. It was her most prized possession." He turned his cornflower gaze on her, his eyes firm. "I am entrusting it to you shall see that this is returned safely to my mistress."

Leonie took the item graciously, clutching it tightly in her pale hands.

"Thank you, Lord Earwyn. I will take great care of it for you."

Chapter 9

"Will you do nothing, Your Majesty?"

Arvyn slammed his fist on the king's sturdy dark oak desk, the abrupt movement disturbing the large pile of untouched paperwork in the corner.

Having returned to the treasure room in the early hours of the morning, the young prince was suffering from a lack of sleep, bags decorating his eyes. His patience was never very good whenever it came to his father, but today had been worse than usual.

His eldest brother, Oleksander, stood unmoving beside the king's chair, his arms regally clasped behind his back. He wore his favourite black and gold tunic that was embroidered in crimson poppies, the national flower of his new wife's homeland. His golden hair was slicked back neatly, allowing his golden eyes to meticulously observe his youngest brother. If it were not the slight twitch of his forehead, no one would notice the displeasure of the stoic heir to the throne as he watched his brother once again argue with their royal father.

Duke Wynford, Duke Orville and Marquis Stewart mimicked the first prince's resolve, maintaining their statuesque positions at the side of the stuffy office as the advisors and guards to the three princes. Daryl clenched his jaw, having expected this as soon as his youngest nephew insisted on inspecting the north.

Cain, the Second Prince, in contrast, fidgeted nervously with the teacup in his hands. He pushed his thin black glasses up his hooked nose quietly, his golden eyes flicking between his red faced father and his tense younger brother, the still air crackling between them.

It was not uncommon for these two members of the royal family to argue; it was common knowledge to most people within the palace to avoid both parties if possible after they met.

"Your Majesty, we are losing the war in the east. Soon, we will be conquered and assimilated into the Glerian Empire. How can you still refuse to send reinforcements?"

"Watch your tongue, boy," the king spat, his golden eyes dark.

He scowled at his youngest son, his knuckles going white as he clutched the finely carved arms of his chair.

The boy in front of him was the spitting image of his own father, even down to the fire in his stubborn gaze. And yet, he had always shared his late mother's love of myths and legends. Had he put as much effort into his swordsmanship as his two elder brothers, then King Oleksander was certain that his youngest son would have been the strongest knight on the continent by now. Indeed, when Rochelle had passed away and her brother had returned from the frontlines for the first time, he was certain that his son would have lived up to his potential.

He ground his teeth, focusing his anger on the young man.

It was no secret that the Glerian Empire in the east had set its sights on the much smaller nation of Vyst. With the very recent fall of the nation of Fleris, Vyst no longer had a safety net between them and the imperial enemy, and it was only a matter of time before war would formally be declared. Even with the Glerian envoy requesting Leonie as the Emperor's fifteenth wife, the king knew that it was just a formality.

The tide of war was brewing.

He slammed his jewelled hand on the desk once again, dislodging yet more of the endless documents waiting for his attention.

"You will watch your tongue, boy," the king roared.

Unhindered, the prince continued, his voice raising as he leant over the desk to stare straight at his father, the thunderous air crackling between them.

"Father, look what happened to Fortorin. If the Empire arrives then we will be executed, our people slaughtered and your head paraded on a spike in the imperial capital. At best, Leonie will be locked in the Emperor's harem as a slave."

"Arvyn," his second brother chided nervously as the eldest watched on silently.

A loud slap echoed around the room.

The study fell to silence, all eyes on the king.

His jaw clenched, his broad hand still raised in the air beside his youngest son's cheek as the imposing man leant over the busy table. The vein on his broad forehead pulsed, his face red.

"Your task was to inspect the northern defences, not go gallivanting off after fairy tales. How dare you lecture me on the safety of this nation, when you cannot even face the reality?"

"Your Majesty, I implore you," Arvyn replied, his golden eyes defiant against the redness of his tanned cheek as he gritted his teeth. "Allow me to find these artefacts. Let me find a way to even the odds."

"Insolent whelp," the king roared, pushing himself from his grand red chair so that he towered over the young man before him. "You know nothing of war. Go back to your books like the disgrace that you are."

Arvyn clenched his fists, preparing to open his mouth once more.

"If I may interject, Your Majesty," the Crown Prince said, moving towards his youngest brother with measured steps. "I see no problem in humouring Arvyn."

The king turned his furious gaze onto his beloved heir.

The eldest prince met his father evenly, his face seemingly devoid of any form of emotion as he stopped beside his brother's shoulder, his head held high.

"As it stands, Your Majesty, our military has been dwindling due to constant conflicts with the nomads in the eastern mountains. Even if we were to ignore the number of men that the Empire has gained in their recent conquests, their own military numbers are at least fifty-thousand, whilst ours is thirty-five thousand. Calling for conscription will hardly help against such a difference in trained numbers, and weapons."

The king sat back in his seat, gesturing for Oleksander to continue.

Oleksander nodded, his eyes ordering his younger brother to return to his seat. Arvyn did as he was bid, grinding his teeth just like his father.

"The church suggests that we increase our prayers and donations to God, to beg for His blessing in this time of crisis. Whilst I will indeed continue to pray, Your Majesty, I suggest instead that we use our finances to hire mercenaries from Burhou and Lordia, and to ensure that all men of fighting age are being trained to wield a weapon."

The king narrowed his gaze on the First Prince.

"Mercenaries are easily bought; the Empire will be able to buy them from us."

The prince inclined his head. "That is true, Your Majesty. Which is why I suggest that we allow Arvyn a little time to hunt for this legendary weapon. We are in a dire situation; we should keep all of our options open."

The king rubbed angrily at his temples, his brow creased.

"I will not grant any military units for this wild ghost hunt."

"Of course, Your Majesty. May I suggest that Duke Wynford select no more than ten men to accompany himself and the prince on this mission? That way, other key figures in the military can focus on training the troops."

The king returned to his seat, his golden scowl still set on his youngest son.

"Very well," the king announced, waving his jewelled hand with a sigh. "I shall give you three months to locate this mythical weapon. If, after that time, your search has not been fruitful, then you and those loyal to you will be exiled from this nation."

"A wise decision, Your Majesty," Oleksander replied, bowing low to his father. "Now, may we return to the matters of state, Your Majesty?"

The king waved his hand, looking back at the documents on his desk as he dismissed his two youngest sons and their bodyguards.

Oleksander nodded his golden head towards the door at his younger brothers, silently retaking his place behind his father, their attention once more on the eternal pile of documents.

"Are you mad?" Arvyn turned to face Cain, his molten eyes full of rage as the door clicked shut between them. "You know that he doesn't give a damn about the eastern border and the Empire. That's something that Oleksander will have to deal with; he has no interest in the war whatsoever."

"Our people are in danger. How can you sit back and let that happen?"

"I'm not," his older brother sighed, massaging his temples. "I am no match for Oleksander's strategy and sword. I trust him wholeheartedly, and you should too."

Arvyn turned on his heel, his fists clenched tightly at his side as he strode down the corridor.

Daryl bowed to the Second Prince and Duke Orville before swiftly marching after his youngest nephew.

One look at the incoming prince sent the innocent courtiers ducking out the way as they caught sight of his unwelcoming gaze, the duke expressionless behind him.

"Magic is a thing of fairy tales. To believe in them is to go against God."

"So I should be grateful I've not been arrested for heresy, is that what you're implying?"

"A little more tact when dealing with the king may be appropriate, Your Highness. He is as stubborn as you."

The prince gritted his teeth.

"Where's Cliona?"

The duke looked at him silently.

"Playing for your sister in the gardens I believe."

Arvyn nodded, calling for his travelling cloak from a passing maid as he diverted his angered steps towards the late queen's private gardens where his sister regularly took her tea.

Chapter 10

Leonie sipped her tea quietly, her golden eyes closed peacefully as she let the soft melody of Cliona's lyre swirl around her.

She ignored the busy chattering of the young court ladies who insisted on joining her in the secluded garden, always on the prowl to advance their family's standing in any way they could. She was used to the vultures; their fake smiles her constant companions.

She turned her head to the sound of heavy footfalls drawing near, the ladies whispering excitedly as the youngest prince came into view.

"Leave us," Arvyn announced crisply, his low voice booming over the peaceful garden as he stopped behind his sister's chair.

The gathered young ladies curtsied politely to the handsome prince, a number of them flashing charming smiles in his direction as they scuttled away.

Cliona stood from her perch on the edge of the limestone fountain, her flowing white skirt rippling in the late afternoon breeze. But, the duke appeared beside her, shaking his head subtly as the prince took a seat opposite his younger sister.

"What's wrong?" Leonie laid her delicate teacup on the wrought iron table in front of her gently, gesturing to her maid to bring a cup for her brother and uncle. "Did you speak with His Majesty?"

"He still has no intention of developing our forces in the east," he sneered, his fist clenched on the table.

"Breathe, Arvyn," she whispered, gently resting her warm hand over his.

He let out a long breath, clenching his fist.

"Now," she smiled, sitting back in her seat. "What did His Majesty say, exactly?"

The prince remained motionless, attempting to control the prominent vein throbbing angrily on his high forehead.

She turned to the faithful duke, stood to attention beside the gentle fountain.

"This might take a while, Uncle. Please make yourself comfortable; we're family after all."

Daryl inclined his head, sitting at one of the empty seats beside the siblings.

Leonie leant forward, smiling at the duke warmly. "Arvyn doesn't seem to be able to tell me, so would you be so kind, Uncle?"

The duke sighed. "His Majesty believes the Sword of Nour to be nothing more than a legend and will not commit any men to finding the items, Your Highness."

"Well, that's not surprising, is it?" She sighed, a soft smile on her lips. "As much as I love you, Arvyn, I didn't truly believe you either until last night."

The prince turned his face away, angrily watching his late mother's favourite yellow roses swaying in the breeze.

"The Crown Prince convinced His Majesty to give Prince Arvyn three months to find the weapon, or be exiled."

She nodded slowly. "I suppose His Majesty has finally lost his patience with you, brother. I must say that you lasted much longer than I thought, though."

"If he acted like a king and defended his borders properly then we wouldn't have to deal with the Empire in the first place."

"Watch your tone, brother," she whispered, indicating to Cliona to continue playing. "You don't want anyone to misconstrue what you're saying."

"Oleksander will fair no better. He knows that the Empire is poised to invade and yet he does nothing to sway His Majesty's hand, even when he knows he is the only one he will listen to."

"Empires will always look to expanding their boundaries," Cliona said softly, her fingers brushing over the lyre strings gently, her crimson eyes meeting the prince's. "That is why the Demon War happened in the first place, and in my experience history has a habit of repeating itself, in one form or another."

"I will not let His Majesty's disinterest destroy this kingdom," he shouted, slamming his fist on the table again.

The princess took a sharp breath in through her nose, attempting to retain her composure.

"Three months is not a long enough time to gather six more items. More so when we have no knowledge as to their locations."

The prince threw back his head at Daryl's words.

"We have one item, at least," Leonie sighed, stroking the large seashell in front of her, not wanting it out of her sight. "So, it must be possible to find them. You must have faith, brother, that God wants you to find the items."

Cliona snorted softly, her long fingers stuttering ever so slightly at the princess's words.

The princess herself did not seem to notice, preoccupied with soothing her brother, but the duke stared at the silver haired woman carefully.

"In the domain of the sirens," Daryl said steadily, addressing Cliona, "you seemed rather well acquainted with Lord Earwyn."

The two siblings blinked, their attention brought to the pale woman silently plucking at her instrument.

"To the extent," the duke continued, his hand resting nonchalantly on the hilt of his sword, "that one would think you knew him personally."

Cliona sighed, closing her crimson eyes.

"You are very perceptive, sir."

The prince stood, his golden gaze narrowed.

"The knowledge of the war between the Demon Army and United Front was purged from the memories of all mortals many centuries ago, at the instruction of the man that you know as Oleksander I. But, my knowledge was left in place and I was locked within the confines of Dunsberg Castle."

"Why?"

She turned her bloody eyes on the prince bitterly.

"History is written by the victor. The Demon Empire won the war, and so sought to obliterate all memory of those who opposed them. A fate, I fear, humanity is repeating through this empire threatening your lands now. Although, on a much smaller scale."

Leonie gasped, clutching the blazing sun pendant around her neck.

"You were alive when King Oleksander reigned?"

Cliona nodded sadly, her fingers flagging.

"How dare you. This is all a farce; you've been manipulating us for your own ends!" The prince hissed at her, ignoring his sister's pleading eyes.

Cliona raised her head, the music frozen in the air as her frail body closed the gap between them in an instant. Her pale face, so serene before now, had turned sour, her square jaw clenched as her dark red eyes seemed to glow, resembling dried blood.

"Believe what you want of me and my past. But know this; the longer you dally here, the closer the empire comes to wiping your family name from this earth and plunging your kingdom into darkness. It was you who sought my knowledge. You have no right to question it now."

"Calm down, Your Highness," the duke said, stretching his strong armoured arm in front of the prince's torso, his mercury eyes still narrowed on the woman. "I do not agree with her methods, but I believe that she is right. The safety of the people is paramount and we cannot delay finding the weapon that will protect them."

"Will it? Will it protect them? Or have you lied about that too?"

Cliona maintained the prince's golden stare. "Whilst our goals are aligned, I am not your enemy."

The prince turned on his heel, striding towards the castle gatehouse.

"We ride for the Orville Forest at dawn."

Chapter 11

It had been five days since the prince had left the capital. He had begun to grow increasingly more restless as he led his small entourage through the dense Orville Forest, led by a local woodcutter they had encountered in the small town of Thornbury. Accompanied by his trusted bodyguard and Cliona, he was determined to complete his task before his deadline.

To Arvyn's dismay, Leonie had also tried to accompany them, disguising herself as a soldier in her attempt to join in her brother's quest. But, unfortunately for her, the duke was much too astute, and foiled her plan for adventure early on. She had been left with a single guard in Thornbury two days prior, with the express orders to return to the capital after the storm relented.

The twisted chestnut trunks moaned as eight horses cantered under their dense canopy, each carrying a heavily armoured figure, their features obscured by a dark cloak and no livery visible. The harsh scent of fresh rainfall filled the air as the raindrops landed on the ruddy undergrowth, muddy puddles littering the well-trodden paths through the south of the ancient woodland.

"Your Highness!" Their guide cried over the wind screaming in his wrinkled face. "We must turn back and take shelter before the storm gets worse!"

The prince blinked against the harsh icy rain, ignoring the pleas of the woodsman from Thornbury. His arms shook relentlessly, although whether from adrenaline or the cold, Arvyn couldn't tell any more.

Daryl gritted his teeth, watching his nephew's back silently.

Since leaving the castle, the prince had hardly spoken to anyone, except to bark orders. Daryl was more than used to the young man's rage filled outbursts, having served him for over a decade. Whilst being known as the most charming and bright of the king's sons, he had, unfortunately, inherited his father's infamous temper.

But never had the prince retained his rage five days after an argument with the king, no matter how great.

"I have to agree, Your Highness," the duke shouted, urging his black mare alongside the prince.

"I don't have time to stop," Arvyn roared, his weight shifting forward in his rain soaked saddle, willing his mount forward.

The duke grunted as the young man he was sworn to protect pulled away, the path narrowing once more. He gently patted his mare's sweat soaked neck, aware that her pace had begun to falter after being ridden sohard for the past two days as they tried to outride the storm.

A loud crack echoed through the dense forest, accompanied by a bright flash of light.

"Prince Arvyn!"

The prince's eyes widened as his loyal mount reared onto her hind legs, her nostrils flaring wildly as a giant sycamore came crashing down a few strides in front of them, the crisp leaves rustling madly.

Arvyn stroked her neck gently, his own heartbeat pounding in his chest. Pulling his hand away, he finally noticed the thick foam that had been covering her white fur for the past few hours, now staining his black leather gloves.

His body crumpled forward against her strong neck, the bitter taste of bile rising in his throat as the exhaustion finally engulfed him.

"I saw a cave a little way back," Daryl shouted over the rain, riding close beside the prince's fretting animal, his own mount dancing as her long black ears flickered.

The prince nodded slowly as he noticed the drenched downtrodden faces of his six loyal guards, each one obediently following his orders without a single complaint.

"It is a fool's errand," he whispered, grabbing the mare's neck as he sat himself back in the hard saddle.

The duke laid his hand on the prince's shoulder, his tone softening. "It is better to rest now to regain our strength, rather than be forced to give up later. There is no shame in waiting."

Arvyn nodded, turning his skittish horse to follow the duke. Although he avoided the gaze of his loyal guards, his golden eyes landed on Cliona as he walked past her. Her eyes were closed, the rain dripping down her long slender nose as she held her face up to the sky. Her pink lips were slightly parted as she allowed the icy air to race through her heaving lungs.

His mare followed the duke's mount slowly, her pale legs splattered with thick, clay-like mud.

The group trudged along the dirt path as it ran alongside the river, the water close to overflowing thanks to the torrential rain pelting on the usually serene surface.

It wasn't long before a cave became visible on the other side of the river. The small crack in the rocky landform was normally obscured from view by an ancient oak, but now the freshly felled tree had revealed the dark space.

The duke urged his mount to the edge of the river bank, her large feet sliding in the loose mud. He dismounted, raising the long black reins over her head. As he inspected the river, he noticed that the fast flowing water was rather shallow. But, upon cautiously taking a single step into the stream, the pebbled ground trembled under his black boot.

"How does it look?"

Daryl turned back to the prince, shaking his head slightly.

"There is a crossing, Your Highness," the old woodsman grumbled, wrapping his grey cloak tightly around him as his shoulders quivered. "But, it's about half an hour back that way."

"We'll die of a chill before then," one of the older guards grumbled, trying to calm his own fretting mount.

The prince sighed, pulling his mare sharply in the mouth. "The longer we delay, the more likely that will happen. Let's head to that crossing."

The horses continued their trudge through the forest, the undergrowth becoming thicker and more tangled as they went, the assailing rain merciless.

Before long, a narrow bridge appeared before them, crossing the tumultuous river. A flint wall railing held rotting wooden slats in place, the wind whistling down the narrow alleyway it created.

Arvyn looked upwards, the overcast sky turning to night through the thick canopy.

He dismounted, carefully testing the integrity of the moss covered planks.

"Allow me, Your Highness," the duke said, appearing beside him.

The prince nodded as Daryl passed his mare's reins to one the guards.

He gently tapped along the floor with his foot, his strong arms holding onto the uneven flint railing as he went. The mossy timbers beneath his black boots were slippery in the harsh rainfall, the stones cold on his hands even through the black gloves. The smell of damp wood and moss mingled with the mud and rain, trying to distract him as he steadily made his way over the creaking boards. The wood had degraded too much in a few areas, and the brave duke feared that he would fall into the rocky river below.

But, luck was on his side and he made it across.

Arvyn nodded to him, the visibility growing worse by the minute as he urged his companions to lead their horses across on foot, one at a time.

Satisfied, the prince crossed last, leading his shattered grey mare.

The duke patted him firmly on the shoulder as the guards lit three torches between them.

They made their way carefully up a narrow dirt track, their footing obscured by the ferns and bracken growing over the path. It had clearly once been well used, but now the only traffic was the animals inhabiting the dismal forest.

The prince pulled back the ivy and bramble curtain over the entrance, peering into the empty cave, his eyes straining in the dark despite the torchlight.

Water dripped along the stalactites, the delicate clear drops rippling in the puddles on the smooth limestone floor, the rhythmic sound echoing over the still cave.

"It looks safe enough, and better than out here," the duke said beside him, handing the reins of his mare to one of the guards as he stepped over the threshold.

Arvyn nodded, his body raked with aches as his adrenaline washed away.

"Remove your wet clothing, Your Highness, before you catch a chill."

The prince did as he was bid, tossing aside his drenched cloak and crimson doublet.

Daryl turned to his five men.

The guards began to remove their heavy iron chestplates and black leather trousers, each one grateful for the thin black cotton underlayer beneath stopping the hide from sticking to their cold legs.

"Nairne, see to the horses. Wilfred and Cuthbert get a couple of fires going and start cooking. Edgar, I want you to check how deep this cave goes."

The prince sighed, his shoulders slumping as the stress and exhaustion raced over his body. He watched as Cliona took a seat on a relatively flat topped rock, her hands wringing the water from her black cloak. In the faint orange glow of the torch, her silver hair looked almost translucent as it tumbled around her pale face, like an expertly crafted spider's web.

She had protested at the prince's request that she change from her flowing white gown into a pair of black breeches and crimson shirt that matched the vague uniform of his soldiers, just as he and the duke had done so as not to draw attention to themselves. But now she was grateful, knowing that the cotton of the uniform would dry quicker than the silk she had always preferred.

"I'm sorry," Arvyn whispered, taking a seat on the rock beside her.

"Actually, I thoroughly enjoyed our ride," she smiled, beginning to plait her wet silvery hair. "I have always loved the rain."

"I meant for snapping at you. I know that you will have your reasons for not telling me your past, and I am in no position to refuse your deal."

She turned her face away, gazing out of the cave entrance.

"Everyone has their secrets. And, it is best that you do not know mine."

He took a deep breath, clenching his jaw as he refrained from probing further.

Chapter 12

The next morning, the rain was still hammering down outside the dank cave, the air filled with the scent of wet soil and leaves.

Arvyn stretched his shoulders, enjoying being free from his cold metal armour for a little while longer. They had decided to give the horses a little longer to rest, until the rain let up, before hastening their pace once again.

But the prince was much too anxious to stay inside the dark cave and had instead started to wander along the edge of the rocks that the dark grotto was carved into. One of the knights named Edgar and their local guide had accompanied him, at his uncle's insistence.

It was not long before his rocky path clinging to the uneven crag began to steeply incline, and so he ran his hand casually along the moss covered wall beside him, his steps steady along the slippery stones. He cast glances over the hill below him as his route led him further into the canopy level of the forest, the path beginning to narrow.

"Forgive me, Your Highness, but I fear we should return to Duke Wynford soon."

He glanced at Edgar, the seasoned knight's face showing no sign of emotion.

"I want to see the view from the top," Arvyn replied firmly, continuing his trudge up the craggy path.

The knight said nothing, although the guide walking between himself and the prince began muttering a prayer as his hands visibly trembled.

"Stop looking down," Edgar said curtly, his hand nudging the man's back as his steps faltered. "Look at the wall or His Highness's boots instead."

"I'm not being paid enough for this," the woodsman mumbled, doing as the knight ordered.

Arvyn ignored them as he halted, his forehead creasing as he realised his fingers had been sliding over a more subtly uneven surface on the wall.

He turned to the wall beside him, his hand rubbing away at the mossy blanket protecting the grey stone beneath.

Just as he had thought, hidden beneath the moist green curtain were strange symbols carved into the stone. As he pulled the blanket further from the cold wall, it revealed a large picture etched into the wall, runic symbols that he now knew as demonic text chiselled around it.

"Fetch Cliona and my uncle; I need her to translate this," the prince ordered, continuing to pull back the moss to see the whole image.

Edgar inclined his head, retreating carefully back towards the base of the crag.

The woodsman leant nervously against the uneven wall behind him, his eyes squeezed shut as he muttered prayer after prayer, tightly clutching a wooden blazing sun in his hand.

After a while, Arvyn stepped as far back from the wall as he could, satisfied that he had revealed the secret carving.

Although much of the cliff they had ascended along had been smoothed down by the harsh weather of the north, this small patch was untouched by the elements. The carefully carved lines were crisp, the foreign letters clearly distinguishable.

In the centre of the cleared space was carved a very unique giant tree that seemed to be made up of three smaller trees entwined together. Although the branches to the left and right were in full bloom as they stretched outward, the middle was barren. A large slash cut through the heart of this carefully twisted tree trunk. Below the intricately knotted roots of the ancient tree was growing a single flower.

It was longer than Arvyn expected before Edgar returned with the pale woman. The knight offered her a hand as they scrambled up the moss-covered rocks towards the prince, taking it steady as the rain continued to beat down on them.

Arvyn scowled, his patience running thin as she stopped beside him.

"I need you to read this," he said curtly, directing her attention to the engraving before them.

She sighed, kneeling on the wet stone to get a closer look, her fingers gently running over the damp surface, pushing away bits of moss that obscured the short passage.

"Each night they appear, bringing lost loved ones near. They are neither heard nor felt, and in the skies they have long dwelt. Where one has fallen we shall reside, within the lightning blessed tree with pride."

The prince furrowed his brow, repeating her words slowly. "What on earth does that mean?"

Cliona stood, stretching her arms up to the rain above her, relishing the gentle droplets dancing over her skin.

"Well, according to the riddle and the images, Your Highness, I believe that we need to find a tree that was once struck by lightning," Edgar said slowly.

"There must be dozens of trees like that in this forest," Arvyn grumbled, running his black gloved hand through his soaked golden hair.

"It cannot be too far away, Your Highness," Daryl replied. "Shall I have the men start their search?"

"What of the other part? 'Where one has fallen'. Where what has fallen?"

The four men pondered for a moment, each one muttering quietly.

"Rain or snow, perhaps? Or leaves? We are in a forest," Edgar muttered.

Cliona sighed, stretching her hands up to the grey sky above her. "Stars."

The prince looked at her, quizzical at first then realisation dawning on his golden face.

"Well done," he said. "But, how do we know where a star has fallen?"

"There's a well not too far from here, Your Highness," the old guide said nervously. "A local legend says that a maiden fell from the stars a long time ago and landed there. Her sisters wept, and their tears created a wishing well that will bless any who drink from its waters. It's just an old story, though, Your Highness."

Arvyn glanced at his uncle before nodding, going to clamber down the rocks back to the cave entrance.

"Lead the way," he said firmly, not checking that the guide was following his descent.

The old duke sighed, gesturing to the man to follow the prince, Edgar and Cliona close behind.

The tired guide led the four of them back over the bridge that they had crossed the evening before, easier now that they were on foot. Despite the now slowing rainfall, the forest air was eerily still, disturbed only by their footsteps and the rhythmic drip of the raindrops landing on the river beside them.

It did not take long before they reached the little wishing well, pale pink daphnes growing in abundance around the stone brick structure. Although the slate roof tried its best to protect the old wooden beams, it was clear that they had been replaced many times over the years, and was once again due fresh timber. A long hemp rope dangled down into the well, attached to a wooden handle along one of the beams.

"Let's take some water," Arvyn said, his eyes scanning the tree line for an oak similar to the depiction.

Edgar slowly turned the winch, pulling the small wooden bucket back to the surface. Inside was a beautiful clear pool of water that seemed to sparkle in the dim sunlight. Daryl filled his empty flask with the water, nodding to the prince.

The small group explored the surrounding area carefully, their boots crunching over the fallen twigs and leaves littering the undisturbed forest floor.

Just as the carving in the crags has depicted, before them stood a trio of oak trees entwined together to create an imposing twisted tree. The branches to either side were heavily burdened with brilliant green leaves and acorns, despite the winter. But, the middle had been stunted by a strike of lightning, the blackened bark of the central trunk a stark contrast to its sister trees.

"This is it," the prince said, kneeling at the base of the tree beside the twisted roots that covered the concealed entrance.

Daryl passed him the small bucket of water from the well, staying close by his nephew's side.

As the prince dripped the glittering liquid over the knotted roots, they began to recede, revealing a small declining passageway, just wide enough for each of them to fit through.

"I'm not going down there," the guide said, shaking his head nervously.

"Return to the cave and tell the others where we have gone. Should you choose this time to desert, know that I will not be lenient on you, or your family."

The frightened woodsman's breath quickened as he met the cold glare of the prince before scampering back down the road.

"I'll go first, Your Highness," Edgar said, getting onto his knees and holding the torch ahead of him as he squeezed sideways through a narrow gap, slightly scuffing his black leather boots as he went.

The prince sighed, holding his breath as he did the same, followed closely by the duke. Cliona rolled her eyes silently, sliding through the gap deftly without crawling on her knees like her male companions.

The narrow tunnel continued for what felt like an eternity, and at one point the prince truly started to fear that his body would be stuck and lost to the cave forever. But, he followed the dim orange glow, steadying his breathing in time with the musical drips.

As the tunnel began to broaden, he brushed down the dust and cobwebs from his black trousers.

His gaze was caught by the unusual floor beneath his boots; instead of the smooth limestone that he had expected, he was greeted by a mossy blanket growing over the stone. Besides that, the prince realised that his eyes were no longer straining to see, but that it seemed to be as bright as day.

He raised his head slowly, his mouth slightly agape.

Before him stretched a small grove of hawthorn trees, the branches littered with tiny ivory flowers that filled the hidden grove with a delicate floral aroma. The soft mossy blanket soon merged into lush grass that reached to the prince's ankles. A handful of birds chirped in a tall apple tree, their tiny bodies hidden by the ripe, juicy vermillion fruit.

A narrow brook flowed past them from a small waterfall atop a ten foot limestone cliff sporting a giant oak tree, the crystal clear water evaporating into mist as it hit the cave wall they had just come through. Upon closer inspection, the stone from which it fell was not a smooth rocky outcropping of the cave, but instead a run-down building, the gnarled oak tree sprouting from the unkempt dark thatch roof.

A door stood ajar to the cottage, with what remained of the pale blue paint peeling away from the once polished wood.

Daryl drew his sword, indicating for the guard to do the same as he stepped cautiously along the cracked cobblestone path towards the derelict structure.

He carefully pushed the door open, the rusted iron hinges screaming after years of disuse.

The inside of the cottage was caked in a dusty grey film, the air thick with the stench of rot and mildew. Yet, despite its clear abandonment, the room was lit by an ethereal orb floating on the ceiling.

A large black marble table sat in the centre of the deceptively spacious room, ten chairs arranged neatly around it. The prince breathed in sharply, his eyes widening at the six figures slouched over the cold table. The figures each wore a fur cloak about their shoulders, their facial features and clothes obscured by their long hair, each one a slightly different shade of brown. Before them was laid an extravagant feast, the skeletal remains of a suckling pig on a silver platter in the centre.

The walls were lined with dark oak bookshelves, reaching from the silver birch floorboards and beyond the dark oak beams that supported the vaulted birch ceiling.

"These people are breathing," Edgar whispered, holding his dagger in front of one figure's nose.

He looked to the duke with concern.

"It'll be a sleeping curse," Cliona said quietly. "Although, I've never actually seen someone under one before."

"And how would we wake them?"

The prince ignored the incredulous look of the guard as he pulled a heavy leather-bound book from the shelf, gently blowing away the thick layer of dust on the cover. He flicked through the pages, watching the strange runic letters on the crisp pages as they passed before his eyes.

"I don't know," Cliona said as she shook her head, leaning against the door frame, her feet not daring to cross the threshold. The old wood was covered in small carvings of flowers, bringing a soft smile to her face.

Her eyes narrowed as they focused on a series of runes etched hastily into the wood, a very faint pale blue glow emanating from them.

"*Look at the world with wonder and peace shall fill your days.*"

"What?"

She turned to the prince as he stood beside her and pointed to the words.

"It sounds much better in the demon tongue, I assure you. But, I believe it may be a hint on how to wake them," she said pointing at the table.

The duke nudged the foot of one of the bodies cautiously, his sword ready in his hand. The slumbering figure shifted, rolling their head so that their pale brown hair revealed their serene expression. The movement dislodged a small wooden orb from their grey hand, the item rolling along the uneven floorboards.

As he watched it, the guard noticed a spherical notch on the ground in front of him. He knelt down slowly, sweeping away the dust. His fingers brushed over thin grooves that seemed to follow a strange pattern.

"Your Highness," he called, bringing the torch nearer to the floor for inspection. "There's an indentation here."

Arvyn picked up the wooden sphere, polishing it with his black sleeve to reveal more runic letters embossed onto the surface, the colour shifting from pale blue to silver depending on how he held it. He looked to the hole before the guard, his golden brows knitted as he knelt beside the lowly knight, pushing the sphere into the floor.

There was an audible click as the orb sunk into the pale floorboard, glowing white. Looking around the room, he noticed five more spherical dents evenly spread in a circle on the dirt covered floor, each one pulsating with a pale blue light.

"Find the five other orbs. Perhaps that will awaken our hosts."

Daryl and the guard nodded, immediately beginning to scour the room for more spherical objects.

Cliona walked to the bookshelf, her fingertip collecting dust as she scraped it along the old leather spines.

"What do you see, Cliona?"

"They're medicinal tomes, mostly. A couple about gardening and a recipe book but nothing you wouldn't expect to see in a cottage like this." Her hand stopped beside a particular book, her fingers resting on the runic title of the tome. "This is the domain of the Fair Lady Avalon, after all. From what I know, she was well versed in potions and curses, so, of course, it would make sense that she could create a sleeping curse. But, I never expected her to pull it off."

"Why not?"

"They were a taboo. Except in medical emergencies when it was crucial to restrain a patient for their own safety, dryads were not to cast sleeping spells."

The guard narrowed his eyes as he looked along the cluttered cabinets lining one of the walls. Dozens of now empty glass jars and containers watched him as he passed, their neatly written labels faded with age.

A single mirror stared at him, his reflection distorted by years of grime and use on the silver surface. It was held together by a stunning carved dark oak frame, the whittled ivy and honeysuckle gilded in silver and gold. A handful of seed pearls, emeralds and topaz sparkled on the ornate surface, out of place in this run-down building. As he looked closer in the cracked surface of the mirror, he noticed a spherical light shining at him from across the room.

He turned, his dark brow knitted as he looked for the item but could not see it.

He looked back in the mirror to find it in the same place, glinting quietly, beckoning him.

Carefully, he lifted the mirror, walking backwards with it in his hands so as to still see the object's reflection, stopping just before the spot on the ancient bookshelf where it glinted. Without looking, he carefully reached for it, using the mirror to direct his movements.

To his surprise, his fingertips grazed the cold silver metal of the orb. But, when he brought it in front of his body, there was nothing in sight.

"Your Highness, I've found another one. But, I can only see it in the mirror."

Previously the prince would have scoffed at such a statement, but now he just nodded, indicating for the soldier to place the orb into one of the nooks in the floor.

The orb glowed brightly when he placed it in the ground, pulsating with light just like the other.

Cliona walked towards the dead hearth, lifting the lid of the heavy iron cauldron hanging over the fire pit. The logs below had long burned to ash and the pot's contents rotted away. The acrid stench that had been trapped within the mouldy pot raced out as the lid was lifted, spiralling around Cliona quickly as nausea washed over her.

A glinting silver orb caught her eye within the cauldron. She covered her nose with her hand, reaching into the rotting sludge to retrieve the object.

"Here," she said, trying hard not to retch as she tossed the item to the prince.

He slotted it into the gap in the birch floorboards carefully, watching as a bright light started to be emitted from the small object.

"Wait," the guard said, his dark brow furrowed in concentration. "There are six orbs. Your Highness found the first one by touching the person at the table. We then found one by looking in the mirror and one by smelling that pot. Could it be as simple as being linked to the senses?"

"There are only five senses; sight, touch, hearing, smell and taste." The prince said, sitting heavily into one of the empty chairs around the table.

The duke walked over to a closed window at the back of the room, sliding the rusted iron bolt back on the wooden shutter, the dark blue paint peeling under his touch as the hinges yawned.

Outside sat a peaceful garden, the steady echo of the distant brook bouncing along the long vibrant green grass. Various purple and blue flowers grew alongside a small silver birch fence, little faces carved delicately into the orbs at the top of the fence posts, each one different from the next. Their almond shaped eyes all seemed to look towards the tall apple tree growing at the far end of the garden.

The large tree had been split in half in its youth, causing the trunk to divert into two separate entities. In their quest for sunlight, the saplings had initially grown away from each other, but later returned to entwine in the middle. From the window, the tree looked like a large heart, the delicate white blossoms decorating the twisted trees. A handful of vibrant crimson apples hung proudly from their branches, glinting in the light.

Daryl was overcome with desire to eat one of the apples, his mouth salivating at the thought of the crisp, succulent flesh of the fruit.

He pushed open the back door, the birch wood smooth under his touch.

The prince watched his uncle stride through the long grass from the window, his arms folded neatly over his chest.

As the duke reached the foot of the tree, his hand stretched upward towards an apple hanging from the lowest branch, plucking it from the thin twig holding it in place. He raised it to his lips, sweet, syrupy juices running down his large chin as his teeth broke through the ripe flesh.

He wiped the loose liquid with his hand, his eyes wondering upward.

A spherical object hung from a branch above him, wrapped neatly in a red cloth to blend in with the crimson apples surrounding it. As the duke pulled on the thin black string holding it in place, a heavy silver orb fell from the cloth into his hand, the markings similar to the orbs they had already discovered.

He held the item above his head as he returned to the cottage, noticing the prince watching him from the window.

"Two more," the prince muttered looking around the room.

"Let's assume our assumption is correct," the duke said as he returned, placing the orb gently into the ground. "We have found the smell, sight, touch and taste, so have hearing left."

The prince crossed his arms, his right hand massaging his temple. "But, what could the sixth be?"

"Look at the world with wonder and peace shall fill your days." Cliona smiled, rushing back towards the door. "It's a line from a song from the realm of dryads. I believe it was to do with their royal family, but I can't be certain. However, I do know that it was banned after the Demon King conquered the realm of Kovira."

She closed her eyes, clenching her fist over her heart as she lowered her head. Her melancholic melody filled the air, her exotic words washing over the three men. She was soon joined by the enchanting song of a flute, the high pitched sound echoing over the derelict cottage as three ethereal figures materialised around Cliona. Their transparent pale blue faces smiled sadly as they joined their voices in harmony with hers, each one laying their hand upon her shoulder.

As their song ended, the figures began to fade once more.

The final figure held out her hand to Cliona, nodding solemnly. As she, too, faded, she left behind a silver orb in her place.

Cliona gently slid it into the floor.

A bright light filled the room, blinding those gathered.

Arvyn lowered his hand as the light began to fade, his eyes blinking in an attempt to regain his vision.

The room was no longer decorated with a thick layer of dust, but instead pristine and well cared for. Sunlight streamed in from the open windows, the shutters freshly painted in a beautiful sky blue. A tangy aroma filled the air as the cauldron bubbled over the fireplace, the lid clattering as the steam tried to escape.

He turned his attention to the great table in the centre of the room, an abundance of rich food decorating the polished silver plates. What he had before perceived as black marble, now he saw as shining constellations in a midnight sky, twinkling and glistening in the new light. It was held in place by a dark oak border, the rough bark still left on. The table legs were twisted trees, leaves, fruit and small animals carved into their dark wood.

But, what caught his eye most was the absence of the six figures around the table, their decorated dark oak chairs now vacant.

He looked over to the sixth and final spherical slot in the floor to find that it had been filled not with a physical silver orb, but instead with a bright ball of pure light.

"To whom do I owe my thanks?"

He gasped as he turned to look in the direction of the voice.

A slender woman stood before him, reaching at least six foot tall. Her long dark green hair was plaited over her bare slender shoulder, pansies in a variety of shades of purple and white littering her hair. Her brown-green skin was rough, pale white freckles littering her cheeks as she smiled at him, her arms welcoming. Her relatively flat chest was covered with dark brown hardened leather, matching her short trousers that only reached a third of the way down her long thighs.

Edgar blushed, turning his back to her.

"I am Arvyn, the Third Prince of Vyst," he said, bowing his head. "To whom am I addressing?"

Her dark green brow furrowed.

"I have not heard of Vyst."

"You have been asleep for a long time. I believe many things have changed."

"I see." Her dark green lips smiled, revealing perfectly straight white teeth. "Well, I am Rowan. I am indebted to you."

She bowed with a flourish.

"These are my companions; Duke Daryl Wynford, my guard Edgar, and my scholar Cliona."

Her smile vanished and her crimson eyes went dark as she looked to Cliona, stood once again by the doorframe.

Cliona stared at the dryad for a moment before turning her back to the room, striding away swiftly.

"Interesting company you keep, Prince of Vyst," Rowan said through gritted teeth.

"Is something wrong?"

The dryad wrinkled her nose, glaring out of the front window.

"She stinks."

"Excuse me?"

"Never mind," she sighed, her disdain replaced quickly with a gentle smile, waving her hand. "The three of you are most welcome in our garden. We must prepare for my sister's return."

The prince smiled, donning his courtly mask as he started to follow through the back door, his eyes briefly glancing towards the front doorway where Cliona disappeared.

He paused beside the duke, grabbing his upper arm as he whispered in his ear. "Send Cliona back to the cave. I doubt they will part with the object we need if she is here."

The duke nodded, briefly dipping out of the front door.

Arvyn followed the dryad with Edgar close behind, the light warm on his golden face. One dryad carefully wrapped a thick pale blue ribbon around the trunk of the heart-shaped tree, whilst the others all busied themselves tending to the blooming flowers, their brown fingers gently soothing the plants that they had not tended to in so long, their lilted voices joined by the delicate song of birds.

Rowan passed a dozen other ribbons of various colours to the first dryad, a smile on her bark-like face.

"I know why it is that you have come," Rowan said quietly, watching her sisters decorate the small garden.

"Then you know what it is that I want."

She nodded slowly, her head held high as she sighed.

"I worry that no human is worthy of such a gift. Particularly humans accompanied by such a monster."

"What do you mean?"

"It is not my place." She shook her head, her face clouded by sadness. "Nevertheless, you did pass Avalon's test, and so by rights I must give you the item that she set aside for the heir of Oleksander."

The dryad turned her red eyes to him, her warm hand grasping his upper arm tightly as she stared at him pleadingly.

"Just, promise me, Prince Arvyn of Vyst, that you shall never give it to her."

He narrowed his eyes, but bowed his head to her nonetheless.

"Thank you." She smiled sadly. "I believe that you will find the entrance to the realm of Lord Nathario in the mountains north of this forest. He always enjoyed forests, much like my sister. I'm afraid that's all the help I have to offer you."

She sighed, stretching her long arms high above her head, her eyes closed as she muttered in the ancient language of the dryads. As she did, her hands began to glow bright blue, a low humming filling the warm air around them.

As she lowered her arms once more, the light in her cupped hands began to dim, and in its place sat a long, thin crystal vial. A viscous vibrant blue liquid was visible beyond the thick frosted glass, small flecks of silver glinting as the dryad moved the vial. The top and bottom were protected by silver, small sapphires encrusting the polished metal.

"When you have found all the other items, return this to my sister's hand, and she will awaken," Rowan breathed, gently passing the potion to Arvyn.

"May I ask what the liquid does?"

"No," Rowan said, turning her back to him as she delicately caressed a yellow chrysanthemum nearby. "Such knowledge is not for humans. It must be returned to my sister in this exact condition."

The prince strode back through the cottage, carefully wrapping the cold crystal vial in a red handkerchief from his pocket.

Chapter 13

A cold mist hung over the trees as the prince and his party made their way back through the Orville Forest. Their well-rested horses had a spring in their step as they made their way over the damp dirt pathways through the trees, the remnants of last night's storm and the morning dew dripping into their shining manes. The sound of their heavy iron shoes was dull against the damp ground, their breath visible in the crisp morning air.

"We'll take the goat path to the mountains, Your Highness," their guide called from the front, his shaggy bay mount setting a slightly slower pace than the prince wanted. "It'll be slow going but the distance is shorter."

The prince nodded, gritting his teeth. He gently patted his chestplate, tapping the breast-pocket where the second object lay sleeping as his mind began to wonder.

The prince leant down to stroke his mount's strong neck, the tension leaving him through her soft fur.

She snorted as a large rock thudded into the tree where his head had just been.

The prince sat bolt upright.

"Bandits!" Shouted Daryl, already drawing his longsword as he brought his horse close to the prince's.

The prince squinted into the tree line, his eyes meeting nothing but a dark fog rolling towards them. The hairs on his neck stood on end, his palms sweating as he tightened his reins. Deep red eyes appeared from the fog, tracking the movement of the horses.

"They're not bandits," the prince said, his voice low as he drew his own weapon, the guards closing in around him.

"Run!" Cliona shouted, kicking her horse forward.

Arvyn pointed his hand forward, the signal to move out, just as two large black creatures jumped at one of the guards. As they leapt from their hiding place, their thick black fur started to glow, lime green spirals of light pulsating over their muscular, square bodies. Their giant paws and triangular muzzles were a solid vibrant green, their long glowing tails shaking as they charged forward.

One's curved white teeth sank into the guard Alfredo's torso with ease, his thick iron armour doing little to protect his ribs as its strong jaw closed down.

The second beast clung onto the panicking horse's neck, steam cutting through the icy air as the ruby blood trickled onto the ground below. The horse stumbled, its knees shaking as its head was pulled towards the floor.

The shrill screams of the horse and rider rang loudly over the still forest, piercing the prince's ears as he urged his mount forward, his companions following close behind.

"What the hell are those things?" The prince spat, his anger threatening to spill from his golden eyes as he continued to urge his horse forward.

"Void beasts," Cliona shouted, her cold red eyes staring straight ahead. "We can't linger; those two should be occupied for a while, but other creatures will no doubt be drawn to the stench of the blood."

"More?" One of the guards shouted, before muttering a quick prayer under his breath.

"Yes, and many are much worse," she continued. "Avalon and her dryads used to keep the monsters at peace in this forest. Without her protection, the void beasts will be awakening without anyone to keep them in check," Cliona shouted behind him.

"What's awoken them? Why now?"

"The more artefacts that we gather, the more magic will be released back into the world. These void beasts must have only had a weak barrier spell placed upon them if their seal broke so soon."

"How far must we go to be safe?"

Only the sound of thunderous hooves deigned to answer the duke's question as they charged hastily north through the forest.

Chapter 14

A loud hum filled the small clearing on the edge of the deciduous tree line, growing high above the Orville Forest on the edge of the Orville Mountains. Tall granite stones stood watch around the circular space, runes carved in various colours glowing all over them. Unlike the grass and weeds that grew beyond the stone circle border, the middle was cut short, creating a gentle blanket beneath their booted feet.

The duke held up his sword, quietly inspecting the handiwork of his whetstone as he perched on top of a large boulder.

He watched as two of the guards silently erected the pale canvas tents, their faces solemn. Daryl knew them as Fredrick and Irving and had overseen them guarding the Third Prince for the past three years, although their service had begun many years prior. But, he had never seen their weathered faces so grim, their sharp eyes dulled by this new venture.

Nairne stood brushing the prince's mare silently. Every couple of strokes, the young man would hold the rough bristles against the mare's neck, burying his head into her soft white fur until only his dark blonde hair was visible.

The prince himself stood on a fallen rock on the edge of the circle, looking out over the valley below, his face a mask. Cliona sat at his feet, gently plucking the delicate strings of her lyre, her long silvery hair draped carelessly over her shoulder.

"Your Grace," their guide said, revealing a bald spot on the top of his sun-kissed head as he removed his dark brown cap. "I can't go any further on your journey, sir."

Daryl continued caressing his blade with the whetstone, his dark eyes focusing on the well-used weapon.

"You see," the man continued, scratching the back of his neck, "I never come this far west, Your Grace. I don't think I can be of any use to you any more."

"His Highness cannot allow you to return."

The man's tanned face began to pale, his hazel eyes landing on the iron sword in the duke's hands.

"Is two gold coins a day not enough? I would have thought that would be plenty for a man in your situation."

The guide's face reddened, his hands shaking from a mix of fear and anger.

"I don't want to die."

"Then you will carry on with us," the duke said, returning his sword to its sheath as he stood, towering over the short guide. "Were you to travel alone through the forest now, no doubt one of those monsters would devour you in moments; I do not believe that you have the skill to dispose of such a beast. And, even if you should make it back to your village unscathed, no one would believe the ramblings of an old man, his family ruined by his drinking habits, who claimed the forest was full of monsters."

The guide squeezed his hat tightly in his sweating palms as he backed away.

The duke sat back on his rock, quietly watching his nephew.

"Your Highness!"

They each turned to face the sound of one of the guards racing towards them on his horse, his partner in tow as a void beast drew closer, green foam dripping from its open jaws. Something hung limp over the pommel of the first guard's saddle as they charged towards the magic barrier.

The guards on the ground dropped what they were doing, one loading a bolt in his crossbow as the other two readied their swords, fear visible on their faces.

The void beast prepared to sink its long claws into the hind of the second horse, just as its back hooves passed beyond the stone circle.

The void beast screeched in pain, reeling backwards as a bright golden light filled the sky.

When he looked again, the prince saw a cloud of black ash in its place, the tiny shards floating back into the forest despite there being no breeze. The chestnut filly's head hung low, her breathing laboured as she favoured her hind right leg.

"I see why you suggested this location, Cliona," the prince said, jumping off his rock. "These beasts seem unable to enter."

"You can thank the dryads for that. Though, I doubt that the magic will have awoken enough to last another attack," she said quietly, her eyes closed as she raised her face to the drizzling rain from above.

Arvyn nodded, heading towards the two returning guards. The first dismounted, careful not to dislodge the cloaked figure slung over his pommel, as his companion leapt from his horse, immediately going to check his mount's injury, concern clear on his hardened face.

"We found this man passed out in the forest, Your Highness. The beasts were closing in on him so we intervened."

The prince lifted the black cloak away, looking at the stranger's unconscious face. His wrinkled forehead was tightly knitted, his parched lips quivering as he muttered in his sleep. Aside from a small scar over his left eyebrow, he was very plain, matching the simple brown and white clothes that he wore. Although his body was long, Arvyn got the impression that this elderly man would snap in a gentle breeze, let alone a void beast.

"Fetch him some food and water."

The duke appeared beside him, gently laying a hand on his shoulder.

"We may not have time for that," he said, nodding towards the forest.

The trees swayed even without a breeze, the ground rumbling.

"Mount up."

"Your Highness!" He turned to see the guard who rode the injured chestnut, his hands covered in her blood. "I don't think my mare will make it."

"We don't have an opening anyway," Daryl said quietly, drawing his sword.

More than a dozen void beats appeared on the edge of the forest, bright green saliva dripping from their open lips, black steam rising from their large nostrils as they circled the perimeter.

The prince nodded, drawing his blade too. "Musician, stay by that rock with our guide and this man."

She gritted her teeth as the guards moved the resting stranger's limp body beside her on the short grassy blanket.

The beasts charged at the invisible barrier, their bodies vaporised by the weakening ancient magic. One after the other the mindless creatures lunged forwards, their glowing bodies disappearing.

But, the magic was not as strong as they had hoped.

After many beasts met their end, the barrier began to waver; the broad lime green paw of a beast slipped through, green blood spurting over the ground as the limb was severed from the creature's body.

Yet still they persisted, clawing with their paws and snapping with their teeth.

"Get ready," Arvyn said, gripping his sword tightly, his heart pounding.

The stones cracked as the barrier shattering into a thousand pale blue shards before disappearing into thin air. The remaining ten void beasts grinned, their green saliva dripping onto the cold ground below their feet as they sprung forward.

Arvyn and his men readied their blades.

The beasts froze in mid-air, their red eyes darting around as their paralysed bodies fell to the ground like lead.

Arvyn looked around, his mouth shut in a tight line as his eyes stayed fixed on the vicious creatures sprawled on the floor.

"That was slightly too close for comfort, I must say," a gentle voice called, diverting the prince's attention.

Beside Cliona stood a slender man, his right arm outstretched towards the creatures, pale grey smoke dissipating around his gnarled fingertips. On closer inspection, in place of the pale skin that the prince had expected to see was a stiff mahogany wood hand, green runes glowing along the fingers and exposed lower arm. His black hood was pushed back, revealing deep cavernous grooves in his pale skin, his white hair flowing freely around his diamond-shaped face.

"I must thank you, stranger," the prince said, turning warily towards him. "I am not certain how we would have fared if you had not acted."

The man smiled calmly, crossing a long arm over his long body as he creaked into a slight bow.

"One should not travel these woods if they are not prepared for such basic void beasts, sir," he offered, his emerald eyes emotionless. "My name is Kimiro, I am a servant to Lord Nathario."

The prince smiled softly as he offered him his hand.

"I am Arvyn, Third Prince of Vyst and descendant of Oleksander I. I am searching for a settlement in this area, known as Ophidium."

Kimiro's black eyes darkened despite his smile as he bowed once again. "Ophidium is a difficult place to find, Your Highness. Perhaps it would be best if I guide you to your destination."

The duke glared at the man, his hand still clutching his beloved sword.

"We are in rather a hurry," the prince replied. "How long will it take to get there?"

"A full day's travel following the river, your Highness. But, it is a location that can only be reached on foot; I would recommend that Your Highness leave your horses behind."

Arvyn inclined his head, his eyes meeting with the duke briefly. "Have our men return to the town with our mounts. I shall write a quick report for them to send to my father. You and Cliona will accompany me to Ophidium."

"Understood, Your Highness," the duke replied, immediately starting to bark orders to the guards.

The prince glanced over to the silver-haired woman, her emotionless eyes gazing sadly at the cracked ancient stones surrounding the clearing.

He cleaned his jaw, reaching for his travelling ink pen and a piece of parchment from his trusted mount's saddle bag.

Chapter 15

Kimiro was surprisingly nimble and quick on his feet for an old man, picking his way through the dense forest undergrowth with ease. He dodged fallen branches deftly, foraging a handful of edible berries occasionally and passing them amongst his three travelling companions, each slightly slower than himself over the rough terrain.

Cliona set her gaze to the elderly man, his dark eyes watching her silently as she stepped carefully towards him, leaving the prince and the duke behind her.

"Is something on your mind, Kimiro?"

"Forgive my impertinence, my lady, but I simply must ask," the old man whispered, ignoring the uncomfortable sensation of the duke's murderous gaze behind him as he led the prince ever deeper through the uncharted area of the Orville Forest. "Why now?

"We have waited long enough," she breathed, unhooking her long cloak from a bramble's thorny clasp as she cast a glance at the prince walking just out of earshot behind them.

"Do these humans understand the extent of the task assigned to them?"

Cliona stared at him, her crimson eyes cold.

He turned away, inclining his head.

"You should remember your place, Kimiro," she said coldly, an old flame flickering over her eyes briefly.

"My apologies, Lady Cliona."

She paused, putting some space between herself and the elderly man, steadying her breathing as the cool air filled her lungs. Her long fingernails dug into the fleshy part of her hands as she closed her eyes, trying to drown out the old man's concerns.

It was not that she didn't agree with him. In fact, the very same worry had been plaguing her since she left the confines of Dunsberg Castle.

"Are you all right with a hike like this? You seem rather pale."

Her eyes flickered to the prince as he came up beside her, offering her his hand. She smiled softly, graciously taking his hand as she fell into step beside him.

"I wish to see this expedition through to the end."

"I suppose you did start this," he said, holding back a low hanging branch for her to pass under.

Cliona watched her feet moving slowly over the branch littered floor, avoiding his cool gaze as they continued onwards.

The small group continued their trek through the dense forest, their footfalls accompanied by the sweet song of birds in the distance. Even after three hours of travelling, their path had continued to ascend up the mountain, the unruly undergrowth making their journey slow and their breathing laboured.

"How much further?" The duke growled, dodging yet another branch as he surged up behind the old guide.

"The entrance to the river is just up ahead, sir," the old man replied calmly, pulling back a dense curtain of foliage.

Light streamed into the cluttered forest, causing all those gathered to blink quickly.

When his eyes had adjusted, Arvyn could not stifle the gasp as he looked over the landscape surrounding him.

The trees parted onto the edge of a wide lake, the azure water sparkling in the midday sunlight.

"This is Lake Ophidium, the gateway to the great city of Ophidium. Please," Kimiro said calmly, extending his hand towards a large birch river boat moored on the edge of the lake.

The duke stepped onto the boat first, cautiously testing the structure of the vessel before nodding to his nephew. The prince helped Cliona on quietly, waiting for her to perch on one of the pale green cushions before climbing on himself. Kimiro followed last, reaching for a long birch pole from the side of the boat which he proceeded to use to push the boat along the serene water.

Exotic white and silver fish swam elegantly below the surface, occasionally breaching the surface. Sleeping at the bottom of the deceptively deep lake lay a sprawling palace, carved entirely from the naturally occurring white howlite decorating the floor of the lake. Tall pillars spiralled towards the surface, the walls shining brightly under the mystical blue light.

"That was the Great Hospital of Ophidium," Kimiro said quietly. "Demons and humans alike would journey here for treatment. It was the centre of medical advancement, and the pride of Lord Nathario."

The prince glanced at the old man, the respect clear in his gentle voice.

"If it was the pride of your lord, then how did it end up at the bottom of a hidden lake in the Orville Forest?"

The old man grinned.

"The great forest may be a place of danger now, but many centuries ago it was a great haven for many races. The continent was united under one ruler, and their capital was not too far from here, in the centre of the forest. The hospital was built on the outskirts of that great city, to make it easy for those in need to reach it." His dark eyes clouded over as he stared unseeing ahead. "When the Demon Lords were sealed away, so too were their people. Those under the protection of Lord Nathario were not hunted or sealed away with him. Instead, our medical knowledge was still needed, and so we were trapped within the Orville Forest so that our skills were still usable by the Demon Empire."

"But, how did the hospital end up under the lake?"

The old man smiled sadly.

"Lord Nathario's sister, Lady Nefera, refused to aid the emperor's vulgar research. He flooded the hospital as a punishment. Our people retreated to our city and refused to tend to any outsiders after that."

He continued pushing the boat along silently.

"I have to ask," the prince said after a moment, "but it seems that many of the followers of the Demon Lords have managed to survive for centuries. How is that possible? Are humans the only ones who age?"

The old man laughed. "Not at all, your Highness. Although humans do traverse their lifespan faster than most species, everything that possesses life must someday die. Before the Demon Lords were sealed, they placed a forbidden magic on their followers so that we would survive until their return. Fortunately for us, the emperor could not rescind the stasis on our ageing without releasing them, so we have been left in peace since then."

"Many would call eternal life a blessing, not a curse," Cliona said quietly.

"Whether you call it a blessing or a curse, the fact remains that we have not aged in two and a half centuries. For my people, any children born since Lord Nathario was locked away have matured, but those born before have been frozen in time. To be trapped in that state for so long is nothing short of torture."

"Perhaps that is why Oleksander did it," Arvyn said quietly. "I know that the Glerian Empire takes many conquered citizens as slaves as a punishment for their nation's refusal to surrender."

They continued their journey in silence, each enjoying a small moment of peace as their vessel glided over the smooth water.

Cliona allowed her fingertips to gently brush over the still surface of the lake,

After a while, she closed her eyes, softly singing a gentle melody.

Fare thee well, lone traveller,
Your bags are packed and farewells said,
As they wish to you good fortune,
And that your journey is none too long.
Dawn is breaking, adventure is waiting,
So let us bid to them our last goodbye.

The ancestors are waiting.
The twilight is breaking.
As we wait for you upon the moonlit hill.

Ride the winds and waters,
As your feet lead you ever on.
For someday, at the fall of day,
You'll feast your eyes upon
The sacred fields of joy and love
Where we'll spend forever more.

The ancestors are waiting.
The twilight is breaking.
As we wait for you upon the moonlit hill.

You'll journey far and journey wide
And yet you must journey still.
Let the moonlight embrace you,
Dance i149heshirlesséd light
As she welcomes you home.

The ancestors are waiting.
The twilight is breaking.

As we wait for you upon the moonlit hill.

Rest for now, lone traveller,
Upon the moonlit hill.
Lay down your sword; lay down your bow,
For your journey is at its end.
But have no fear for your loved ones are near
And rejoice with open arms.

The ancestors were waiting.
The twilight is breaking
As we dance with you upon the moonlit hill.

Kimiro smiled softly, sadness clouding his gaze as he steered the boat forward.

"Correct me if I'm wrong," the prince said after a while, "but I believe I hear the sound of a waterfall."

"You are correct, Your Highness," the old man replied, his rhythm unreeling. "Have no fear. I will guide you safely to the city of Ophidium."

Arvyn and his uncle shared a nervous glance.

Cliona looked out across the water, the gentle current steadily becoming stronger. But, both she and Kimiro was the picture of tranquility, the oncoming thunder doing little to shatter their steady resolve.

Arvyn swallowed his fear, looking out over the landscape before them.

A dense forest of trees, identical to those surrounding the lake, stretched out over the horizon before them, the sweet sound of high pitched birds echoing over the peaceful landscape. His breath became heavier as the thunderous cliff drew nearer, the boat speeding towards the edge.

He could see his uncle tensing beside him, his hands clutching tightly on the edge of the birch vessel.

Arvyn involuntarily squeezed his eyes shut, silently offering a prayer to anyone who would listen.

Cliona laughed, turning her head up to the sky as the old man deftly navigated the vessel along the truculent waterway. The small boat twisted along the jagged route, water splashing across the people inside.

The river soon slowed once more, as Kimiro began to hum softly.

The prince slowly opened his eyes, breathing in as he gazed at the sight that greeted him.

A howlite wall created a narrow path through the centre of the waterfall, guiding Kimiro gracefully away from the tumultuous rapids and instead down a smooth passage. This channel descended the mountain slowly, allowing the boat to travel at a steady pace as its passengers marvelled at the untouched landscape.

From beside the lake, it had seemed as though the mountain was perfectly flat, and yet this new vantage point revealed the ravine splitting this portion of the mountain in two. Silvery sedimentary rocks lined the ravine beneath the vibrant blanket of trees.

But, even more breathtaking was the large sprawling city stretching alongside the calm azure river at the base of the ravine. Only a small portion could be seen from the top of the waterfall, as much of the flat land below was guarded by tall stacks and arches, formed millennia ago.

The visible circular houses were made of the same grey stone that watched over them. The walls themselves were painted white whilst their conical roofs blended into the cliffs around them. A number of small fishing boats splashed about along the meandering river, the riverbed visible even from high above.

"Welcome to Ophidium, Your Highness."

"There are more people than I expected," he said quietly, leaning over the boat to get a closer look. "Your people seem to have fared better than the sirens we encountered."

"We are protected here; we have been blessed to not face the same adversity as our allies. Due to the fame of the Great Hospital, we were not hunted to the same extent as the others."

As the waterway began to flatten out at the bottom of the cliff, dozens of people lined the sandy banks, their tanned faces smiling as they waved towards the strangers. One of the smaller fishing boats paddled towards them, with a young man adorning the prince and his companions with vibrant floral necklaces, each one filling the air with a sweet scent.

At the end of the river stood a tall rectangular building stretching over the entire width of the river. A pair of intricately carved warrior statues stood either side of the river, as it flowed beneath the roof of the building. The carved man and woman stood watch over the steady river, their eyes inlaid with black onyx. A flock of large white ibis took flight as their vessel drew nearer, clearing their path to a white howlite staircase that led from the riverbed to a tall archway.

At the top of the steps stood an olive-skinned woman, her head held high as she watched Kimiro walk a few paces ahead of the strangers towards her. Her black hair was tightly woven, lapis-lazuli beads holding the delicate braids in place. Her dark eyes were heavily lined with thick black kohl, her large lips darkened with a deep red paint. She wore a rather revealing white dress that left little to the imagination thanks to the thin cotton material, not dissimilar to that of the sirens. The material was held in place by intricately woven gold braids wrapping around her waist. Her long, muscular arms were adorned with golden arm bands, matching the large golden circlet perched atop her head, shaped like a cobra with eyes of lapis lazuli.

Kimiro bowed before the tall woman, before he quickly whispered into her ear.

She inclined her head, a subtle smile gracing her finely chiselled face as he took his place behind her.

"Welcome, travellers. I am Lady Nefera, the current guardian of Ophidium."

The prince bowed, returning a polite smile.

"I am Prince Arvyn, Third Prince of the kingdom of Vyst and descendant of Oleksander I. This is my uncle, Duke Daryl Wynford, and my companion Cliona. We appreciate your hospitality."

"You are most welcome, Your Highness. Kimiro informs me that you intend to release Lord Nathario."

Arvyn blinked, unable to recall when he had told the elderly man of his plans.

"That is correct, my lady. As we understand it, there is an item that we require from this city to do so. Do you perhaps know its whereabouts?"

"I do," she replied, her eyes weighing the prince carefully. "However, you must complete a task for me before I grant such a precious relic to you."

The prince smiled politely. "Of course."

She nodded, extending her hand to point towards a cave at the edge of the ravine.

"My people are unfortunately plagued by a vicious creature that dwells somewhere within those caverns. It stalks our city at night and has abducted a number of my citizens from their homes. Dispose of this creature and I shall grant you the item you seek."

Daryl scowled, stepping forward. "May I ask what sort of creature you are speaking about?"

Her dark eyes appraised him silently.

"We call it the Serpentarus. No one who has seen it returns to speak of it. But from what we can tell from the tracks it leaves behind, it is bipedal with four very sharp talons. We have found large black feathers," Nefera said gravely, indicating the length of her forearm. "We never hear it. Only the screams of our dying brethren."

"And it lives in the caves, you say?"

The tall woman inclined her head.

"Very well," the prince replied, holding his head high. "We shall find your monster for you in the morning."

"Then I shall have rooms and a fine meal prepared for you, as pre-emptive thanks from the people here."

She held out a long slender arm, summoning a pair of young women, dressed similarly to their mistress, but with much fewer golden decorations.

"We are most appreciative, my lady."

She watched as he and the duke went to follow her trusted maids.

Cliona hesitated for a moment, her crimson eyes meeting Nefera's as she passed her.

Chapter 16

Cliona stepped quietly into the warm pool, slipping the soft white robe from her bare shoulders. She descended the blue and white tiled steps into the women's bath, carefully taking her place along the edge of the pool.

Even after countless years of healing, the once-broken skin on her scarred back was still tender as the warm water grazed the surface.

"May I join you, my lady?"

She turned to see Nefera standing above her, letting her own golden robe drop to the floor at her feet, a maid racing to collect it. Another young maid silently sprinkled blue and white flower petals and scented salts into the crystal spring water.

The slender woman entered the bathing pool gracefully, sitting quite close beside Cliona.

Nefera cupped the water in her olive hands, delicately splashing it over the black snake tattoo coiled around her left shoulder.

"I honestly never expected to see you here again," Nefera said quietly once the maids had bowed and left the room. "Or at least, I had given up hope."

"I'm sorry," Cliona whispered, lowering herself into the water so that only her head was above the surface. "Things did not go according to plan."

"I had assumed as much."

"Your people seem to have fared well enough," Cliona whispered, unplaiting her long silver hair.

"The prestige of the hospital and university is to thank for that, I suppose. You could say that we were given amnesty, as a reward for treating our enemies' wounded."

Nefera did nothing to hide the bitterness from her normally dulcet voice, her black eyes filled with malice as memories raced before her mind.

"I'm sorry, Nefera," Cliona whispered, her eyes focusing on the spiral lapis-lazui patterns on the high vaulted ceiling. "This should never have happened."

"No, it shouldn't have."

Cliona closed her eyes, lowering her head under the surface, her silver hair almost translucent under the water as it fanned out around her.

Nefera looked directly at her companion, her black eyes unwavering as Cliona resurfaced.

"So what do you plan to do next?"

"I don't know," Cliona whispered, her long arms wrapping around her torso.

"Was the sacrifice of my brother for nothing? Did my people die for nothing?"

Cliona met her gaze.

It had been centuries since they had seen each other. Whilst Cliona had been left to rot in the confines of Dunsberg Castle under the careful watch of General Desmond's descendants, the young woman before her had bloomed into a true beauty.

Even when Cliona first met her as a child, Nefera had been the epitome of elegance, silently watching her family slaughtered by the Imperial Demon Army as she protected her younger brother. She had always borne her burdens with quiet grace, never once allowing her judgement to be clouded by her pain.

But, here she was, unsuccessfully fighting back tears of anger.

"Prince Arvyn will break the seal, Nefera. After that, it is up to them; I will have no more say over their lives."

"I don't pretend to know Nathario's mind. He was not exactly someone who ever shared his thoughts. But, I do know that his faith in you was unwavering, even at the end," Nefera said bitterly as she rubbed at her eyes. "I trust you and I trust my brother. We did not see eye to eye with the war, but I cannot dispute that he was a genius. I have to believe that he foresaw something that I cannot."

Nefera grabbed Cliona's hands, her dark eyes beseeching.

"Nathario made many mistakes in his life. But one I know he never regretted was following your orders. He trusted you with every fibre of his being, and so I will continue to trust in you too."

Cliona turned her face away, wrapping her long arms around her.

"I'll get Nathario back, Nefera. I swear."

"Please do," the tall woman replied, standing from the bath. "Else you will no longer have my people to call your allies, even if you were once our saviour."

Chapter 17

After spending their first night in an actual bed for almost two weeks, the prince and his two companions woke well rested, their aching muscles soothed by the small comforts offered by Lady Nefera's hospitality.

Still, the fatigue attempted to take over once more as Arvyn and Daryl followed the four warriors that their host had offered to accompany them to the cave entrance, having left Cliona at the city for safety.

They walked quickly, the rocky terrain hardly deterring the barefoot warriors.

Just like all the other inhabitants of this city, these three men and one woman were rather slender in build compared to the average person, although their graceful and precise movements hinted at a hidden strength. Each one sported a rather simple black snakeskin tattoo around their eyes, whilst three bands of scales were tattooed onto their left upper arm, marking them as high ranking warriors according to the servants. Unlike the soft, thin cotton attire that the other city dwellers had worn, these four wore simple hardened scale armour, just enough to cover their modesty whilst still allowing them absolute freedom of movement.

They glided gracefully over the uneven terrain leading away from the river, unhindered by their short spears, half the size of the spears that Arvyn and his uncle were accustomed to. The duke was fascinated by these strange weapons; on one end was an iron spearhead, not dissimilar to those that the guards in the capital were assigned, although slightly more rudimentary in design. But, it was the unusual semi-circular shaped blade that decorated the opposite end that had caught the bodyguard's attention.

They climbed carefully over the grey scree that guarded the wide entrance to the cave, the dark red stains of blood on the floor welcoming them to the Serpentarus's lair.

"Shall we light some torches?" The prince said quietly, struggling to get a peek into the dark cave.

"That may alert its presence, Your Highness, but I see no other way," Daryl mumbled.

One of the warriors placed a large hand on the duke's armoured shoulder, shaking his head. Another brought out a pair of thin golden braided bracelets from the black leather pouch at his hip, handing one to each of them.

"Lady Nefera gifted these to you whilst you accompany us. They allow the wearer to see in dark spaces, to some extent."

Sure enough, upon tightening them onto their wrists, the pair of visitors became able to see into the dark cave as though it were dimly lit.

The female warrior waved them forward, her body practically crawling over the jagged stones, her black eyes darting into the shadows as they slowly followed the blood trail deeper into the cave.

Most of the turns they encountered in the intricate cave network were rather small, with some barely big enough for a small toddler to crawl through, whilst others would be able to fit three horses abreast quite easily. Although they were thankful for the crimson smears illuminating their path, it did not go unnoticed that the creature they were stalking had stuck to the larger of these tunnels.

Nor the numerous humanoid bones scattered across the floor the deeper in that they went.

"Your Highness," the duke said quietly, his muscles forever tense as they traversed the underground caves. "Should this Serpentarus seem too dangerous, I ask that you retreat at once."

Arvyn gritted his teeth, nodding solemnly to his uncle.

As much as he had tried to deny it, he was not designed for these gruelling missions away from the home comforts he had grown up with. Yes, the concept of adventure had always called to him as he was continuing his mother's research, but he was finding the reality much less romantic than he had envisioned.

He winced as he heard an undeniable crunch under his black boot. Looking down, he saw the fragmented remains of a child's lower mandible beneath his feet.

"We must be getting close."

Arvyn nodded, resting his hand on the hilt of his still untested sword.

The group trod carefully as they entered a grand chamber, much larger than those they had already traversed. Unlike the rest of the cave, the floor here was smooth, as though something had scraped it until it had become even.

Curiously, there were no bones or blood here.

Water steadily dripped down from a cream stalagmite onto a wide stalactite, the two almost touching. Curtains of ivory minerals dripped down the walls of this cave, as though thousands of candles had been left to drip wax for too long. Aside from the entry way that they were standing at, and a small area on the left wall, these stone icicles painted the otherwise dark grey walls.

Lying in front of this barren segment of wall was a mountainous pile of black and white feathers. From a glance, the smallest of these quills measured almost as large as the prince's forearm, the largest that he could see almost reaching as tall as himself.

One long, white scaled leg draped out over the nest of stones and bones. It had three taloned toes, with a fourth at the back of its thin foot for balance. Each of these talons curved gently, not dissimilar to the curved sword blades that Arvyn had seen in Ophidius. The tips were sharpened into a razor point, fading from black to white.

The mound rhythmically moved up and down, blissfully unaware of the intruders.

The four warriors spoke amongst themselves with silent hand signals. They nodded to each other, satisfied, and the three men dispersed around the edge of the room, sticking to the shadows. The woman turned to the two foreigners, her black eyes devoid of any emotion as she tried to communicate the same way with them.

The prince smiled awkwardly in confusion, whilst the duke, more accustomed to this sort of work than his royal counterpart, nodded silently.

"They will be a distraction. We will stop it from leaving."

Arvyn nodded, trusting his seasoned uncle.

The female warrior made eye contact with the prince, tapping her chest and then the snake tattoo on her shoulder, before crouching silently in the shadows.

The duke gestured for himself and his nephew to crouch too.

They watched as one of the warriors slunk closer, stopping just short of the slumbering beast.

He took a deep breath, lifting his spear in the air.

Just as he prepared to throw it at the creature, the ebony feathers whipped up, revealing a large black eye nestled on fiery gold skin, watching the warrior. Within seconds, the feathered monster swung out its scaled leg at the intruder, slamming the man into the opposite wall.

Arvyn's heart raced, watching the stoic warrior slump against the cold wall.

The woman screamed in rage, drawing her obsidian dagger from the black braided belt around her muscular waist, her knuckles going pale as she clutched the weapon tightly. Her body sprung forward like a taut coil as she slashed at the snake tattoo on her shoulder.

Had Arvyn had the luxury to observe the fierce woman carefully, he would have seen the deep purple dagger absorbing the woman's blood offering, causing a tiny black spark to flash over her brawny shoulder.

She ripped at her chest, extracting her true serpentine form from her flimsy human skin, her black scales blending into the dark cave.

The other two warriors followed suit, leaving their limp human skins in their wake as they both charged at the monster, their unique weapons forgotten on the floor.

Arvyn and Daryl ran to the limp warrior, lifting his unconscious body between the two of them whilst the Serpentarus was distracted. His body was surprisingly heavy, and the pair struggled to stop his knees from scraping over the rough cave floor to the entrance of the chamber.

"Stay behind me, Your Highness," the duke said curtly, unsheathing his sword quickly as he turned back towards the fight. "If we are likely to lose, you must run."

The prince gritted his teeth, following his uncle into the fray.

Feathers and claws engulfed the group as they fought against the gargantuan bird. One of the snakes wrapped his broad body around the creature's long, white scaled legs. But, the bird was too quick; it freed one leg, using its razor-like talons to rip the snake from its grasp. It struck out at him, its giant foot grinding into the warrior's chest and sending him sliding across the uneven floor, slamming him against the wall.

Arvyn charged forward with his sword raised whilst the Serpentarus's back was turned, but it was too quick, whipping its feathered body to face the new danger. Its long tail feathers rustled with the movement as its body bashed into the prince, knocking him off balance.

Its golden curved beak ripped through Daryl's armour as he pushed the prince out of the way.

Seeing an opening, the nimble female snake coiled herself around the Serpentarus's large body, sinking her long pointed fangs into the soft flesh through the feathers. Although the creature tried to shake her, she clung on with her powerful jaws and tightly coiled body.

The beast squawked in pain as its body began to go limp, the toxic venom making its way around through the Serpentarus's blood. To be safe, the warrior wrapped her body tighter around the feathered creature until, finally, it fell limp to the floor.

Arvyn sunk to the floor, agony raking through his body with every breath he took as he leant against the cold cave wall. He wiped his brow, his golden hair soaked in sweat as his hands shook. Looking over at his companions, he was certain that, despite the ribs he believed to be broken and the various minor flesh wounds, he was by no means the most scathed from that encounter.

Now transformed back into a human, the three snake warriors set about bandaging each other's wounds. One of the men hissed as the woman wrapped his leg in a rudimentary splint, the other man staunching the heavy blood flow from a gaping slash wound on his comrade's shoulder. Each of them looked worse for wear, deep red badges of honour colouring their olive skin.

The duke slumped to the ground beside Arvyn. His chest shuddered with every breath he took, his hand weakly fumbling with the straps on his well-worn chestplate. Once removed, his hand pressed down on a slightly darker patch of his black shirt, his fingers quickly growing sticky with blood.

"Uncle!" The prince called hoarsely, applying pressure to the wound. "We need to get you back to the city, quickly."

The duke grunted, pushing himself into a sitting position.

"I'm perfectly fine, your Highness; this is just a small flesh wound."

Just as the golden haired prince prepared to protest at his uncle's stubbornness, he heard a soft shuffling sound coming from within the large mound of rubble, bones and feathers that had served as the creature's nest.

Arvyn rose to his feet, his legs threatening to buckle as the adrenaline evaporated from his bruised body. He clutched his sword tightly, knowing full well that neither he nor his companions would survive another bout of combat.

Carefully leaning over the edge of the coarse nest, his eyes widened as he met the dark gaze of a small child, no older than five years old. His ebony hair was dishevelled around his round tanned face, his cheeks red from tears.

He slunk away from the prince, clutching his small knees tightly to his chest.

Beside the boy lay two other young children sleeping on the bumpy floor of the nest. Each one was adorned in violet bruises, a few bloodstains decorating their dirtied white tunics.

"It's all right; I'm not here to hurt you," Arvyn said softly, his deep voice trying to mimic how his mother would soothe him as a child.

The boy hissed, the sound waking his two fellow abductees.

The largest child rubbed his eyes sleepily, nudging the slightly smaller girl beside him.

"We should return these children to their families quickly," Arvyn said to the female warrior appearing beside him. "Their parents must be worried sick."

"They have no parents. Once the eggs have hatched, children are the responsibility of the community," she explained before addressing the children. "Which part of the city are you from?"

The girl sheepishly slid her hand into the older warrior's, looking down at the floor. The youngest ran and hugged the muscular leg of the woman, tears falling freely from his black eyes.

The bigger boy sighed, scratching the back of his head. "We're from the eastern artisan's quarter."

"How long have you been here?"

"Probably a week or so. The big bird gave us some of its food," he said, his teeth clenched. "It tasted horrible and made us feel sick, but it's better than going hungry."

"Hungry," the youngest one whimpered, accompanied by a perfectly timed rumble from his stomach.

"Well, let's get you back so you can have something nice to eat."

The warrior smiled, lifting the youngest child onto her hip with ease, taking the girl's hand. Her eyes winced briefly in pain as the boy got himself settled, nuzzling his face into her warm, bruised shoulder. The older boy threw back his shoulders, walking proudly beside her despite his small limp.

The group made their way out of the dark cave slowly. The female warrior carried the two small children, the older boy close on her heels as they traversed the uneven rocky terrain. The other warrior helped his seriously injured comrade. Although the bleeding seemed to have stopped thanks to his emergency care, he had still lost a considerable amount of blood and his bone was still protruding the skin, although hidden by the tight white bandages. The prince offered his shoulder to his uncle, but the stoic man refused, insisting it was a mere scratch.

The cave began to grow brighter, their eyes slowly adjusting to the now dim light that greeted them fondly. Daryl went to cover his eyes instinctively, but the movement sent a jarring pain through his chest, forcing him swiftly to his knees.

"Daryl!"

The prince was quickly kneeling by his side, his eyes wide. He helped him lie on the ground carefully, noticing that the wound on the duke's chest was still bleeding, despite Daryl's assurance. He applied pressure onto the wound once again, gritting his teeth.

"We need to get him back to the city immediately," the female warrior said, releasing the young girl's hand as she readjusting the now sleeping child on her hip. "Asim,

I will care for Eskaq. You run to the city. We need help carrying our wounded and need a medical team ready when we arrive."

The burly warrior sat down his injured comrade on a rock, taking off down the hill towards the river.

The female warrior carefully passed the sleeping child to her injured comrade before kneeling beside the duke. The two older children also sat beside him, their young faces intrigued as she deftly cut the black shirt away from the duke's unconscious body.

By the time that help finally arrived, the seasoned knight had lost consciousness. The warriors quickly staunched the blood using the tattered remains of his shirt now that he was not awake to protest, before wrapping his torso tightly in their remaining bandages. With the help of the handful of townspeople that the warrior had managed to gather, the small band made their way back to the palace quickly, their path lined with grateful citizens.

At some point, the children were reunited with their family, but Arvyn was too worried about Daryl and in too much pain himself to notice.

"Kimiro," Nefera called, gesturing towards the two men carrying Daryl's limp body as they drew near the palace. "See that he is properly treated."

The old man bowed, gesturing for two guards to relieve the townspeople of the broad man's heavy body.

The prince smiled, trying to hide the pain he felt as he ascended the steps slowly towards Nerefa and Cliona.

"As my brother hoped for, I see that you are adequate, for a human." Nefera said softly when the prince drew near, her black eyes filled with an uncharacteristic softness as she gazed over the citizens.

She extended her hand to Arvyn, a cautious smile on her full lips as she gently dropped a golden arm band into the prince's open palm.

The delicate ornament was made of tightly woven braids of gold, the cold object glistening in the golden sunlight. Thin tendrils of pale blue metal were interlaced with the gold, the exotic material seeming to pulsate in time with the prince's steady heartbeat.

"This was my brother's most valued possession; a gift from our mother before she was slaughtered by the Imperial Demon Army. She was infamously well versed in poisons and venoms; this protects its wearer from any harm that would be caused by such toxins. Return it to Nathario during the ritual."

"Thank you, Lady Nefera."

Arvyn wearily followed a servant into the palace, his legs threatening to buckle.

Nefera held her head high as she looked at the joyous people dancing at the bottom of the palace steps.

"Thank you," she whispered to Cliona beside her.

Nefera absently wiped away at her tears with her hand, rubbing her palms together to hide the black kohl smudged on her olive skin as she strode back to the palace.

Chapter 18

After three days of rest in the comforts of the serpent city, the prince and his two companions left Ophidium, their spirits higher than when their journey had first begun fourteen days ago. Accompanying them was a jovial old merchant and his son, permitted to visit the town of Thornbury to trade by Lady Nefera. His well-used wooden cart was filled with vibrant cotton sheets, ornate gold jewellery and a few intricately carved ivory ornaments.

Kimiro also insisted on joining the prince's expedition, adamant that he had to be present when his master Nathario was released.

Arvyn managed to give himself a small rest whilst reclining in the back of the laden wagon. Thankfully the road, although barely used for the past few centuries, had been well maintained by Nefera's people as they awaited the day they could once again welcome visitors.

Finally, the once-sharpened points of Thornbury's tall wooden palisade began to come into view after three days of peaceful travel.

Once upon a time, there would have been dozens of guards adorning the twenty-foot wooden palisade, clad in sturdy armour and well-cared-for weapons. Now, aside from the two guards lounging against the eternally open gate rotting on its rusted hinges, Cliona could not see a single sentinel.

There was, however, a single horse and rider waiting just off the side of the dirt road, looking in the direction of the cart. Although his nondescript clothing did its best to hide his identity, Daryl recognised him as one of his subordinates immediately.

Clearly noticing the prince and the duke, the soldier trotted up to ride his mount beside the cart.

"Greetings, Your Highness," Wilfred said quietly, inclining his head. "We had begun to fear that you had met trouble on the road. I was getting ready to send a search party."

"There was a situation that we had to take care of. Did the report get sent?"

"Yes, Your Highness. We have yet to receive a response from His Majesty, but if the rumours of a coordinated nomad assault are to be believed, then I am not surprised."

"I'm not expecting one. His Majesty does not expect this expedition to be a success."

"I understand, Your Highness," Wilfred mumbled. "We have organised rooms in the *Scarlet Skelly* for you to rest in, Your Highness."

"Are they aware of my status?"

The knight paused for a moment.

"No, Your Highness. Although the innkeeper is aware that we are waiting for our employer, I believe that she thinks of us as wandering mercenaries."

"Good. Better than drawing unwanted attention. See to it that our companions know to address me as Sir Arvyn Walters, if required."

"Yes, sir."

The soldier wavered as his horse walked alongside the prince.

"What is it that you wish to say?"

"My apologies, sir. But, I feel that I should warn you that you have a guest waiting for you at the tavern."

Arvyn's golden eyes narrowed on the soldier, squirming under his firm gaze.

"Princess Eleanora apparently came down with an illness when we left her. She has remained in Thornbury claiming to be indisposed since then, and has since been joined by two women she had employed as maids. As I am aware, her identity is still not known."

The prince's jaw clenched, causing the guard to flinch involuntarily. Daryl put his hand on Arvyn's shoulder calmly.

"Her Highness has always been one to do as she pleases; you both take after your mother, after all. We should not be surprised by her actions."

Arvyn started to reply but stopped himself as the cart rolled to a halt in front of the two town guards.

The first, his eyes closed, leant lazily against the wall, his arms folded over his drab maroon uniform. Where there should have been a simple iron helmet, there was instead a mop of greasy blonde hair, the same shade that messily covered the lower half of his diamond face. His spear had been discarded behind him, the iron tip starting to rust from years of mistreatment.

"State your business," he sighed, not bothering to open his eyes.

"We are here to trade," the merchant said loudly, indicating to the crates of luxury goods behind him.

The second guard spat to the side, grabbing his equally dishevelled spear from its perch against the palisade. He scratched the back of his balding head as he yawned, sauntering over to the cart.

His dark blue eyes lit up when he noticed Cliona sat in the back, her hood half obscuring her pale face.

She looked down quietly at her hands, her long fingernails digging into the flesh of her palms as she chewed the inside of her cheek. Arvyn tensed beside her, clenching his jaw.

"You have some very high quality goods here," he sneered, revealing a mouth of cracked yellow teeth.

"Yes," the merchant said firmly. "We have fabrics, jewellery and ornaments to sell. All of the finest quality."

"Yeah, yeah," the guard grumbled, brushing off the old merchant as he shamelessly watched the hooded woman. "I think fifteen gold coins should do it. What do you reckon, Bert?"

Daryl scoffed, drawing the guard's glare.

"Or, we can take the girl instead," the guard sneered, his hand stretching up towards Cliona's arm. "I'd prefer that."

The prince leant over his female companion, his golden eyes blazing as he gripped onto the guard's bare wrist. He pulled the man closer to him, lifting him off his feet and eliciting a yelp from the local.

Cliona simply looked down at her hands.

"We will ignore this offence and will enter without charge." Arvyn pulled the man closer before pushing him firmly off the end of the cart onto the floor. "Drive on."

The elderly merchant urged the horse forward slowly, tipping his hat to the guard standing dumbfounded by the gate.

"So much for a low profile," Cliona whispered, her eyelids closed gently.

"This sort of corruption sickens me," he muttered, his sour eyes glaring over the ramshackle town.

"Unfortunately this is rather tame, my lord," Kimiro said quietly. "As I am aware, a number of towns and villages on the eastern border fare much worse than Thornbury."

"When our current business is over we will return to discipline this town."

Daryl turned his attention to the scenery, his grey eyes absorbing the views that the derelict town had to offer.

Although many houses were in need of repair, Thornbury was by no means unpleasant to ride through for the most part. The ground floor of the houses were constructed from the grey granite that could be found in abundance in the nearby Orville Mountains, whilst locally sourced shards of flint were embedded into the white walls for the rest of the building. The oak shutters were open for most houses, letting the warm late afternoon sun bathe their rooms. Well-trimmed planters rested under the window ledges on the ground floor for each house, the colourful wildflowers swaying in the gentle breeze.

Despite the picturesque buildings, it was evident that the town itself was not as affluent as it first appeared. Whilst the local people smiled at the passing strangers, their open smiles did not touch their eyes. Their clothes, whilst neat and seemingly well-cared for, were three years out of fashion at least, and a number of the children were dressed in clothes either much too big or too small for their slender frames.

The cart stopped just in front of a large, four storied building that towered over all the others. Its smooth stone walls had been painted white, although a few areas had begun to crack and peel. Dark timber struts embellished the walls. Ivy had begun to sprout on the western wall, desperately fighting for entry through the clear windows. Just as with the houses, well-tended plants slept underneath the closed windows. But, unlike the delicate pastel wildflowers that decorated the rest of the town, these black wooden window boxes were home to dark red and golden yarrow flowers, their pungent aroma making it difficult to ignore their existence.

Arvyn jumped out of the cart, pulling his black hood close over his face and arranging it to carefully conceal the detailed hilt of his golden sword. He headed impatiently walked towards the heavy oak door, painted black with a very thick layer of paint. An oversized human skull was nailed into the wood, the smooth bone dyed crimson.

As he walked into the room, he was greeted by the heady scent of beer and ale, swirling around him as his eyes adjusted to the slightly dim room.

The busy room was filled with hefty wooden tables and chairs, almost every one already occupied by locals after a long day's work. A buxom woman stood behind the long bar across the room, her thick hands deftly cleaning a wooden tankard before filling it from a well-used clay pitcher. A broad smile was painted on her square face below her rosy cheeks, her dark green eyes lovingly watching over her raucous customers. A pair of young men darted between the tables, refilling tankards from large clay pitchers.

"Are you the proprietor of this inn?"

She raised a slender blonde eyebrow at the cold duke as he stood before her with his two companions, each one's face obscured from view.

"Aye," she smiled, revealing a single gap in her broad grin as she glanced up and down. "If you're here for a room, we're full. If you're here for ale, find a seat."

Arvyn laid a small pouch on the table in front of her, his voice low.

"My sister has been staying here. I am sure she has not been an easy customer so this is extra for her upkeep. And for your silence."

The innkeeper sceptically reached for the plain black leather pouch, her round eyes growing larger as she peered at the numerous gold coins before her.

"I assume you mean Miss Leonie," she said quietly, slipping the pouch into a pocket on her dark grey skirt, hidden beneath a slightly grubby white apron. "I'll escort you up to her personally."

The woman shouted to one of the young men to sit at the bar, before stepping out slowly from behind the counter. As she moved, Arvyn couldn't help but notice the unusual sway of her shoulders as she walked with a not so slight limp. Every other step came down with a thud as she lifted her long plain skirt slightly off the uneven grey stone floor.

Arvyn caught himself when he realised he was staring, clenching his jaw in embarrassment.

The woman pretended not to notice, her smile hardly fading as she led the way up the creaking stairs.

"We only have six guest rooms here; we're a locals' tavern. Travellers normally go to the *Amber Sword* or *Black Horse* nearer the gates. But, Miss Leonie insisted on staying here. She's not left the room, mind, so none of my regulars have noticed. The two men with her have been ordering food and wine for her every day."

Arvyn fought the urge to rub his temples as the thought of dealing with the hurricane that was Leonie dawned on him.

"She has always been rather stubborn, for which I must apologise," he muttered quietly.

"Ah, she's been a good lodger, sir," the innkeeper said cheerfully. "Pays on time and keeps to herself. Can't ask more than that, really. Here we are."

The woman knocked loudly on the thick wooden door before heading back down the stairs.

After a few moments, the heavy door opened a little crack, revealing the delicate face of Leonie's youngest new maid. Her blue eyes looked nervously at the four hooded figures behind the innkeeper.

But then her eyes caught sight of Wilfred joining them and she seemed to relax, opening the door slightly more.

"May we come in?"

The maid opened the door fully, revealing a large but simple room. It had four single beds arranged neatly against the right wall, each with a small wooden trunk at the foot of the wooden bedpost. The two windows, small in Arvyn's eyes, at the far end of the room were thrown open, sunlight streaming in through the coarse white curtains.

Lying on her stomach on one of the beds was the golden haired princess, her pale legs kicking in the air as she intently read the book in front of her. Daryl and Wilfred politely looked away as they realised she was in nothing but her white nightgown despite it still being the afternoon.

The prince gritted his teeth.

"This doesn't look like home, Leonie."

The girl's head shot towards the door, her golden eyes wide for a moment before being replaced with a genuine smile as she leapt towards him.

"Arvyn!"

He stood stiffly as she wrapped her arms around him, pressing her head against his cold black cloak.

"I told you to return to the capital. Father will kill me for kidnapping you."

"Don't worry, brother," she smiled, looking up at him. "I sent a letter telling him I'm staying at Varnika Abbey for a while; he thinks that I'm preparing my soul before my marriage."

She smiled, stepping away from him.

"My lady," the older maid said quietly, draping a grey cloak over her shoulders carefully in an attempt to hide the nightgown.

"Cliona, you will stay here with Leonie for the night. Daryl and I shall share with the guards," the prince said coldly, turning for the door. "Take some time to freshen up; I intend to be on the road in the morning."

The men left, closing the door softly behind them.

"You must be exhausted, Cliona! I'll call for a bath, and Hana and Lila can give you a massage too," Leonie smiled.

Cliona sighed, sitting herself on the edge of one of the neatly made beds. "That's not necessary, but thank you."

Leonie pouted, lying back on her bed. She lifted her arms out before her, stretching out her fingertips as she breathed a content sigh.

"Edgar told me about the dryad's cave," she said quietly. "I wish I could have seen such a beautiful grove."

"No doubt you will," Cliona replied. "If we succeed, I'm sure that groves will grow all over the world again."

The princess smiled. "How much longer do you think it'll take? To find the items, I mean."

Cliona sighed, turning her crimson gaze firmly on the young princess.

"Did Edgar also tell you of the void beasts that have reawakened in the forest? The further down this path that your brother travels, the more danger he will face. Perhaps it is best if you do return to the capital."

Leonie glared at the silver haired woman, her voice harsh.

"I am just as much an heir of Oleksander as Arvyn. Why does he get to…?"

Cliona cut through her protests. "Thanks to the suppression of women by the church in this land, you have no way of protecting yourself. You cannot swing a sword or raise a bow. Nor can you cast magic or possess an innate aura. Tell me, what use will you be when the bloodshed finally starts?"

"I don't know. But how will I know unless I'm given a chance to try?"

Cliona sighed lying back on her own bed. "I admire your courage, but resolve alone will not protect you from what is to come."

Leonie glared at her for a while, before silently returning to her book.

Chapter 19

The earthy taste of the deep crimson wine lingered as Leonie put her crude wooden goblet back onto the table in the centre of the room. She was oblivious to the various glances of the tavern's other patrons as her doe-like golden eyes happily absorbed the words from the romantic novel in front of her.

Thankfully her temporary bodyguard, Markus, sat beside her, the hefty black leather wrapped hilt of his longsword clearly visible on the table in front of him as he, too, read silently. Whilst his charge, only three years younger than him, enjoyed her cheerful novel *The Thorn Princess*, the young knight meticulously studied *The Lawful Practice of Being a True Knight*, which, just like the princess, he had discovered in the Thornbury Market two days ago.

The pair was so absorbed in their reading that they both only offered a cursory glance as a fresh faced Cliona and the two maids joined them.

"I know that my brother won't tell me even if I asked," Leonie said quietly, raising her glass to her lips as her eyes remained on the page, "but did you find any more artefacts, Cliona? I forgot to ask."

"We found one more after the dryads, yes. Your brother is keeping it safe with the others."

Cliona nodded slowly, closing her book with a smile.

"I suppose that's better than none. Although, if it has taken almost three weeks to find three items, I worry that we will run out of time."

Cliona said nothing as the innkeeper personally brought over more goblets and a bottle of the princess's favourite wine.

"Do you at least have any ideas on where to look?"

"Leonie," a familiar voice gruffly grumbled behind her. "You would do well not to involve yourself with my affairs further."

The prince sat in the only remaining chair at his sister's table whilst his bodyguard grabbed a seat from the next table along.

"But, I want to help. I was given one of the items."

"Enough, Leonie. I have already lost good men on this venture; I will not lose you too. Tomorrow, I will personally escort you to the abbey, where you will stay until my mission is complete, just like you told Father."

Leonie pouted quietly, not wanting to cause a scene in such a public space. Besides, she was close enough to her brother to tell when his notorious temper was beginning to flare up.

The group sat in silence as the two servers brought out stew and bread to their table, refilling the empty glasses.

The room went quiet as the door flung open, revealing two tall guards carrying one of their comrades between them, his limp knees trailing along the hard floor. Blood smeared along the ground in their wake.

"Where's Doctor Salter?"

A dark haired man quickly pushed his thin spectacles up his nose at the sound of the panicked guard's voice. He unbuttoned and rolled up his cream shirt sleeves quickly as he made his way towards the blood-soaked newcomers.

"The sewers?"

The guards nodded, both clearly out of breath as they lay their companion on a now vacant table before collapsing into their own chairs.

"Those damned bandits," one of them spat through rasping breaths, clutching his wounded side. "We don't have the resources to deal with them."

"If Lord Clayton doesn't deal with them soon, we might not have a town any more."

"Easy," the innkeeper said dryly as she gestured to her staff to serve the guards whilst she helped the doctor. "Let's not make any assumptions, Milo."

Arvyn stood quietly, standing in front of them. "Where are these bandits?"

The guard looked the plainly dressed traveller up and down, his exhausted gaze lingering on the fine gold sword at his waist.

"Are you a mercenary?"

"Something like that," the prince muttered, his eyes narrowed on the limp body on the table. "Tell me where to find them."

The man stood slowly, reaching two heads taller than the young prince.

"Lord Clayton won't pay you."

"I'm not seeking payment," Arvyn said firmly, his golden eyes steadily filling with rage. "Just tell me where to find them."

Daryl stood behind him, his grey eyes appraising the battered armour of the burly guard.

The guard sighed, falling back into his seat.

"They're hiding in the sewers that run under the old part of the town. Jonah will show you the way," he said, nodding to the other guard who was in slightly better condition. "But don't say I didn't warn you; they're ruthless masters at ambushing."

Arvyn inclined his head before turning to his uncle.

"Have Markus rejoin the unit; Kimiro can guard Leonie. The rest of us will deal with these vermin."

"Yes, sir," Daryl replied, turning to bark orders at his knights, each one quickly finishing their golden ale before returning upstairs to retrieve their armour.

The prince looked down at the young man on the table, his breathing ragged. An unusual slash wound on his chest caught his eye, a sticky black sludge bubbling from the torn flesh. He stepped closer to inspect it.

The doctor caught his wrist, clearing his throat.

"I suggest you don't touch that," he said monotonously. "Last time, my apprentice's fingers began to melt when he touched it. I have no idea what in God's name could have caused it, but I can tell you that nothing good can come from such a weapon."

Arvyn sighed, taking a step back.

"I have seen this before," Cliona whispered, standing close beside Arvyn.

He met her steady gaze as she nodded.

The knights returned, wearing their inconspicuous iron armour, the royal cockatrice emblazoned on the sturdy chestplates. Nairne quickly started to help the prince into a spare set of armour, as both Daryl's and his armour had been damaged beyond repair thanks to the Serpentarus. Whilst it did not fit as comfortably as his previous set, Arvyn knew that he had little right to complain when the local guards were adorned only in hardened leather.

Cliona ignored the excited whispers of the nearby locals as she unwrapped her thin white skirt from her waist, revealing the thick white cotton trousers that she had bartered from Lady Nefera. She pulled on an unusual black and gold jacket over her white bodice, deftly fastening the golden buttons. Her hands expertly lifted her long silver hair back into a tight bun using the thick black ribbon passed to her by one of Leonie's maids.

"Kimiro, I am entrusting my sister to you," the prince said, his cold golden eyes staring at the elderly man as Edgar tightened the armour strap under his armpit. "I want you to take her back to your hometown should the situation here worsen."

"Understood, sir."

"Arvyn, be careful," Leonie said, her voice cracking as she fought back tears, her eyes fixed on the black ichor oozing from the guard's wound.

The prince nodded, an exasperated smile on his golden face as he, Cliona and his six knights followed the battered guard into the town dimly lit by the early evening sun.

The streets, busy with merchants only a few hours ago, were desolate as the group travelled quickly towards the west of Thornbury town.

"Why are the streets so quiet?"

The guard gritted his teeth at the prince's question.

"Most people hide from the thieves and drunkards that come out at night. The old town's not quite so bad, but the south side is the worst for it. Unless you want to be stabbed or kidnapped, you stay inside, if you know what's good for you. We were actually chasing a hooded thief in the sewers when we got attacked; he must have been one of the bandits."

Arvyn clenched his fists tightly, realising that neither he nor his brothers had ever truly seen the land that they ruled.

They marched in silence until they got to a large bridge, the sandy stone arching over the dainty River Thorne. The river trickled slowly under the ancient stone bridge, the riverbank three quarters higher than the water thanks to years of measly rainfall.

The guard jumped down the riverbank from the unkempt cobblestone road, his cracked black boots splashing in the shallow river as he landed.

Prince Arvyn nodded, and his small troop of knights followed, all disappearing under the wide stone bridge.

The guard stopped in front of an old, rusted black iron gate, the water trickling down the steps beyond the rusted metal grate.

"Down here," he said, pulling the gate from its weary hinges as the knights lit a few torches between them. "It's the old sewers. It's not been used in a long time so it's not well maintained; a few of the tunnels have had cave-ins so I'd be careful. Keep to the wall on your left at every turn and you'll find where the bandits ambushed us. I'll head back to the guard house and try to send some backup for you. If Captain Julien is willing to help, that is."

The torch light cast a dim orange glow over the clay tiled tunnels as the group disappeared into the darkness, small creatures scurrying out of sight as the torch light drew near to them.

Arvyn gritted his teeth as his feet sloshed through the thick, pungent liquid lining the floor. How the town guards, with their clearly rotting leather armour and cracked boots, could stomach such a place was beyond him. Just the thought of the sewage touching his skin was enough to make him stifle retching, let alone having it seep into old boots.

He looked to Cliona, her bare fingertips trailing along the glazed tiled walls as she walked behind the knights.

"I remember hearing that this was being built," she mused quietly. "It was just after the demons were sealed away. To think that the architecture is only just still standing."

"What was here before?"

"Daudanus. Loosely translated from the demon-tongue, it means 'City of the Dead'."

"So, you mean it was a cemetery?"

She smiled at Markus, her crimson eyes seeming to sparkle in the dim light.

"No, it was a magnificent city. The buildings were made of a stone that was once native to the demon realm. I can't remember the name, but it was pure white under the sun, and looked like a rainbow under the moonlight. Some even said that it was so rare to find because it came from the moonlit hill itself."

"What's the moonlit hill?"

A flicker of sadness flashed over her face as Markus watched her, intrigued.

"The moonlit hill is where a demon's soul returns to rest after the body dies."

"That all sounds like something from a dream," Cuthbert mumbled, not believing her.

"So do dryads and magical beasts, but here we are," Edgar said, ruffling the younger knight's black hair.

The group continued down the dark tunnels, sticking to the left-hand side as the guard had recommended. Slowly, the clay tiles began to grow in more disrepair, the air growing more putrid with every step they took. After a while, so many tiles were missing from the arched ceiling that, aside from the stench, it had begun to feel more like being in the rotting burrow of an animal than an ancient sewer.

Eventually, they came across a pristine portcullis, crimson tendrils strangling the black iron bars like ivy. The ancient defence was being held open by a large pile of rubble, a handful of rats scurrying back into the small holes of the mound.

Arvyn borrowed the torch from one of the guards, peering down the dark path ahead. But, as much as he squinted, his eyes could not make sense of his surroundings through the dense shadows.

He returned the torch, nodding to his bodyguard. "We'll continue for now, but be on alert."

The duke ducked under the portcullis first, noticing that his movements were still slightly stiff after the skirmish with the Serpentarus. But he gritted his teeth, holding the torch for Cuthbert as he followed the senior knight silently, waiting for the rest of their party to join them.

They had not long wandered beyond the portcullis when the path they were taking began to incline slightly, the water fading away as the ground transformed into cracked cobblestone, not dissimilar to the town above. The packed-dirt walls began to change, large pillars of grey stone now lining the walls.

Markus almost dropped his raised torch as he lifted it towards one of the walls. Having expected to see stone or dirt, the young knight was unprepared to be greeted instead by row upon row of human bones. Five skulls intermittently lined the centre of the wall, their dark eye orbits staring silently into the dingy tunnel.

Wilfred, under the duke's silent order, quietly lit one of the thick black sconces that decorated the walls. Despite having been unlit for centuries, the ancient oil began to burn brightly, the other scones simultaneously bathing the corridor in light.

A barely audible gasp whispered through the group as more walls of skeletal remains greeted them, as far as the eye could see.

"What is this place?"

Markus subconsciously clutched at the subtle religious pendant he wore on a chain around his neck, a good luck charm given to him by a sweetheart before he became a Wynford Knight.

As their surroundings finally came into view, Arvyn finally noticed three fresh corpses lying on the floor ahead of them, each one wearing the same tattered uniform of the Thornbury guards, strewn across the cobbled floor just ahead of them.

"Stay alert," Daryl ordered, drawing his sword as he turned over one of the corpses with his boot.

The man, no older than thirty, stared back at him with lifeless black eyes, half of his face seemingly already rotted away. On closer inspection, the same thick black slime seemed to ooze out of his cracked jaw bone, similar to the injury he saw in the tavern.

"Cliona," the prince called. "You said you recognise this sort of wound."

She knelt on the ground behind the body, her pale hands draped over her now grey trousers.

"It is a toxin," she said quietly, inspecting the slash on the corpse. "One that only the most ancient liches can secrete, although the older the lich, the more potent the poison. To put it simply, it burns through all organic material, except bone, that it comes into contact with, including blood. I'm told it is an incredibly painful way to die."

Arvyn was silent for a moment, swallowing his disgust at the putrid stench being emitted from the already decaying body.

"We should keep moving, Your Highness," Markus suggested as his voice slightly trembled.

The prince nodded, turning to walk further down the corridor when his foot landed on something firm.

His golden eyes grew wide as he looked down to find an intact skull below his foot, a pair of glowing crimson orbs staring up at him from the empty eye sockets.

"Trespassers," the skull hissed in a thick, guttural accent as its body reassembled from the various remains on the ground in front of the prince. "Trespassers must die."

The duke drew his sword, pulling Arvyn behind him. The knights quickly followed suit as they fanned out in a semi-circle behind the duke. Markus, having not yet seen such a mythical creature, fumbled with the hilt of his sword, allowing it to slip from his quaking fingers onto the cobbled floor below.

The perfectly articulated skeleton grinned, a strange black mist tumbling from its grimacing mouth as it took a step forward, its arms outstretched.

Two more skeletons began to shake on the ground beside it, black threads of magic stitching them meticulously back together as their boney feet stepped towards the prince and his companions.

Arvyn turned to look behind them, only to find two more undead figures creeping towards them. Just as with the three in front of them, these two were slowly emitting a thick black gas from their open jaws, their crimson eyes burning as they grew closer.

"We have business in Daudanus," Cliona bellowed firmly. "You will allow us to pass, or face your master's wrath."

The skeletons looked to each other, the first one tilting its head slightly to the left as it appeared to listen.

After a moment, the skeletons' crimson eyes began to fade into black, the black smoke dissipating. Four of the figures began to fall once more to the floor, their separated bones rolling off to the side of the corridor.

"Master shall see," the main skeleton replied, bending down to the floor.

As its skeletal hand touched the cold cobblestone, a circle of glowing black runes appeared on the floor surrounding the travellers and single remaining skeleton, filling the space around them with a pitch black fog.

Chapter 20

As the black fog began to clear, Arvyn and his companions found themselves lying on the cold ground, their hands bound tightly behind their backs.

"Ah, finally! You're awake!"

Arvyn looked up towards the voice, his head still foggy from the obnoxious fumes.

A small child sat cross legged in front of him, their vibrant ruby eyes glistening excitedly as they met the prince's.

He could barely contain his disgust as his eyes were drawn to the left side of the child's face. The tanned flesh of the child's cheek was rotting away, revealing the smooth bone of their mandible beneath it. Black sludge-like pus seeped from the hole, filling the room with the stench of decay.

The child smiled broadly at the stranger's discomfort, their two canines filed down into sharpened points. They leant forwards, resting their decaying face on a closed fist.

"I couldn't wait for you to wake up! Now we can go play!"

Arvyn fought a shudder at the child's menacing voice.

"Is this how you treat your guests? Who are you?"

"Oh, how rude! You think you're guests?"

The child sprang backwards into a somersault, landing elegantly on their feet. They held their arms out in a flourish, their pale green bob bouncing around their diamond face as they looked up to the air.

"You are not guests. You are here to play. And I love to play."

The child turned their burning crimson gaze back to the prince, the smile stretching even further on their face.

Black flames erupted in their hands as they let out a high pitched laugh, sending a shiver down the prince. As the aggressive flames began to subside, two circular silver blades appeared in their hands, black leather bound tightly over the centre of the weapon to create a handhold.

"Wynne," a deep voice called from the side, their face obscured by the shadow cast by their crimson hood. "I shall have them transported to the theatre."

The child pouted, throwing the strange weapons on the floor as they crossed their arms, sitting back on the sandy floor. As they did so, the weapons dissipated into the same black flames that had spawned them.

"You're no fun."

"I am merely following Master's protocol," the stranger said monotonously, stretching their long arms, hidden by their billowing cloak, before them.

As they did so, a series of glowing red circles began to appear on the floor around the bound intruders. A series of red and black runes began to etch themselves in the ground between the two outermost rings. Black smoke once again began to fill the area, making the prince's head feel heavy just like before.

But, when he opened his eyes, the two figures were still in front of him.

As he shifted his weight, he realised he was stood on loose sand, not the hard sandstone floor from before. He was able to move his arms freely, the harsh leather bindings suddenly removed. However, so too was his sword.

The sound of cheering and chanting hit his ears as the smoke slowly began to thin.

Arvyn and his companions found themselves in the centre of a large arena. The sandy ground that they stood on was enclosed by fifteen foot high walls made of smooth sandstone, topped with evenly spaced black iron spikes. Embedded into the north side of the arena were three iron-studded black stone doors, each one reaching almost to the top of the wall.

The pit itself was longer than it was wide, with the length divided in two by a deep ravine. Six tall sandstone pillars had once stood tall in the centre of the arena, but now the remains of all but two littered the orange floor.

Beyond the walls sat row upon row of spectators, each one cheering loudly from the stands. From his position, Arvyn could make out their pale skeletal frames, each one with crimson eyes staring into the pit expectantly.

The hooded figure stood tall in front of them, the child giggling excitedly sat at their feet.

A hush fell across the crowd as the hooded figured raised a long arm into the air.

"By the ancient laws of Daudanus, those who invoke the name of the Master must prove that they are worthy of His attention."

As the crowds began cheering again, the figure turned to face the prince and his companions, a pair of deep crimson eyes glowing through the shadows of the hood.

"You must defeat the adversaries that I provide, or else your souls shall be forfeit."

Daryl glanced at the prince, who merely nodded back to him.

"We accept your challenge," Arvyn said clearly.

The child, still sat cross-legged on the floor in front of him, giggled.

"Oh, you think you have a choice? By invoking the Master's name, your fate was already sealed."

"You shall have five minutes to select your weapons before I open the gate," the tall figure said quietly, a pair of magic circles appearing under each of the challengers. "Come, Wynne."

"Good luck, humans," the child giggled, enveloped in smoke.

In place of the two strange figures was a tall weapons rack, adorned in various different armaments, some of which even Daryl had never seen before.

"Cliona, you and His Highness will stay in the centre. The rest of us shall spread out in a circle around you," the old bodyguard announced firmly, reaching for a one-handed longsword and large circular shield from the rack in front of him.

The prince reached for a sword, his golden brow furrowed as he glanced at Cliona. "Do you know anything about what enemies we might face?"

She sighed, stepping towards the rack herself. Her pale fingertips brushed over the weapons gently, finally landing on a long staff, runes carved into the wood.

"If it is a series of skeletons then that plan may work, but I doubt that such a simple strategy will be possible for other enemies. The undead take gladiator fights very seriously; we can expect a strong opponent or two."

"If it's more of those void beasts then we will need range," Cuthbert said, selecting an old longbow and quiver of twenty or so arrows from the rack. After a brief hesitation, he also grabbed a single-handed axe.

Wilfred selected a bow and dagger, Nierne a long spear, and Edgar and Markus a shield and sword.

The prince hesitated, knowing that he was not as skilled in combat as the knights surrounding him. After a moment, he decided that it was best to use a weapon that he had some experience with, and so he selected the only other sword on the rack.

As he did so, the rack disappeared.

A loud gong sang above them as the colossal gate at the edge of the pit began to rise.

"Whatever happens," Daryl said firmly, "do not be afraid of whatever greets us."

Arvyn closed his eyes in a brief prayer, his hands gripping the sword in front of him as he faced the gate.

* * *

Wynne leant forward in his sandstone throne, his knuckles going white as he watched the strangers huddle nervously around the weapons rack in the arena below.

"I want to play too," he smiled, rocking back and forth. "Let me play, Ambrosia."

"Our job is to observe and judge the threat of the intruders, not to defeat them ourselves."

"But, you know I could do it. Why can't I play?"

The woman sighed, raising her hand to open the gate with a magic circle. As soon as the tell-tale runes appeared on the vast iron gateway, a servant banged the gong, signifying to the crowd that the fight was about to begin.

"I am quite aware. The Master started to imbue a lot of his magic into you, after all. It's just a pity he did not correct that attitude of yours whilst he was at it; it has become most tedious after all these years."

The boy folded his arms, pouting.

"What was the point in it all if I never get to show off how strong the Master made me?"

His dissatisfaction was short lived. He raced to the edge of the viewing box, his smile wide with excitement once again as the crowd cheered from the side-lines. The boy clapped his hands, sitting on the narrow sandstone railing to the box, his legs crossed.

As the gate creaked open, six large quadruped figures skulked out of the darkness, their muscular black bodies littered with glowing lime green spirals. Each one wore a thick red collar, now unclipped from the dense iron chains they were accustomed to. Their sickly green saliva dripped from their elongated muzzles as they paced the outside of the arena, their quick eyes fixed on the humans in front of them.

The knights below formed a tight circle around the girl, the two armed with bows shooting at the void beasts. Whilst the arrows hit their marks, the beast merely foamed more, their vibrant green paws drawing them nearer and nearer.

"Interesting," Ambrosia muttered, joining the boy at the railing, her eyes glowing crimson beneath her hood.

The strangers below drew their swords, slashing at the oncoming void beasts, all the while dodging their dripping green jaws.

Wynne glanced at her, confused at why her dull voice was suddenly laced with colour.

"Tell me, what do you see down there, Wynne?"

He smiled, turning his big scarlet eyes back on the fight. "I see blood, lots of it. I want to bathe in it."

"Not with your eyes, you dolt," Ambrosia spat, scuffing the top of his head with her black-gloved fist. "Use the sight that the Master granted you. Or are you incapable of even doing that much?"

Wynne glared at her, his red eyes beginning to glow as he unleashed the dark magic that General Floki had started to weave into his soul. As he did so, the world went dark, the walls and furniture around him becoming simple grey outlines. The woman in front of him became a thin wall of dark red energy, thanks to the intense magic that General Floki had imbued her soul with. Looking at his own hands, Wynne could see that he was the same vibrant shade of crimson, although there were patches devoid of any colour.

He held his arm angrily, once again cursing the demons that interrupted his enlightenment ritual and leaving him as neither a skeleton nor a lich.

The boy turned his gaze over the pit below them.

A small gasp escaped from his mouth as he caught sight of what had intrigued Ambrosia so much.

In the pit, Wynne could make out the four remaining void beasts from their menacing pale green shapes, and the faint red outline of the skeletons cheering in the stands. But, the intruders emitted an unfamiliar pale red aura that seemed to pulsate in and out of view. The more he tried to focus on the source of the aura, the more unclear the scene before him was, with each of the humanoid figures completely engulfed within the smoke.

"What is that?"

"Unlike the dark red magic that the Master gifted us, humans possess a much paler shade of red. It should be a single block colour, like with most other creatures. But, demons possess innate auras that merge between two or three different colours. Think of it as a magical fingerprint showing their ancestry and strength. For a human's aura to swirl in such a manner, they are either directly descended from a very powerful demon, or have been in contact with one recently."

"Does that mean you know how strong they are? Which one is the strongest?"

Ambrosia narrowed her eyes, trying to find the root of the majestic colours swirling in the pit. "Perhaps the

Master could tell, but I am not so skilled. Besides, if my theory is correct then the owner of this aura is much more powerful than I am, perhaps even more so than the Master. We must test it thoroughly."

Wynne licked his lips, summoning his circular chakram blades once again. He leant forward over the railing, ready to jump into the ring.

"No, Wynne," she said firmly, grabbing him by the scruff of the neck. "Let the beasts do the work."

"Argh! I never get to play!"

He threw his chakrams on the floor, crossing his skinny arms angrily.

"This is an unknown entity of unknown potential. It is safer and easier for us to evaluate their strength by staying here."

Ambrosia raised her hand towards the arena, her fist closed tightly. Unlike most of her incantations, she began to mutter under her breath, summoning a thick black sphere in the centre of the arena. She opened her gloved hand, the smoke dissipating.

In its place was a giant creature, towering above the prince and his companions. The quadrupedal beast had blackened leathery skin and a long tail that flickered as it walked, it's broad, clawed feet sinking slightly into the sandy ground of the arena. It possessed three distinct heads, each one belonging to a different creature. The giant white tiger snarled at the humans before it, its golden eyes tracking the prey as it moved forward. Beside it, the draconic head snapped its jaws impatiently, a thick black ichor dripping from between the sharpened teeth, melting the sand as it lumbered slowly forward. The third head belonged to a humanoid creature with mottled purple skin, its black eyes focused on the prince and his companions and mouth sewn shut. The visible black threads that held the creature together pulsed with Ambrosia's crimson magic as it breathed heavily.

Ambrosia leant against the sandstone railing, her crimson eyes glowing as she watched her treasured chimaera stumble towards the outsiders. Arvyn stood shaking beside the duke, adrenaline coursing through his veins as his chest heaved against the exertion. Steam dripped from his sword along with the thick black blood from the void beasts.

His golden eyes watched the monstrous creature before them, its snarling head ripping through the thick skin of yet another void beast.

"How the hell do we defeat that thing?"

"With brute force, Your Highness," his uncle replied, tightening his grip on the leather hilt of his sword. "We must attack together. Distract the heads whilst attacking from behind."

"Wait," Cliona called from behind them, her body completely unscathed thanks to the soldiers around her. "Wait and watch the chimaera. The dragon's jaws are dripping with venom. The tiger seems to be doing most of the damage. The giant doesn't do much, so I can only assume it is giving the other heads orders somehow."

"And how does this help?" The prince spat through gritted teeth as yet another void beast charged towards him, his guards deftly disposing of the creature.

Cliona closed her eyes, her voice steady.

"Blind the giant first. Disabling its eyes would probably be best. Then attack the dragon or the tiger. It doesn't appear to have any wings, but I wouldn't be surprised if it could fly because of the dragon so be ready for it to take flight."

Daryl and Arvyn nodded to each other.

"Wait for the creature to look at us," Daryl said firmly to the soldiers with bows. "Then aim for the giant's eyes."

"Yes sir."

"Steady," Daryl shouted as the draconic head turned its attention towards the weak humans.

The giant turned its black eyes onto the prince.

The soldiers released a volley of arrows at the chimaera, just as the beast began its charge towards them. It screamed as the arrows hit their target, its stride faltering for a moment. But, it continued to close the gap, black blood oozing from the damaged purple orbits of the giant's head. Nierne deftly threw his spear into the open mouth of the dragon, the crude weapon lodging into the back of the creature's throat.

It thrashed its head, the sickly black venom splashing over the sand before it.

Edgar and Markus planted their feet into the sandy ground, raising their borrowed shields in front of their bodies as the chimaera continued to charge towards them. The prince and the duke stood just behind them, their swords ready.

Just as the beast was about to slam into the shield, a shrill sound rang throughout the arena, the chimaera becoming engulfed by a dense black smoke as it disappeared.

"Oh thank God," Cuthbert muttered, crossing himself as the creature disappeared.

Ambrosia stood tall before them, her arms folded tightly over her chest as her crimson eyes stared at the humans before her. The petulant child remained cross legged at her feet, his face turned away as he pouted.

"I have seen enough," the woman announced, lifting her arm high in the air. "It would not do for my pet to be mutilated even more. Besides," she smiled, her full red lips visible below the shadow of her hood as she muttered, "I am not stupid enough to challenge such an aura that could perhaps test even the Master."

Arvyn let out a sigh, passing his sword to Edgar to wipe.

"I am Ambrosia, acting Lord of the Undead until our master General Floki returns. You are already acquainted with the Master's second apprentice, Wynne."

The child glared at the prince before bouncing to his feet, falling into an exaggerated bow, his crimson eyes burning.

"I am Prince Arvyn of Vyst, descendent of Oleksander I. My companions and I were sent to investigate the deaths of some local guards in the sewers. From what we've seen of the corpses, your poison seems to be involved."

Ambrosia looked down at Wynne, her eyes cold.

The boy raised his hands in the air, shaking his head. "Don't look at me; I just practiced on the bodies the patrols found."

Daryl sighed, rubbing his temples. "And where did you find these bodies?"

"In the tunnels," Wynne whined, folding his arms and avoiding the duke's gaze.

"Wynne will show you where he found them so that you may be on your way."

"There is one more thing that we need to ask," Arvyn said, lowering his voice as he glanced at the distant skeletons leaving the stadium.

Ambrosia snapped her long gloved fingers, summoning a thick black fog around the group.

"This barrier dampens any sound as well as hides those inside from view. So, what is it you wish to request?"

Arvyn watched her carefully, his hand resting on the hilt of his sword, now sleeping once more at his hip.

"I want your master's artefact; the one that is needed to bring him back," the prince said calmly.

Her eyes snapped to the prince coldly.

"And what right would you have to claim such precious treasures?" She hissed, her eyes glowing as she spoke.

"I am a descendant of Oleksander I, and have already gathered three of the others."

"What would you do with the relics?"

Arvyn's brow creased as he looked at her, confusion clear on his face. "I intend to bring them back."

She let out a loud, short laugh, her hands on her hips.

"You expect me to believe that a child of that bastard would ever truly appear to resurrect the Eight Generals?" He turned her cold gaze on him once more. "I will give you another chance to tell the truth, as you bested my chimaera."

"His Highness would not lie about such a thing," the duke said firmly, his hand resting on the hilt of his trusty sword, now returned to him.

She glanced at Cliona over the old knight's shoulder. She held her silver head high, meeting the undead woman's gaze steadily.

"Perhaps you should use your magic to analyse his lineage, Lady Ambrosia," Cliona said firmly, her crimson eyes cold. "I believe that you possess the elven magic to do that, at least."

"A wonderful idea," the skeleton woman smirked, her hand pulling a simple obsidian dagger from the belt at her waist. "Give me your hand, human, and I shall see if you are truly who you claim to be."

Daryl stepped in front of his nephew, his eyes cold. "You will not harm His Highness."

Arvyn laid a hand on his uncle's shoulder, his eyes still trained on Ambrosia.

"My golden eyes and golden hair mark me as a direct descendant of Oleksander I, and the fact that I have already acquired the items from the sirens, dryads and serpents should be enough to prove my identity."

"Aw," Wynne cooed, his hands cupping his decaying face as his eyes glinted. "The poor little human is scared of a little blood."

"You need only prick your finger with this dagger; I will be able to learn the truth from a single drop of blood. Although," Ambrosia continued, her voice dripping with malice, "if you are indeed lying then I will have no choice but to dispose of you. Perhaps I shall allow Wynne to use you as he pleases."

The pair laughed.

Arvyn turned to face Cliona. She nodded, her face expressionless.

He sighed, holding out his hand to the woman. She took his hand in hers, quickly pricking the tip of his right thumb and squeezing the flesh to draw a small pool of blood with the ancient dagger.

As she did so, she muttered a few words that Arvyn couldn't make out, his hand swallowed in her black smoke as her eyes glowed with her magic.

"Well, I suppose that you are to be trusted after all. With this, anyway," she smirked, the smoke dissipating as she released his hand, taking a step backwards.

Her slender hands stretched up to the black fur trimmed crimson hood, carefully pushing the velvet fabric away from her face.

It was clear from her finely chiselled features and high carriage that she had once been the sheer image of beauty. Her hooded ruby eyes were full of life, her full lips painted a shade of red to match their unique hue. A small, pert nose sat in the centre of her dark skinned face, delicate freckles decorating her velvety skin.

But, the left side of her face was not unlike her younger companion; her once perfect skin had long since rotted away, revealing her carefully sculpted cheek bone and the corner of her mandibles.

Not once did her gaze falter as the prince observed her, fascinated by the undead woman before him.

She smiled, sorrow lingering over her plump lips as she held out her hands, a grey fog enveloping them.

Arvyn looked down at her hands. As the smoke dissipated, a chunky golden arm ring lay carefully in her palms, rubies glaring at him from the twisted circlet.

"This was a gift given to the Master by his own master, long before he created me. It was his most cherished possession." She met the prince's eyes firmly. "Should anything happen to my Master or his treasure, I will personally see to it that your soul is seized as forfeit."

The prince bowed his head.

"I understand, my lady."

She nodded, handing the cold golden band to the prince.

"One more thing; take Wynne to the surface with you, as an insurance policy for the Master's arm ring. And," she grinned, resting her hand on her ample hip, "I'm tired of this runt's belly aching. Might do him some good spending some time with humans for a change. Listen to them, Wynne, and become better for the Master."

The boy scowled at her, crossing his arms.

"Plus, dear Wynne," Ambrosia said softly, "perhaps one of your new companions would agree to spar with you."

His eyes lit up, his sharpened teeth glinting as he smiled.

The prince fought back a shudder.

"Well, if we are in agreement then, Lady Ambrosia, we shall take our leave. We will head to the bandit camp first and then finish collecting the items."

Ambrosia pulled her hood back over her face before snapping her fingers, dismissing the fog once more.

"I shall eagerly await the Master's return."

Chapter 21

Wynne led the prince and his companions expertly through the maze of tiled tunnels. Even though their nostrils had become accustomed to the putrid stench of the sewers, their hardened leather expedition boots were slowly tiring, no longer able to defend them from the stale waters that swirled around their ankles.

"Here," Wynne said after a while, pointing to a rapidly decaying body lying face down in the centre of a dingy pathway. "This is where we normally find them."

The boy leant against the curved wall of the tunnel, lifting his foot flat against the cracked tiles whilst folding his arms over his chest. He cocked his head to the side as his piercing eyes watched the prince closely.

Arvyn and Daryl both knelt beside the body, carefully turning the guard over using the tips of their swords.

The man wore the same tattered uniform of the local guards, but beyond that there was little left to establish his identity. Most of his face had been slowly eroded by the same tar-like toxin that they had seen before, the purple slime still glistening on his leathery skin.

"How often do they appear?"

"Depends, I guess. Every week, but normally two or three times a week. I guess it depends on how often they get caught by the humans further up."

"What are the humans there doing?"

"Beats me," the boy shrugged. "We don't bother getting involved with humans unless they come into our territory."

"Your Highness, this man's weapon is missing."

"They never have anything of value on them. No trinkets or weapons that we can use, anyway. Honestly, they're just clogging up the waterway."

The prince bit his tongue, his molten eyes focusing on the stiff corpse lying before him as he stood, brushing down his black trousers.

"We'll follow the tunnel. Be on the lookout for an ambush."

Daryl relayed the prince's orders to the rest of the guards.

"Cliona," Arvyn said softly, standing beside her. "If it gets dangerous further ahead, I want you to get yourself back to the tavern."

She tilted her head slightly to the side, watching him quietly. "Understood."

Satisfied, the small group continued trudging down the tunnel, their soiled boots growing heavier with each step.

It wasn't long before the tunnel before them became bathed in a dim orange glow. The sound of crying bounced over the grimy tiles around them.

"This is it," Wynne licked his lips as they curled into a grin, his eyes glowing. "I can sense their life sources."

Cliona cast him a stern glance.

"How many?"

The boy closed his eyes, his lips twitching as he counted quickly. "About fifty, maybe more. Most are faint and close together; only about ten decent ones I reckon."

"Amazing," Nierne muttered, stringing his bow.

The duke nodded to the prince as they both drew their swords.

* * *

"Please, sir," the final man waivered, dropping his rusted sword to the floor, "have mercy. We were only doing as the boss said."

Daryl appeared behind him, his sword pressed against his back.

"Who is your boss?"

"Big Albert," he said, pointing to the burly corpse on the floor. "He got an offer from some local lord to move people from here to the Glerian Empire. Women and children, mostly; said he was paying to get them to safety, or something."

"And you truly believed that these people wanted to be ripped from their homeland?"

The prince clenched his jaw, his fists clenching at his sides.

"Aw, may I play with him when you're done?" Wynne sneered, jumping into a crouch before the battered man. He tilted his head, his rotting face clearly visible as his eyes stared unblinking at the frightened human. "The other's don't have enough strength left to be any fun, but this one still has a bit of life in him."

The man's eyes widened as he trembled, his frightened gaze focused on Wynne's rotting face.

"No," the duke growled, grabbing the boy by the scruff of his neck. "We do not harm prisoners."

Wynne crossed his arms and scowled, tucking his knees under his chest. Daryl laid him on the floor behind him, making sure to stand between the prisoner and the boy.

"Daryl, take Wynne, Nierne and Markus, and check that there are no more bandits anywhere. Have the able assist those who cannot walk on their own. We will return them to the surface and then pay this local lord a visit."

As his men left to do his bidding, a strange hooded figure caught the prince's eye, their well-worn black robe obscuring their face as they waited before one of the nearby cages silently.

"Greetings, Your Highness," a deep female voice said softly as the figure bowed their head slowly. "The Seeker invites you to speak with them."

Arvyn's golden brow furrowed, his hand on the cold hilt of his trusty sword.

"And who," he growled, his blood still boiling from the bandits, "is this Seeker?"

Cliona glanced at the hooded figure briefly, her voice low as she laid her hand on the prince's shoulder. "A servant to a very ancient being tasked to guide travellers. I had not expected to find them here. If they have chosen to visit you then it is best not to keep them waiting."

The prince sheathed his sword, allowing himself to be led by the stranger, Cliona following closely behind.

The figure led them through row upon row of cramped iron cells, each one home to between three and five emancipated figures. Their dull eyes glared through the cold bars as they passed, their exhausted forms slinking into the recesses of their barred crates.

Arvyn clenched his hands and ground his teeth, trying not to catch the eyes of the caged inhabitants.

Finally, they stopped in front of a small cage, the bars covered by a coarse black fabric. The figure's long billowing sleeves exposed their dark hands as they lifted the black canvas, somehow revealing a large room hidden within the miniscule cage.

Although the room was very dimly lit, silver stars glinted on the walls and ceiling of the space, seeming to revolve slowly. The air was heavy with musky incense, so thick that Arvyn fought back the urgent desire to cough. The room was barren aside from a mound of plump black and pale blue cushions arranged neatly in the centre.

Upon these pillows sat a small hooded figure, an unlit black candle waiting before them.

Their footsteps echoed over the packed dirt floor as they headed forward.

The figure was sat cross-legged in the centre of the room, their head bowed as they ground small crimson toadstools in a large black bowl with a pestle. Their features were hidden by the thick black bear-skin cloak draped over their hunched shoulders, a single long tendril of silver hair visible.

"Seeker, to you I beseech," Cliona whispered, sitting on her knees before the hooded figure, her crimson eyes closed as she pressed her forehead to the floor. "I bring to you one who seeks knowledge beyond his reach."

The hooded figure raised their pale face to the newcomers, their silver eyes glazed over as they stared at Arvyn.

He shivered, deciding to mimic Cliona and show the same reverence to the strange being before him.

"Speak true, dear child, what knowledge is it that you seek? The Land of Sight is no longer a well-trodden peak. A great many dangers shall you face, if we grant you passage to the spirit's place. Be sure that your desires are for more than just fun, for our magic cannot be undone."

Cliona turned to Arvyn, her eyes lowered. "The Seeker is bound by an ancient curse; they cannot hear nor speak except in verse."

The prince nodded, his voice slow as his mind searched for the right words.

"Seeker, I wish to find the path to a relic from the war. I seek the secrets of the Temple of Nour."

The Seeker paused their grinding, their silver eyes turning to look at Cliona. The girl said nothing, merely looking down at her hands clasped neatly in front of her.

"Such a name I have not heard for centuries past. Knowledge of the Temple of Nour is no small ask."

"My kingdom is in peril and the people are at risk unless I know more. I beg you; please show me how to locate the Temple of Nour."

The Seeker sighed.

"We regret that the knowledge that you seek, lies far beyond even our reach. You must journey to the Land of

Sight alone, if you truly wish for these answers to be known. But, for the veil to be crossed by one who is still full of life, one must provide a great sacrifice." The Seeker rasped, their pale eyes still settled on Cliona. "The Land of Sight holds many mysteries to behold, but the price for such knowledge is yet to be told."

The prince nodded slowly.

The Seeker held out a wrinkled black hand, their long fingernails painted silver. Cliona lifted the prince's hand, placing it in the palm of the hooded figure.

The Seeker's hushed words swirled around Arvyn, leaving icy trails over his golden skin. They spoke with the voice of hundreds of people, each one filled with malice and sorrow, with joy and despair. Their grip tightened on his warm hand as they pulled a simple obsidian dagger from their cloak, the jagged blade mirroring the night sky.

The coldness of the blade was quickly replaced by sticky warmth as a line of blood beaded on his large palm. Although the Seeker held his hand firmly in place, the prince did not flinch, but instead gritted his teeth, clenching his other hand tightly. They sprinkled a fine pale blue powder into his fresh wound.

The skin bubbled and oozed, thick white foam spreading over his body from the wound.

"Do not lose sight of what you seek," they whispered, a sorrowful smile dancing on their lips as Arvyn's eyes were shrouded in darkness, "or else forever you will sleep."

Chapter 22

Arvyn lifted his hand slowly to his throbbing forehead.

Where am I?

As he opened his eyes, he was greeted by a small pond, the shallow crystal-clear pool the most beautiful sapphire shade that he had ever seen. Fresh water gently danced into the pond over a series of white marble stones, the movement causing the pale pink lilies blooming on the water's surface to carefully sway. The pond was enclosed entirely by a wall of white climbing flowers, the delicate petals emitting a calming fragrance.

He was sat on the white marble edge of the tranquil pool, his legs dangled in the cool water, the warm sun caressing his cheeks.

The air was blissfully still.

When did I last feel so at peace?

As his eyes focused on the wall ahead of him, he noticed a small wooden door, hidden by the overgrown tendrils of pure white roses and delicate cream jasmine. The refreshing scents danced around him, seemingly growing stronger now that he had noticed their presence.

Arvyn, a log forgotten voice called softly.

He turned his head to face the hooded owner.

A tall, blonde haired woman stood before him, leaning heavily on a gnarled cane made of black wood, silver wire wrapped loosely around it. Her body was shrouded in a thick silver cloak, the fabric shimmering in the sunlight as they slowly opened the door.

The sounds of women crying and men screaming in agony echoed from the empty space beyond. Sword song surrounded him, the thrumming of unfamiliar explosions accompanying them.

He stood, raising his hand to his face. As he did so, the tranquil pond began to emit a dense silver mist, twisting its icy tendrils around his legs.

Stay with us, his mother's gentle voice whispered. *Relax with me; you need only know peace here.*

He took a deep breath, his steps heavy as the misty tendril tried to keep him in place.

There is something I must do, he thought, his mind racing for the answer. *There is something I must find.*

Suddenly, he was in a large oval room. Eight thrones sat around a central circle, all but one occupied by a motionless figure shrouded in shadow. The more that the prince squinted, trying to make out their cold faces, the more they faded from his view.

"You gave me your oath!"

He turned to see a tall woman being dragged into the room by a dark humanoid shadow, her black arms bound tightly behind her back by the creature. Although Arvyn could not focus on her features, a pair of long, curved silver horns sprouted clearly from her short silver hair, betraying her as a demon.

The faceless shadow behind her covered her mouth with its hand. The woman kicked against it, as a golden-haired figure appeared before her, carefully lifting a long two-headed sapphire snake towards her chest. She bit down on the shadow's hand, her face crumpled in pain as the snake's silver fangs sunk into the soft flesh of her breast.

She screamed, black tears dripping down her pale grey cheeks.

The shadow threw her to the ground, dissipating as the skin on her exposed arms quickly faded from an ombre grey and black to a pale peach, spreading over her entire body as her horns dropped to the floor.

The prince gasped as her features came into view, her hollow red eyes meeting his.

Cliona.

He went to step towards her, his arm reaching for her hunched body, but the mist swallowed him.

His hand instinctively covered his face, her distraught screams ringing in his ears.

When he opened his eyes once more, he was standing in the middle of a field, clad in his unscratched golden ceremonial armour that he had once been so proud of.

Hundreds of men were engaged in combat around him, but Arvyn was mesmerised as he watched his eldest brother, the Crown Prince Oleksander, cutting down swathes of dwarves before him, his golden vanguard never far away. His impressive greatsword sliced cleanly through their squat forms, the elegant movements of his brother's skilled body splattering their fresh crimson blood over his muddy canvas.

Arvyn unsheathed his sword, swinging it towards the oncoming figures beside his brother, only to find that his weapon went through his target, his opponent unharmed by the ethereal blade.

He returned to his senses as the earth shook beneath him, forcing him to his knees. He looked around, seeing a hunched lilac giant stumbling through his brother's army, a small dark figure sat on the creature's left shoulder. The soldiers seemed to disintegrate in the monstrous creature's wake as it charged towards the Crown Prince. It swung its iron-studded club before it, colliding through swathes of soldiers with each strike.

"We must retreat Your Highness!"

"I should have listened to that damned fool," Oleksander spat, gripping into his sword as his Generals panicked. "What the hell are these monsters?"

"Flee, Your Highness!"

Arvyn turned to see one of the Generals valiantly charge towards the beast's legs as it closed the gap. The creature didn't miss a stride as it slammed its foot onto the man, leaving behind a footprint of blood and bone.

The lilac-skinned giant stopped abruptly just before the prince, crouching down onto its bare knees. It reached up to the small figure on its shoulder, lifting a tall dark-haired dwarf towards them.

"Who here claims to be the spawn of Oleksander?"

"I am. Speak; what are your demands?"

The dwarf grinned, jumping off of the giant's palm.

"Ye aura bears no resemblance," the dwarf laughed, waving his hand to the giant. "Ye're hardly worth me time."

The giant raised its closed fist.

Oleksander!

No words left Arvyn's lips as he tried to move towards his brother, his legs held in place by the icy mist.

For a moment, the prince thought that the monster's strike had missed its mark, as he watched his older brother's body stand unflinching. But, as his golden eyes refused to look away, he noted that Oleander was a head shorter than before, dark blood seeping into his armour, the stoic body crumpling forward.

Nausea flooded through him as the head of his eldest brother landed at his feet, dark red liquid splattering over his mud-soaked black boots. Oleksander's golden eyes stared motionless at his younger brother, his mouth propped open with fear.

The young prince's hands hesitantly stretched towards his brother's fine golden hair.

The fighting around him faded with the mist, screams of dying men and horses echoing through the haze, laced with the cackle of the dark-haired dwarf.

Oleksander's head remained in Arvyn's shaking hands.

Although he knew that this was just a vision projected by the Seeker, deep down he doubted that this was a mere illusion. Something told him that what he had just witnesses was more than fiction.

Is this what you truly want? Is the knowledge that you seek worth this? A voice whispered in his ear, a cold black hand cupping his chin gently from behind.

I must find the Temple of Nour. I must protect my people and my family. I have to prevent this fate.

The voice chuckled, the hands tightening around his throat, their long fingernails scraping over the stubble starting to grow on his chin.

This is no fate, the voice whispered. *Oleksander's issue is one less.*

Voices whispered around him in a dozen languages, interlaced with screams and cries.

He covered his ears as he recognised his older brother's voice amongst them.

A short shadowy figure emerged from the mist, its visage hidden by a dripping cloak of blood. It lifted its arm, pointing into the mist in front of them.

A black door appeared. Silver brambles and briars held the ebony wood tightly shut, a pale white light seeping out from behind it.

The path ahead is soaked in yet more blood, the voices hissed. *If you continue down this road, Death shall greet you, like all those who have walked here before you.*

Arvyn raised his head, unashamed by the tears glistening over his golden eyes as he gently laid his brother's still warm head onto the cold ground before pushing himself onto his feet.

Will my people be safe if I stop here?

The figure smiled, its elongated canines visible beneath the shadow of its hood.

The war began long before you were born, child of Oleksander, and many more are yet to die for peace. Fight or not, that will not change. But, the victor perhaps shall.

Arvyn stared straight ahead, his eyes firm.

I must protect my people.

The figure smiled at the prince as the brambles slowly slithered away from the door, allowing it to creak open. One of the brambles snapped forward, coiling tightly around the prince's body. The thorns embedded themselves deeper into his skin as he squirmed, gritting his teeth. A single tendril slithered over his face, circling slowly around his left eye.

He screamed as the thorns burst through the soft tissue of his eyeball, scraping over his eye orbit as it gouged the golden eye, a symbol of being descended from Oleksander I, from his skull.

Warmth radiated from the wound, blood trickling down his left cheek as the thorns receded, his hands quickly going to cradle his bloody wound.

The figure turned their back on the prince, fading into the mist.

Do not regret your choice.

He fell to his knees, greeted by a gentle blanket of undergrowth. A gentle rain caressed his face, washing away the blood on his cheek. His nose was filled with the scent of fresh rain, fragrant flowers and damp moss. The thrumming of crickets and other insects echoed around him as the sweet calls of hidden birds danced in the trees over the rainfall.

As he tried to steady his breathing, he became aware of how thick the air surrounding him was. His skin swelled from the warmth of the air, even despite the cool downpour. He noticed that all he wore was a thin black shirt and black trousers, his armour nowhere to be seen. Even so, the heat was unbearable.

Coming to his senses, he cast his gaze around him.

Arvyn sat at the base of a large ancient tree, the buttress roots providing a little shelter from the cool rain. Aside from that, there was little he could see, thanks to the dense overgrown canopy towering above him. A few stray strands of sunlight broke through the leafy dome, but not enough to ease the strain on his damaged eyesight.

He wearily pushed himself onto his feet, the nausea still coursing through his body.

I must find the temple, he thought, stumbling forward amongst the trees, carefully stepping over the dishevelled roots that littered the ground.

He walked for what felt like hours over the uneven, slippery ground until he came to the edge of a large obsidian rock standing tall amongst the tree. The base of the rock was overgrown with vines and brambles, the black surface smooth except for a small rune carved into the surface.

He raised his hand, trying to get a better look at the carving.

The ground began to tremble below him, forcing him to his knees. When it subsided, he looked up to find a path had appeared behind the monument, the trees cut in two.

He could just about make out a strange triangular shape in the distance, surrounded closely by the towering trees.

Arvyn squinted, his eye refusing to focus on the shape in the distance as fog invaded his vision.

Hundreds of voices twisting with pain cried out through the fog as it began to envelope him, his vision blurring.

Save us. Free us. Kill them. Help us. Avenge us.
Kill them all.

* * *

"Your Highness!"

Arvyn groggily opened his eye, his head pounding as his blurry vision tried to focus on his dim surroundings. A shadow obscured the vision from his left eye; the socket throbbing with pain as he tried to open it.

His breathing grew rapid as his hand shakily reached to his head, feeling the stiff bandages wrapped around his eye tightly, nausea bubbling in his stomach as he realised that he would forever bear the scar of meeting the Seeker.

How much of that was real?

"How do you feel, Your Highness?"

The face of his loyal uncle appeared before him. It seemed that his face had aged ten years, the wrinkles on his brow much deeper than before, his worried eyes weary.

"How long was I unconscious?" The prince replied, his voice hoarse as he tried to sit himself up.

"About eight hours," Daryl replied, helping his young master carefully. "Are you trying to make me join your mother, Your Highness? How could you be so reckless?"

The prince sighed, his hand running through his hair. "What exactly happened?"

The duke looked at him, his greying brow furrowing.

"You visited one of the slaves with Cliona. Cuthbert found you unconscious beside the cell afterwards and brought you straight here. She said that you had been granted a vision. That's when your eyeball exploded! If we had not been there to stem the bleeding, I dread to think what would have happened!"

Arvyn closed his eye as he remembered the strange cloaked figure and the blue powder that stung his hand. But, when he looked down at his palm there was no mark to remind him of the event.

"It was an unsettling vision," the prince mumbled, the image of his brother being beheaded flashing before his eyes. "I fear that we will not see Oleksander again, uncle."

Daryl stared at him silently, holding his youngest nephew's hand tightly.

The prince sighed after a while, sitting up slowly as his ears rang.

"Where is Cliona?"

The duke avoided Arvyn's gaze, looking over his own shoulder.

"She and Wynne went to check that we cleared all of the cells."

"I see," the prince mumbled, standing slowly. "Summon them back; we're returning to the surface immediately."

"Yes, your Highness."

Chapter 23

Having spent close to a day in the putrid sewers of the small town, the prince and his group were bombarded by the grateful townsfolk as they returned with the victims from the slave auction. But, with one look at his freshly mauled face, Leonie insisted on Arvyn receiving a visit from the local physicians.

And so, having changed into a fresh dark green dress provided begrudgingly by Leonie's maids, Cliona sat silently in the dark corner of the tavern. Her slender fingers wrapped tightly around the warm clay cup of spiced wine, the welcome heat seeping into her pale hands as her eyes lingered on the smooth surface.

Wynne drummed his fingers on the oak table impatiently beside her, his hidden face leaning heavily against his other hand.

He sighed loudly.

"You promised you would train me," the boy muttered, swapping his head to his other hand.

"After I have told them the truth. They deserve that much, at least," she sighed softly, closing her eyes.

"They're going to die anyway," he mumbled, slamming his shoulders against the cracked wooden wall behind him, folding his arms in front of his chest. "That's all humans are ever good for."

Cliona turned her glowing eyes onto him.

"As your temporary master, I shall pretend that I did not hear such an unsavoury remark."

The boy held her gaze for a moment, his jaw twitching. But he quickly lowered his eyes, slumping back in his seat. He drew a small obsidian dagger from his pocket, slamming the crooked blade into the table.

Cliona sighed, noticing the prince and his trusted companions steadily descending the stairs, his gaze searching for hers.

"Humans are fragile," she whispered, "but they still have a role to play. You must learn that each life you use is precious; do not waste such help so easily, or you will be granted none in the future."

"I don't understand," he whined.

Cliona slowly raised her warm cup to her lips as the prince, his sister, the duke and the guards all arrived at the table, Kimiro following a few paces behind as he carried a tray of filled glasses diligently. Arvyn took the seat opposite Cliona, his golden gaze cold beside the tight black bandage that covered his recently lost eye.

"I demand an explanation."

She looked down silently at her slender fingers, tightly gripping the vessel in her hand.

"Two hundred and seventy-three."

The prince's fair brow creased at her soft words.

Cliona lifted her eyes slowly, her ruby eyes seeming to swirl with flecks of black and gold.

"Two hundred and seventy-three years. That is how long I have been waiting for a descendant of Oleksander to successfully break the seal."

"What seal?" Leonie gently laid her trembling hand over her brother's, looking nervously between him and Cliona.

"The seal keeping the demons at bay," Arvyn spat.

Cliona met his gaze firmly.

Leonie's lips trembled at the ensuing silence, her delicate fingers tightly clutching at the religious pendant around her neck, the golden sun cold under her smooth skin.

"In war, history is written by the victorious army. Those on the side of defeat are often cast into shadow or painted as monstrous villains."

"I suggest that you stop playing games and speak plainly," the duke replied firmly, his hands gripped tightly together on the table.

Her glowing crimson eyes snapped to the duke.

"This world was the final battleground for the Demon War, between the Liberty Faction, Imperial Faction and Chaos Faction. The so-called god that you worship," she spat, her eyes honed onto the flaming sun pendant caressing the hollow of Leonie's neck, "is nothing more than the bastard who led the Imperial Faction. Your ancestor Oleksander was nothing more than the emperor's pathetic lackey. If we had not tried to broker a truce then this world and all its inhabitants would have been obliterated centuries ago by the fighting."

Arvyn grabbed her shoulders firmly from across the table, his face twisted in pain.

"How long do you intend on lying to me?"

As he did so, Wynne swiftly appeared behind him, holding his crude dagger at the prince's neck. His blood red eyes glinting in the dim light of the suddenly silent tavern, his Cheshire smile glowing.

"Enough."

Cliona held up her hand to Wynne.

The boy tutted, flourishing his dagger as he slid it back into its sheath at his hip before slowly returning to his seat. The duke stood behind the prince, his broad hand silently resting on his young nephew's shoulder.

"Perhaps this is a conversation best had behind closed doors," Leonie whispered, forcing a smile as she stood.

"Who are you really? I demand the truth now!" Arvyn hissed, ignoring his sister as his stare locked onto Cliona, his fists squeezed tightly closed as tears threatened to dampen his cheeks. "Do I not have a right to know? A right to know why you have been playing me from the start?"

Cliona looked at him, a chilling smile on her pale face, her glowing red eyes filled with pain as she pushed herself from her seat, standing tall as she addressed the silent room.

"Apologies for the commotion; the drinks are on me tonight!"

A cheer erupted from the tavern patrons as Cliona nodded to the flustered innkeeper from across the room. She waved her hand as she calmly returned to her seat, her eyes fixing on Arvyn's.

"I tried for the first few decades to convince humans that demons were more than a fairy tale; that we needed to fight them. But I was just met with hostility and pity. Thanks to Oleksander's power erasing the memory of humanity, I was branded as a madwoman and locked away in Dunsberg Castle on his orders."

"Why were you locked away for almost three hundred years?"

The duke laid his other hand gently on the princess's shoulder, trying to hush her as her beloved brother seethed beside her.

"I was on the losing side," Cliona replied bitterly.

"So, are there more? Demons hiding amongst humans, I mean?"

"They were slaughtered when their masters were captured. Those that you have met, and have yet to meet, were the civilians residing on this land, for the most part. They were hidden away by their masters before they could be captured by the Imperial Army, to keep them safe. The few that were once warriors have been protecting their people whilst they wait for their masters to return."

"So," Arvyn glared, "you're just using us to restart your civil war."

Cliona shook her head slowly.

"The war never truly ended. Until there is peace for all races across the realms then I refuse to admit defeat; I know that the thousands that have died for the Liberty Army feel the same."

A hush fell over the table.

"Pardon me, sir," a young boy squeaked, appearing beside the table, his hands fidgeting with a crumpled brown cap in front of him as he popped a little bow. "I'm looking for the people who defeated the bandits, if you please."

Daryl turned to him, a soft smile on his weather-beaten face.

"That's us, lad; how can we help?"

The boy shoved his small shoulders backwards, his head held high as he repeated his master's words in a slow, monotonous voice. "You are summoned to the manor of Baron Clayton, to receive a reward for the kindness that you have shown this town. He asks that you visit the castle in the morning for your reward."

He breathed, bowing slightly once more as he turned on his heel.

Arvyn sighed heavily, his outstretched arms leaning against the table as he did so, his gaze cast onto the rough oak table below him.

"We will continue this discussion later, but know that I will not tolerate any more lies."

Cliona inclined her head slowly.

Chapter 24

The next morning, the group travelled in silence through the streets, forcing smiles as the local people greeted them warmly. A few children brought freshly cut flowers to Leonie, which she promptly placed in her long golden hair. An elderly man, reunited with his two granddaughters, offered the travellers a warm, hearty meal on their return.

Arvyn continued in silence, his golden face as gloomy as the clouds above him as he ignored the oncoming townspeople.

"I must know," Leonie whispered to Cliona as she appeared beside her. "How was it that you did not suffer the same fate as the other demons?"

The pale woman kept walking, the long green skirts slowing her stride.

"And, how have you survived for almost three centuries? I didn't even think our kingdom was that old! Do demons just live for that long?"

Cliona glanced at the golden princess from under her long black eyelashes, her slender fingers digging into the palms of her hands at her sides.

"I don't think that your brother would be pleased to see you asking me such questions, Your Highness."

Leonie's brow furrowed as she cast a glance towards her brother, marching a good distance ahead of them.

"I am here of my own accord," the girl grumbled. "I don't think that this is a burden that my brother should ever have even attempted to shoulder alone. Even if Father would not listen, I wish he would have confided in me."

"Unfortunately, there is little for you to do at this moment." Cliona glanced at the girl beside her briefly. "But, remember that warriors are not the only necessity in times of war."

Cliona cast a sad smile at the princess before striding off ahead of her, allowing the still morning air to surround her.

Before long the imposing abode of Baron Clayton appeared before them, the dark grey stone walls towering overhead as they neared the twenty-foot-high stone wall. Unlike the town perimeter itself, the gates to the local baron's residence were carefully watched by four well-armed guards, the dark iron portcullis lowered behind them.

Upon seeing the group, one of the guards shouted for the gates to be raised.

They passed carefully under the portcullis, aware of the eyes warily watching them from beyond the hidden arrow slits as they entered the castle courtyard.

The cobblestone courtyard was crowded by dozens of off-duty soldiers lounging around, their eyes fixed on the newcomers walking towards the castle. Atop these stone steps stood a tall man surveying the scene. Despite only being in his thirties, his spine was hunched over as he leaned on a tall black cane. He seemed rather broad, although the thick bear skin cloak arranged carefully over his shoulders greatly contributed to that. His hazel eyes scowled as he watched the band of adventurers stroll closer towards him.

"Welcome, fair travellers!" The man called dryly as they reached the bottom step. "I, Baron Yuriel Clayton, welcome you to my humble abode."

"We are grateful for your invitation," Arvyn replied, his voice devoid of any emotion as he closed the gap between them, his companions following close behind. "Shall we continue this inside?"

The baron smiled, gritting his teeth and clutching at the golden eagle on top of his cane as he inclined his head to the unkempt group before him. He led the way through his castle slowly, the tapping of his cane and uneven footfalls filling the otherwise silent air.

The more they walked through the brightly lit hallways, with elaborate tapestries and carefully carved ornaments lining the walls and display cabinets, the more Arvyn clenched his jaw, thinking back once again to the dishevelled citizens just outside this castle's gates. He watched as the handful of servants that they passed scurried to the walls when their master entered, lowering their gaunt faces to avoid his ire.

Baron Clayton seemed to pay no attention to them, instead holding his head high as he entered his great hall and headed to the slight dais at the end of the room. A lone dark oak chair stood there, draped in red velvet that matched the plump cushions strewn around the chair's base. He snapped his long fingers as he took his seat, summoning a pair of identical girls half his age, who proceeded to sit at his feet.

"You have caused me quite the spot of bother," the baron said coldly despite his smile, his eyes channelled on Arvyn. "Tell me, how do you plan on compensating me?"

"Could you elaborate, sir?"

The man's lips twitched upwards as he gripped onto his cane.

"The group of mercenaries that you so kindly disposed of had kept the people in line. There were no more drunken brawls in the streets at night, no more midnight murders, no more women claiming assault and compensation from my coffers. You see, the people in this town could hardly be called civilised; policing such a territory had placed a significant strain on our local economy and resources. When those ruffians arrived, the guards were no longer needed to quell such insignificant disputes."

"And where were you redeploying these resources to, sir?"

The noble smirked, his arms gesturing around the hall. "I have been investing in the local businesses, of course."

Arvyn glowered at the baron, his fingers twitching at his side. He glanced briefly at Daryl beside him, who remained motionless but for the small vein pulsing on his broad forehead.

After a few moments, the baron snapped his fingers to a servant standing in the shadows, sending the young boy quickly from the room. The man leant forward in his seat, his gaze appraising the travellers before him. Arvyn's jaw twitched as the man's eyes lingered on his younger sister, only to be interrupted by the return of the servant boy and three adults.

Two men carried a small wooden chest in between them, the domed roof of the chest itself open to reveal the glistening contents within. Only a small fraction of the chest's crimson lining was visible thanks to the pile of gold coins inside, a handful of rubies mixed into the loot.

Following a few steps behind them was a young blonde teenager, her pale green eyes clearly puffy even from a distance. She walked barefoot across the cold stone ground, a small silver chain loosely fastened around her left ankle that jingled as she walked. She wore a very plain white dress that looked more like a nightgown than attire for the public.

"Baron Clayton," Cliona said clearly, her cold crimson eyes trained onto his smirking face. "You truly think that this is suitable pay for our services?"

Arvyn clenched his jaw tightly, his hand twitching above the hilt of his sword as he watched his companion stride calmly towards the dais, Wynne shadowing her closely.

The baron smirked as Cliona drew nearer, his two guards behind his throne not even bothering to unsheathe their swords at her movement.

"I hope that you will accept this generous gift. Of course, were you to come into my employ then you would receive much more, my dear."

Cliona stood inches away from the baron, draping her long arm on the back of his gilded seat as she leant in close, ignoring his wandering eyes as she brought her lips to his ear.

"You sicken me."

The baron's eyes widened as her crimson irises began to swirl. His body grew cold as he stared into her petrifying gaze, unable to look away as a cold fear grappled him. She lifted him from his seat with a single hand wrapped around his neck, not even flinching as the two guards fumbled for their swords.

"Enough," Arvyn said firmly, his hand gripping tightly on the hilt of his blade as lightning flashed over the room.

Cliona glanced at him over the baron's shoulder.

A sudden bout of thunder echoed over the tense hall as rain began to charge into the pristine glass windows.

She sighed, settling on tossing the baron to the ground before calmly stepping over his bewildered body as he whimpered from the impact.

Her eyes met Arvyn's steadily.

"One thing that I am sure we can agree on, Your Highness," Cliona said clearly as she passed him. "The corruption of this kingdom must be annihilated."

Arvyn said nothing, his cold golden eye watching the crippled man frozen on the floor, the blood draining from his ruddy cheeks as he realised he was in the presence of royalty.

The prince nodded to the duke, offering his arm to his frightened sister before they followed after Cliona towards the door.

"Have these men arrested, and his assets seized," the duke shouted clearly to his men. "Any persons being held against their will are to be released and returned home with compensation where possible."

"Yes, sir!"

He turned to look at the disgraced baron. Wynne had crouched down beside him, saying nothing as he grinned down at him. The boy reached for the gnarled obsidian dagger from his pocket, envisioning dragging it slowly over the baron's frightened face.

"Be grateful that my master sees you as insignificant, human," the boy whispered, slowly running the cold blade over the man's cheek with just enough pressure to draw a line of blood.

He giggled, standing abruptly and stretching up to the sky.

"Your master is calling," the duke said calmly, ignoring the instinctive disgust that he felt every time he looked at the boy. "Leave this to my men."

Wynne's red eyes glinted as he skipped towards the door, still giggling. He paused just before he crossed the threshold, casting a final glance back to the baron.

"I hope we get to play soon."

Chapter 25

The rain hammered down around the party as they trudged wearily along the unkempt dirt road west away from the small town. They had dallied only long enough to gather their belongings from the tavern before continuing on their journey, unwilling to spend longer in the corrupt town.

Leonie pulled her coarse cloak closer about her golden hair, her shoulders trembling beneath the relentless cold bite of the rain. Daryl glanced at her, his grip tightening on the reins of his mount as he urged her alongside the princess.

"Perhaps it would be best for you to return to the capital now, Your Highness. Our road seems more perilous than expected."

"No," she whispered, "I am perfectly fine, uncle."

The old knight clenched his jaw.

"You are as stubborn as your father and brother, Your Highness. What good could come from risking yourself in this way?"

"I have no intention of returning alone. We both know that Arvyn will do something even more reckless if he were completely left to his own devices; isn't that why you are risking yourself on this journey too? Besides," she smiled, her golden eyes glinting, "it is much more thrilling riding through a storm like this than making polite conversation with the likes of Angelica Hortensia."

He let out a sigh, turning his gaze once more to the prince riding silently ahead of him, his forehead seemingly permanently creased.

"Your Highness," Daryl called as he urged his horse beside the prince, "I don't think it would be wise to continue much further in this weather. Perhaps it would be best to rest a while?"

Arvyn ran his fingers through his thick hair as he followed the duke's eyes towards Leonie, her cheerful facade briefly returning when she noticed his gaze.

"We will rest at the next place we see," the prince replied, his voice cold.

The duke nodded, continuing along beside his young master in silence.

It wasn't long before the group came upon a small derelict structure left abandoned on the side of the well-travelled road.

"We'll wait for the rain to pass here," Arvyn said firmly, riding his horse through the open passageway and into the rundown building.

The pale grey stone architecture had long been shrouded by the dense undergrowth. Dark green fingers of vines and brambles clawed deep into the porous stone, tearing the once sturdy bricks in two. Although swathes of the once wooden roof had since rotted away, there was enough cover to allow the group a small respite from the bitter wind and rain.

The prince dismounted, tying his trusted steed to a nearby branch as he removed the animal's sodden black leather saddle.

Although much of the detail of this clearly once ornate building had been eaten away by the elements, a handful of tiny wide-eyed faces peered from their perches on the cornices above. Their small humanoid faces were framed with delicately carved leaves of oak, beech and ash, all glazed with a deep viridian hue.

Cliona fought against her trembling body as nausea took hold of her as she crossed the crumbled threshold. Her eyes immediately went to those of the large petrified figure, squatting atop a crumbling stone pillar at the far end of the room.

"Are you all right?" Leonie laid her hand on her arm gently, the concern clear on her gentle face.

"Of course," Cliona said, knowing full well that her trembling voice hardly sounded convincing. "I'm just tired, I suppose."

Leonie opened her mouth to ask more but then thought better of it and instead offered her a gentle smile. "It'll be over soon."

Cliona watched the girl settle herself beside her brother quietly as he and the duke looked over the map of the region, the others tending to the horses quietly.

Her feet slowly took her towards the figure. Gently, she lifted her fingers to brush over the square face of the sprite before her, his leafy features still perfectly sculpted after all of these years. His piercing eyes, now devoid of their iridescent colour, still seemed to see through her very soul.

"Who is it?"

She turned to see Wynne appear beside her, nonchalantly draping his arm over the broken pillar beside them as he picked at his teeth with his obsidian dagger.

"He was a great sprite shaman named Kawokanna, native to this world long before humans. He defied an imperial decree and so his people had to pay the price for his actions."

The boy looked at her sideways, his signature smile missing.

"The emperor sounds truly demonic."

Cliona inhaled sharply, turning her head to see a large robed figure crouched in a crumbling alcove to the side.

The creature craned its head to the side, much further than possible for any human. From beneath the shadow of their deep violet hood, she could just make out a large toothy grin, a black substance oozing from between the sharpened points. As her mind hoped against it, she saw the lime green rune appear on its forehead, white light crackling from the freshly exposed flesh beneath the lines. Although she could not see them, she knew that the creature's emerald eyes were locked onto hers and spines were starting to protrude from its back as the scent of its intent to kill flooded the room.

Cliona turned on her heel quickly, dragging Wynne with her.

"We need to continue," she said firmly to the prince, reaching for the reins of her mount quickly. "There are creatures hiding in these shadows that you do not wish to meet."

"Of course, a rest would be a luxury we can ill afford," the prince hissed at her.

"If you wish to meet an anthraen horde then I suggest you do as I say. Now."

The prince furrowed his brow but obliged, sending Daryl to quickly bark orders to his men.

"Wynne," Cliona ordered firmly. "Find the fastest route northwest. Search for areas without any heartbeats and avoid them."

The undead boy nodded, closing his crimson eyes as he searched the surrounding areas silently. "Found it."

The group mounted their horses quickly as the hooded creature crawled forward on gangly limbs from the shadows, its grinning mouth wide open.

Leonie screamed, her high pitched voice echoing over damaged walls. Her brother pulled her onto his horse, charging through the entrance as fast as he could.

"What is that thing?" Wynne shouted, as they raced their horses through the forest.

"An anthraen scout," Kimiro shouted back. "They're husks of the sprites that originally inhabited this world, before the emperor cursed them."

"How the hell was this realm colonised by humans with those things running around?"

"They were supposedly eradicated," the old man shouted back. "The Imperial Demon Army itself led the mission."

Cliona bit her lip, drawing blood, as she urged her horse towards the clearing ahead.

Chapter 26

The next four hours felt like an eternity as the horses galloped down the wooded road, the rain relentlessly splashing over their already cold faces. Their muscles ached. Their backsides were numb from the saddles. Their horses were foaming with sweat.

And still the prince had not given the order to slow the pace; until the last half an hour, each time he turned his head he would catch a glimpse of the spindly figure keeping pace behind them. Although it had seemed to have begun to lag behind since then, his gut told him to keep moving, feeling that the luminescent green mark on the creature's forehead was still trailing them.

Lightning flashed once more over the open sky ahead of them, revealing a small wooden signpost just before a fork in the road. One sign, well cared for and freshly carved, read *Varnika, 22 miles*, whilst the prince could just make out the words *Dransmead, 6 miles* on the other moss covered panel.

He tightened his reins, urging his horse down the shorter path, away from the forest, his muscles screaming for relief.

It wasn't long before a tall flint wall appeared before them, the wooden arched gate cut into the wall open.

As he slowed his mount through the gateway, he looked back once more.

The creature was nowhere to be seen.

"I believe we lost it," Arvyn breathed, allowing his exhausted mount to stretch his dripping neck low to the ground. He dismounted gratefully, stumbling as his aching legs struggled to readjust to life outside the saddle.

The prince quickly covered the horse with a blanket from his own saddlebag before handing the reins to Cuthbert and helping his sister to the floor.

"Come inside, quickly," an elderly woman called from an open doorway, holding a small glowing lantern in her gnarled hands. "You will catch a chill out here!"

The prince nodded to his companions, gesturing to Edgar and Markus to escort the horses into the stables.

He was bathed in warmth as soon as his weary body crossed the creaky threshold of the house. The heat stung his icy skin as it rushed over him, sending a shiver over his spine as he realised just how sodden his clothes were.

Leonie stepped through behind him, immediately clutching onto his arm as her teeth chattered.

The room was much larger than it had appeared from outside, with half a dozen tables occupying the dark wood floor. Each table was strewn with parchments and glass bottles, herbs hanging from the oak beams above. Aside from the rough red bricks that lined the roaring fireplace, the room was entirely made of whitewashed stone, the bright light of the freshly lit sconces reflecting off the pale paint. A large cast iron cooking pot hung from a spit across the fire, the closed lid hardly effective at stopping the fragrant aroma of roasting beef with rosemary, sage and thyme from filling the room.

"Goodness," the elderly woman said, turning her back to them as she added another log to her fire. "Come, come sit here; warm yourselves before you catch a chill."

Leonie smiled, her golden eyes drooping from exhaustion as her brother led her further into the room.

The siblings sat themselves on the low sofa facing the fire, the plump black cushions embracing them warmly.

"Now tell me," the old woman asked softly as she lifted the cast iron lid from the pot, "what brings twelve travellers to my humble abode, *hmm*? And in such a storm, no less!"

"We are travelling to Varnika," the prince replied.

"That's still three day's travel from here, dear. You'd best rest here until the rain lets up, else you're likely to catch ill."

"Thank you, but we are in a hurry. Once we have rested for a while, we will be on our way."

"Nonsense!" The old woman turned sharply back to him, waving her dripping ladle around as she spoke. "You have two women, a child and an elderly man travelling with you; this is hardly the weather to even venture to Varnika from here! I insist that you rest yourselves."

Leonie tugged on her brother's sleeve silently, her weary eyes searching his.

Arvyn sighed. "One night should be acceptable."

"Excellent!" The old woman grinned and clapped her hands. "I shall prepare the guest rooms. Oh my, it's been so long since I had company!"

"Allow me to assist you," Kimiro said softly, offering her a small bow.

The old woman laughed.

Wynne perched himself as close to the fire as possible. "I don't sense those creatures nearby now."

"Thank god," Edgar replied, sitting on the floor and leaning heavily against the wall.

"It seems to be one thing after another. How many more artefacts do we need, Your Highness?"

Arvyn ran his hand through his wet hair, his eyes fixed on Cliona.

She stood with her back to him, her fingers trailing over the loose parchments strewn on one of the tables.

"Three," the duke replied, clearing his throat. "And then we must locate this Temple of Nour on top of that."

"And no doubt more of those creatures."

"Or something even worse."

Silence filled the room as each of them wondered why they had started this in the first place.

Wynne stretched into the air, his signature grin spread on his lips once more as he jumped up and practically skipped towards Cliona. He reached up and draped an arm over her shoulder, his eyes darting over the sheets that had captivated her gaze.

It wasn't long before his expression hardened.

"Is that what I think it is?" Wynne hissed, his voice too low for the others to make out.

Cliona nodded, her hands carefully raising the sheet that had caught both of their eyes.

Curious, the prince extracted himself from his now dozing sister.

Across the table lay dozens upon dozens of aged sheets of parchments littered with strange symbols that he didn't recognise. But, a handful of the sketches were identical, down to the minutest detail, to the items that he and his companions had already gathered.

He reached for the three items that he did not recognise.

"Oh, don't mind those," the old woman said, leaning over the wooden balcony above to look at them. "Just the ramblings of a lonely old woman, those are."

Although her plump face showed a warm smile, her apricot eyes seemed to grow wary.

"Can you read these?"

Arvyn waved the three sheets in her direction.

The old woman laughed. "Well, of course, I can't, dear! No, those are the ravings of my great, great grandmother, bless her. They've been passed down through the women of my family like some sacred heirloom. I have no idea what they are no matter how hard I study them, but I just don't have the heart to get rid of them just yet."

"Do you know what language they are in?"

"Some ancient forgotten script," the old woman replied, making her way towards the inquisitive prince. "The women of my family have always been herbal healers, using the gifts of nature to help others. I suppose they are recipes of some sort."

"You are a beastkin, are you not?"

The woman's eyes snapped to Kimiro, now standing on the bottom step behind her, his face expressionless.

"So what if I am?" She replied, her voice cold.

She clenched her fists tightly, fighting against the rage building inside her.

"What generation are you?"

"You should leave whilst I'm still being nice," the old woman snarled.

"Allow me to apologise," Arvyn said firmly, inclining his head slightly, "but we cannot do that. I assume that you are familiar with some of the creatures that lurk near here? The," he paused, turning to Cliona, "what did you call them?"

"Anthraens."

The prince turned back to the woman, his golden eye firm.

"What do you want from me?"

Arvyn held up the three sheets in his hand towards her. "What do you know of these items? Do you know where to locate them?"

The woman scowled, opening her mouth.

"That's enough, Marianna," a high pitched voice called from the balcony upstairs.

A small child, no older than seven, perched on top of the wooden banister. A gentle smile spread over her pale pink lips as she sipped from a delicate silver teacup. Her pale blue and pale green heterochromatic eyes quickly scanned the room below her.

"Please forgive her impertinence, Your Highness. We live a solitary life here; my maid is no longer accustomed to welcoming guests, and I'm afraid we have not been fond of humans for quite some time."

"Lady Jenevra!"

"Enough," the girl snapped, stamping her foot. "You've done enough. Leave us, you old hag."

"But my lady!"

"Now," the girl shouted, pouting with her hands on her hips.

The old woman glared at the prince, making her way quickly up the stairs as the girl skipped down them, her rose gold curls bouncing as she placed herself on the sofa beside the now sleeping princess.

"Now, what precisely do you wish to know about those artefacts?"

"I want to know where to find them."

The girl looked at the prince silently before her eyes danced over his weary companions.

After a moment, she smiled, flicking one of her pigtails behind her shoulder.

"These are merely ancient relics that I have been researching; how would I know of their locations?"

Arvyn rubbed his temples, clenching his jaw.

"I am a descendant of Oleksander I, searching for the seven ancient artefacts. I have already located four of the items."

"You're no fun," the girl pouted, crossing her arms in front of her chest.

She laid her teacup on the table before gathering the three sketches he pointed to, laying them on the low table before the fire and sitting back down.

"Well, this one," she sighed, taking the sketch of a book decorated with constellations, "is rather easy, once you reach the Convent of Selis, about two days east from here. There is a statue that will tell you how to find Damaris' book, but I don't know any more than that. This one though," she said, her pale brow twitching slightly as she gestured to the sketch of a small handheld mirror, "will be more of a challenge. From what I know, there is no guardian to this artefact any more, but finding the cave it resides in is a feat in itself. All I know is that it is somewhere near the coastal town of Alcano."

"And the third?"

She smiled, revealing two neat rows of pearl-white teeth.

"That depends on why you want to find it. You don't strike me as someone with scholarly curiosity, and no prince would travel through anthraen territory for something so dull."

"We are headed for the Temple of Nour."

The young girl's eyes snapped sharply to Arvyn's, her surprise quickly masked by her smile once again.

"Well, it has indeed been an age since I heard that name," she muttered, taking a sip of her tea. "I see, so the time has come then."

She thought quietly for a moment.

"Answer me one question first."

After a while she raised her hand, holding her palm upwards. As it began to glow with a gentle white light, a thin floral golden pattern appeared on her pale skin.

Hovering above her palm appeared a plain golden monocle.

"I was told to hold onto this until someone came to request it," she said softly, a sad smile tugging at her rosy lips.

She stood, quietly placing it in Arvyn's hand.

"You are welcome to stay until the morning, but then I bid you to make haste, else the anthraens will surround you. I shall provide you with a map to the final two objects. After that, you should travel to Dunsberg; I'm not too sure of its exact location, but I know that the Temple of Nour is located somewhere in that region so that the descendants of Axiolia could keep watch of them."

"Thank you," Arvyn replied.

"I will only accept that sentiment when my kin has been returned to me."

The duke furrowed his brow, watching the girl carefully.

"Is there not some task that we must do for you? We have yet to receive an item so easily."

The girl smiled, taking a sip of her tea calmly.

"There was a task I was supposed to set," she replied, watching the fire. "But, in all honesty, I'm bored of my role as guardian. When Arun returns I can be free to roam again. Why would I try to prevent that?"

The prince nodded, sleepily settling himself in one of the chairs beside her, his muscles aching as he allowed himself to finally doze off.

Chapter 27

Knock. Knock.

"Yes, yes, I'm coming," Sister Brianna called as she fumbled with the large ring of keys in her hand. "Please, wait a moment."

The lock clicked and she slowly pulled open the heavy oak door, the wood scraping over the uneven cobblestones below, adding to the black mark even more.

"Welcome to the Convent of Selis. How may I help you this afternoon?"

She pushed her thick spectacles further up her hooked nose as she smiled to greet the guests. It was no secret that the convent was dangerously low on funds with the recent increase in taxes to the king making matters even more difficult for the devoted residents. She knew that they needed any of the scarce visitors to make a sizeable donation if they were going to keep their doors open.

"Their Royal Highnesses Prince Arvyn and Princess Eleanora wish for a tour of the premises," Daryl said formally, offering the middle-aged nun a small bow. "I hope that we are not intruding, Sister."

"N-not at all," Sister Brianna stammered, her hazel eyes wide as she allowed the party of twelve through the convent gate and into the empty courtyard. "I shall fetch Mother Aneesa. Please wait here for a moment."

She quickly picked up the skirts of her black habit and walked briskly towards the Abbess' office, hoping that she would not be scolded for running again.

Cliona watched her go, her tense posture not going unnoticed by the princess beside her.

"I suppose considering what you've said that you are not religious, Cliona?"

"The god that you worship had a hand in the imprisonment of myself and my closest allies, and slaughtered thousands of innocents."

The princess smiled, sadly touching the pendant around her neck.

"I suppose you're right. Perhaps he isn't the kindest of gods."

"My lady has omitted to tell you that demons do not have a particular deity that they worship, only an idea of an afterlife," Kimiro said softly to the princess. "The deities of my people, however, are neither good nor evil entities. Rather, they merely exist to observe life and get involved when they see fit. Humanity is rather unique in their devotion to a single entity, but I supposed you have the Demon Emperor to thank for that."

It wasn't long before Sister Brianna returned with an older woman in tow, business smiles plastered on their rather gaunt faces.

"Good afternoon, Your Highnesses," one of the women said as she curtsied, the golden rope sewn onto the hem of her white wimple denoting her as the abbess. "I would be honoured to guide you around our humble convent."

"Thank you. My sister has been asking to visit a church so often on our journey to Alcano that I have had to relent."

"We are most grateful for your interest," Mother Aneesa said softly, her wrinkled eyes looking over the strangers cautiously. "However, I must humbly request that you leave some of your companions here in the courtyard. You are in no danger here, I assure you, but my sisters and I are unused to so many men within our walls."

"Of course; how careless of me. But I must insist that we shall take our uncle and my sister's maid with us."

The abbess inclined her head, worried about her anticipated donation should she quibble further. And with that, she gestured for the four of them to follow her.

"I must say," she began, nodding to the handful of nuns that they passed through the whitewashed corridor, "we were very sad to hear of Prince Oleksander. Our prayers have been with the Royal Family, and we shall continue to pray for the King's safety and happiness."

Leonie's golden brow furrowed as she looked at the old woman. "What do you mean?"

The nun inhaled, her eyes blinking rapidly as she looked between the prince and princess.

"Have you not yet heard, Your Highness?"

"Heard what? Arvyn, what's happened to Oleksander?"

Leonie turned to face her brother, clutching onto his arm tightly. Arvyn clenched his jaw, closing his eye as he avoided her frantic gaze.

The nun crossed herself before bowing her head solemnly to the princess before her.

"I apologise, Your Highness; I assumed that word had already reached you. The First Prince fell in battle three days ago; he is in the arms of God now."

Leonie's eyes glistened as she looked at the nun, her face paling as her legs threatened to give way. Her brother's arm wrapped around her shoulders tightly, keeping her steady as she tried to fight back tears.

"Did you know?" She whispered, her royal resolve weakening.

"I didn't want to tell you until I was certain," her brother replied, his brow furrowed as he bit back his own tears.

She hit him in the chest with closed fists, biting her cheek so hard that it bled as she tried to calm the anger building inside her.

"Perhaps Her Highness should rest a while," the abbess said softly, her gnarled hands wrapped around her rose quartz prayer beads. "We will gladly offer her a room to stay in until she is settled."

Leonie stood straighter, angrily wiping at her damp eyes, her fingernails digging into her palms as she tried to smile at the old woman. "That won't be necessary. Please continue."

The nun glanced at the prince, who merely nodded his head slowly.

They continued on in silence but for the abbess occasionally pointing out paintings or sculptures donated by wealthy patrons in the past. Leonie nodded along silently, but the abbess could not help but be disheartened by the prince's clear disinterest. Yet, her smile continued as she gestured to another piece of the convent's collection, much smaller now than it had been even ten years ago.

"This is our oldest donation, dating back to Lady Selis de Soro, who founded our humble Convent of Selis. Our holy lady protected many women and children during our kingdom's turbulent past."

The old woman smiled as she bowed her head before the sculpture, her grooved fingers brushing expertly over the carved ebony prayer beads in her hands.

Cliona stepped forward, her crimson eyes fixed on the delicately carved white marble.

The delicate features of a young woman stood serenely before them, her eyes forlornly gazing before her. A thin veil had been carved over her face, so expertly chiselled that her charming features were still clearly visible. Her delicate lips held no smile, yet her slender arms stretched out welcomingly. She wore a flowing gown that reached down to the floor, plain but for the handful of camellia flowers decorating the carved fabric draped loosely around her waist. The marble of her gown seemed to flow straight into the pedestal at her feet, cementing her to the convent floor for eternity.

"It's beautiful," Leonie breathed, smiling at the abbess. "I am surprised that it is not better known."

"Yes; it is the pride of our convent, Your Highness. I believe that this is the likeness of the woman who saved Lady Selis's life."

Arvyn met Cliona's gaze as she nodded.

"I believe that my sister wishes to admire this piece for a while longer. Duke Wynford, would you be as kind as to discuss a donation with the abbess? We must ensure that such a beautiful work does not fall to ruin in these harsh times."

"Bless you, Your Highness. We are eternally grateful."

The duke bowed, allowing the elated abbess to escort him to her office.

"This is the statue that Lady Jenevra mentioned, is it not?"

"I am almost certain of it," Cliona replied. "Now to find the book."

"Perhaps there is a key and a lock somewhere?"

"Someone would have found it by now if that were the case."

Sister Brianna stood awkwardly behind them, clearing her throat.

Leonie smiled at her softly. "Oh dear, I feel as though I am really rather parched from all this travelling and excitement. Would you be so kind as to fetch me some water?"

The nun curtsied, practically sprinting away from the three strangers.

"We can't move the statue," the prince said, kneeling at its feet to inspect the floor. "The base is carved from one piece of stone, directly into the wall and floor."

"A button then, perhaps? Or a lever?"

"Look to see if there's an inscription of any sort," Arvyn said firmly, looking behind the statue. "We won't have long before the nun comes back."

Cliona looked once more at the tranquil face. A pang of guilt flashed through her as she remembered the woman in front of her being so full of life, always enthralled by her father's research, not so timid and forlorn as this carving.

"I've always hated his damn puzzles," Cliona muttered, pressing a few of the stone bricks behind the statue in vain.

Leonie's brow creased as she stood as close to the statue as possible, her eyes following those of the marble woman's. She gasped, pointing to the ceiling.

Arvyn followed his sister's hand to see a very small engraving of seven camellia flowers in one of the stones, a line of foreign runes etched in a circle around it.

"Cliona, what does this say?"

She followed the princess's gaze too and sighed. "It's a riddle. *The more you take, the more are left in your wake.*"

The siblings looked at each other for a moment, pondering.

"Age?"

"That wouldn't make sense as a key, Leonie. What about lives?"

"Damaris was a scholar and a pacifist, for the most part. I doubt it would be so morbid," Cliona replied.

"Friends, then?"

"Why would you leave friends in your wake?"

"Footsteps?"

Cliona and Arvyn looked at the princess.

"Perhaps," the prince said quietly. "But how many?"

"There are seven camellias. So why don't we try seven steps from the statue?"

"Count out seven steps from the statue and walk in a circle until we find it," Arvyn said, starting to count out the steps directly in front of the statue.

It wasn't long before they discovered an old stone tile on the floor, engraved with a tiny camellia flower.

"Now what? The nun will be back soon; we need to hurry."

Arvyn knelt down next to the tile, pulling his dagger from its hiding place in his boot and smashing at the ornate tile with its hilt.

"Arvyn!"

"Be quiet, Leonie, or you'll alert them."

The princess bit her lip, looking around fretfully as she hissed at her brother. "You can't just go smashing up a convent!"

Arvyn ignored her, pulling the fragments of smashed tile away from the hollow space below. He reached in with his hand, feeling for a lever or a key to open some hidden door. He was surprised to feel a velvet cloth instead, wrapped tightly around a heavy rectangular object, much too large to fit through the small hole that he had made.

"Cliona, give me a hand."

She stepped forward, crouching on the floor beside him. Together they pulled at the thin tile covering the hidden compartment, dust crumbling onto the fabric below.

Finally, the prince pulled the small parcel towards him, carefully removing the pale blue velvet wrapping. Inside was a large black leather book, the cover littered with a cacophony of embroidered flowers.

"Your Highness!"

The abbess couldn't help but shout when she saw the cracked floor.

Arvyn stood swiftly, passing the book to Cliona. "I apologise, Mother Aneesa. I shall send for a skilled craftsman immediately. Uncle, double whatever you just paid her; that should cover the damages and then some."

With that, the royal siblings rushed from the room, Cliona and the duke following close behind them.

Sister Brianna returned with a tray and three wooden cups of water, letting out a gasp when she saw the damaged floor.

"Do not speak of this to the sisters," Aneesa warned quietly, her normally kind eyes firm as she crossed herself. "I have a feeling that we do not want to get involved in this incident any further."

Chapter 28

The sun shone through the thick morning mist, the delicate dewdrops sparkling in the pale rays.

Cliona turned her face to the sun, her crimson eyes closed as her soft skin drank in the once familiar warmth, her long legs draped over the jagged edge of the cliff. Her long black skirt billowed loosely around her legs as the crystal blue sea slowly came into view.

It had taken them a week of travelling to reach the chalky cliffs of Alcano, the weather seeming to improve the nearer to the coast they went. The arduous journey had finally taken its toll on the princess's sheltered body, and so Cliona and Leonie had stayed at the top of the twenty foot cliff whilst the prince and his men scoured the shoreline below for signs of a cave or ancient ruin. Although they had set up a tent for the princess's comfort, she insisted on resting on the lush grass beside Cliona, listening to the dulcet sound of the sea below.

"Cliona?"

She turned to see Leonie lying on her side, her head resting on the crook of her elbow.

"Yes?"

"What was your home like?"

"Why are you interested?"

"Well, before I followed Arvyn, I'd never actually left the capital. The world is so much bigger and different to what I thought. I want to learn more about it, and about the other worlds out there."

Cliona sighed, watching the soldiers scrambling over the dishevelled rocks at the base of the cliff below them. "I've visited many places, all very different from this realm."

"Tell me about where you grew up."

A sad smile crossed over her pale face, her crimson eyes clouding over slightly as she watched Markus start to scale back up the cliff face with the rope.

"My people lived in the northern mountains of the Demon Realm. It was much warmer than this realm, and the days were much longer."

"Do you miss it? Your homeland, I mean."

Cliona was silent, her gaze focusing on a world long forgotten.

"I apologise. I didn't mean to bring up any sad memories."

"It was a cruel place," she whispered. "The monsters that you have seen here are nothing compared to those native to my homeland."

Cliona lent forwards to help Markus pull himself over the edge of the cliff.

"His Highness asks that you join him on the shore, Cliona," he said, bending over double as he tried to catch his breath. "We believe that we have found the cave entrance but need you to translate an inscription. I will stay with you, Your Highness, until His Highness and His Grace return."

"Of course," the princess smiled, lying back against the lush grass once more. "I suppose it would be futile to complain about being left behind this time."

"I apologise, Your Highness," the guard replied, clearly uncomfortable to be guarding the princess alone, his eyes unsure of where to look.

Cliona stood slowly, stretching her arms high in the air above her before heading to the rope.

Daryl waited at the base of the cliff as she carefully made her way down to the shoreline.

"His Highness requires you to inspect an inscription," the duke said as she drew near him.

She inclined her head, following him to the entrance of a small cave.

A pungent wall of musty sea salt washed over Cliona as she followed closely behind Daryl. She slowly brushed her fingertips over the slippery surface of the irregular stone walls, a slight trail left in their wake. The rhythmic echoes of water dripping from the cream stalactites above their heads kept the pair company as they made their way deep into the dark sea cave, Daryl's burning torch offering a slight respite from the cool air as they wandered down the uneven pathway.

"I had called for you to translate some text," Arvyn said when he saw the orange glow of Daryl's torch approaching. "But it seems that may be unnecessary now."

Still, the prince waited until Cliona and his uncle were beside him, perched on a damp boulder covered in a dense blanket of emerald green moss. He stood as they drew near, straightening his black leather doublet subconsciously.

"I rubbed away some of the moss and found the door myself."

He raised his leather gloved hand slowly against the rough surface of the damp driftwood door inlaid in the grey limestone walls, pushing it open slowly.

Silence fell over the three of them as they stepped into a serene chamber, water cascading steadily over the walls to either side of them, a clear layer of glass all that was keeping the saltwater at bay. Through these panes, the trio could see fields of vibrant coloured coral and an array of bright-coloured fish darting between the underwater flora.

Even more spectacular than the alien world they had entered was that of the open chamber before them.

In truth, it was not a particularly large space, big enough to fit two round tables with four chairs each, and a little bit of space around them. But, the high vaulted dome ceiling above them was inlaid in geometric design made entirely of different seashells; iridescent mother of pearl, jet black mussel shells and the larger, delicate pink of queen scallop shells. The walls, too, were lined with these majestic seashells. As they stepped forward, it was clear that the floor was made of a clear cut mirror that expertly reflected the ceiling above.

Directly opposite them was a large marble statue, not dissimilar in style to the elven maid in the Convent of Selis. This woman, however, was carved completely nude, her long wavy locks flowing freely about her shoulders as though there were a gentle breeze. She stood proudly, watching over the sleeping grotto from her tall alcove. The walls that surrounded her were encrusted in row upon row of pale purple amethysts.

Strangest of all was the object strewn across the centre of the floor, a thick layer of dark brown fur attempting to mask it from view.

Arvyn and Daryl drew their swords, stepping towards the mound cautiously.

The duke gently nudged it with the tip of his sword, his muscles as tense as a coiled spring.

And yet, nothing happened.

Slowly, he lifted the fur away from the pile.

As he did so, he instinctively covered his nose from the foul stench that erupted from the rotting corpse, his body reflexively threatening to vomit as he quickly moved away.

Cliona tensed her jaw as she crouched beside it, covering her own face with her hand as the prince and his uncle stepped further away. Her eyes narrowed as a shiny object in one of the clawed hands caught her gaze.

Carefully, she pried the queen scallop away, handing it directly to Arvyn behind her.

He inspected it quickly, opening the tiny silver clasp keeping the two halves of the scallop shut. Inside was the portrait of a beautiful woman with raven black hair and turquoise eyes, her tranquil smile charming the prince through the paint. Opposite it lay a crystal clear mirror, the edge held in place with tiny white pearl beads.

The prince passed the small handheld mirror to Daryl quickly, wiping his hands on his black trousers as soon as he did so, his skin crawling as the stench of rotting flesh once again hit his nose.

"It seems that the residual magic had started to weaken here too early," she said softly, covering the two humanoid forms back over with the seal pelts. "I only hope that these were not the last two selkies, or else Malachy will surely go berserk when he awakens."

"What are selkies?"

She sighed, straightening her back. "Similar to your tales of sirens and merfolk, I suppose. They come from an aquatic realm, where they wear skins of creatures similar to seals when in the water and resemble humans on land."

The prince turned to leave the chamber.

"It seems that with each passing day I am realising just how vast the world outside of my father's kingdom truly is."

Chapter 29

The buxom innkeeper's wife laid the final steaming bowl of forever stew on the old wooden table, her rosy cheeks seeming to grow as she smiled at the large party. Although their clothes were dirty and their faces lined with weariness, she was hopeful that they would turn into well-paying patrons. They had, after all, become few and far between thanks to the recent rumours of nearby attacks.

"Can I get you anything else, gentlemen?"

"That will be all, thank you," Kimiro smiled, the soldiers at their table already starting to dig into the robust meal in front of them.

Leonie wrinkled her nose at the pungent smell of the peasant dish, but picked up her crude wooden spoon all the same. She glanced over at her brother, his arms crossed in front of him as he sat lost in thought.

She supposed that they must have been a strange sight. From the way that many of the locals were keeping their distance, the princess assumed that they mistook the unkempt and weary travellers to be mercenaries. Not that she minded too much; just as Cliona had been too tired from the recent events to dine with them, the princess had no desire to be social. If it weren't for the hunger pangs that plagued her, she too would have retired for the evening.

"Your Highness?"

Arvyn turned around to see an unexpected but welcome face.

"Duke Orville?" The man, dressed in much simpler clothes than Arvyn was used to seeing him in, bowed low. "What brings you so far north?"

The young duke's hazel eyes darted over the crowded tavern as he lowered his voice. "Perhaps this discussion is best kept from local ears."

The prince nodded, indicating that they should talk outside as he stood.

"I will be back soon," he said to his sister, her eyes unable to hide her concern.

Thankfully, the cobbled street was quiet outside, and the trio were able to settle themselves against the uneven grey stone wall of the tavern.

"I trust that news of the First Prince has reached you, Your Highness." Arvyn nodded, clenching his jaw as he saw the vision of his eldest brother's head rolling from his body once more. "His Majesty had only sent the first and fourth division to the battle with the First Prince. As soon as the news reached him, he mobilised the entire rest of the military under the Second Prince's command. We have been engaged in almost constant skirmishes for the last month. I was sent to Dunsberg retrieve some rare medical supplies for our physicians."

"So Cain is also in the area?"

"Yes, Your Highness." Jules nodded, lowering his voice even more. "Our forces have yet to be victorious. His Highness has requested more aid from His Majesty, but I fear that they will arrive too late, if they come at all. These monsters are like nothing we have ever faced."

Daryl and Arvyn glanced at each other.

"I have business at Dunsberg Castle," Arvyn said. "Tell my brother that I will join him after my business is done. Perhaps together we can have some success."

Just then, Leonie came running towards them, her golden eyes frantically searching. When she noticed her brother and the two dukes, she rushed towards them.

"Greetings, Your Highness," the young duke said warmly, falling into a smooth bow.

She didn't even spare him a glance, instead grabbing her brother's hand.

"Quickly," she breathed, pulling him back towards the tavern. "I went to check on Cliona, but she wasn't there. But, I found this note."

Arvyn's face darkened as he skimmed the hastily written letter that his sister threw at him.

Do not test the Will of God.

The prince turned on his heel and raced back to the tavern, his uncle and sister close behind him.

Duke Orville looked on silently, running his hand through his chestnut hair as he went to finish the errand given to him by the Second Prince.

Chapter 30

"Where is she?"

"Your Highness," Marquis Hugo said loudly, his booming voice hiding the surprise in his dark eyes as he turned suddenly towards the clattering of his castle gate being forcefully open. "I was not aware that you would be visiting us so late in the day."

"Shut up," the prince shouted as he slammed into the marquis's body, knocking him to the ground. He drew his sword, the blade reflecting the dim light of the courtyard torches.

The duke glanced at his nephew as he too drew his blade, nodding to his soldiers to do the same.

The soldiers of Dunsberg Castle, most unarmed, watched on silently, glancing between the prince and their lord. A handful of the maids running errands in the courtyard quickly scurried away from the commotion, watching from the shadows.

Arvyn walked towards the robust lord, unceremoniously sprawled on the floor before him, his white nightshirt and thick black bearskin cloak failing to offer him any shred of dignity. Lord Hugo's eyes scanned the dimly lit courtyard for his guards, but none moved in the presence of the Third Prince and his armed entourage.

His gaze caught that of his wife and eldest daughter, both watching with wide eyes from the girl's bedroom, their loose hair framing their ghostly faces.

With each of the prince's measured steps, the once renowned knight crawled backwards, until finally he reached the cold grey wall of his keep.

"Do you even know what will happen if you awaken those demons? It is against the Will of God!"

"How dare you question me?"

Arvyn lowered his sword until it was touching the bare hollow of the lord's neck.

"Your Highness," Daryl said quietly, stepping close to the prince's side.

The beastly lord snarled at the duke, black eyes boring into the golden prince.

"That monster will bring about the destruction of the world," Hugo spat. "Surely you must see that it is God's Will that she disappear?"

Arvyn grimaced, pushing down on his sword.

"I hope that you rot in the deepest pits of hell,"

Hugo's eyes flashed with surprise, his large hands reaching for his neck as the prince retracted his blade. Bright red liquid oozed from the small wound, staining his thick fingers.

Arvyn spun around, walking quickly away from the flailing lord, his face dark as he ignored the screams and wails coming from the open window.

"Find Cliona. Now."

Edgar and Markus sprung into action as their comrades stood bewildered for a moment. They held their swords ready as they charged to the wooden door guarded by three soldiers, prepared to draw blood on their prince's orders. But, their opponents simply held up their hands, stepping to the side as they drew near. One fumbled with the keys in his hand, his shaking hands struggling to unlock the door to the secret garden.

The door swung open just as the prince reached it, his stride not breaking as he marched through the small walled garden where he first spoke to Cliona.

Two more guards stood to attention, attempting to block the black iron studded dark oak door from view.

"Move," Arvyn growled, his thirsty sword still in his right hand.

The pair glanced at each other before doing as they were commanded by the golden prince, desperate to avoid his murderous gaze.

His heavy footfalls echoed through his ears as he raced down the long spiral staircase, the well-worn stone slabs slowing him slightly.

As the path evened out, he clenched his jaw, tightening his grip on his sword.

In the centre of the room, the vibrant gemstones set into the black stone monolith seemed to pulse. The now golden ancient runes carved into the stone's smooth surface shimmered, almost inaudible whispers swirling around them.

At its base, Cliona lay unconscious.

Arvyn hurriedly knelt beside her.

Her face seemed almost peaceful, her pale skin seeming to glimmer in the dim light of the crypt. And yet, her skin felt like ice, her breathing shallow. She had been dressed once again in a flowing white gown, silver runes embroidered onto the bodice. Before, he would have thought nothing of such fine needlework, but now he was certain that they were a restraint on her already dwindled power.

His eyes were drawn to the thin black tube sticking out of a vein in her right arm, connecting her to the monolith itself.

The prince ripped it from her arm, causing a rush of black liquid to shoot from the tube, staining them both. The small incision on her arm beaded black.

Her crimson eyes fluttered open, her pupils struggling to focus for a moment.

"Hugo is dead," he whispered.

She nodded, sitting up slowly beside him, her eyes closed.

"We need to get to the temple," her hoarse voice whispered. "They will know you've killed the guardian they placed here soon enough."

"How are we supposed to do that when we don't know where it is?"

Cliona smirked, her crimson eyes brightly glowing for the first time since they had met.

She stood slowly, the weakness of her knees dissipating steadily. She reached for the tube on the floor, carefully pouring a little of the ebony liquid onto her hand before pressing her palm onto the cold stone's surface.

"Drink of me, that I may locate that which I seek," she whispered.

The stone absorbed the dark blood, the ground starting to quake as the gemstones shot out bright beams of light onto the ground before them, creating a strange, dotted image.

"Is that a constellation?"

"Yes. We know that the temple is somewhere not too far from here, so all we have to do is to find the area where the stars align in the exact same way as this star chart. It is a trick the reconnaissance units in the Imperial Army use often."

Arvyn ran his fingers through his golden hair.

"I believe that will be easier said than done."

"Well, we'd best get started then, descendent of Oleksander," she grinned.

Chapter 31

It was not hard for the group to discover the whereabouts of the Second Prince's war camp. With close to eight thousand soldiers, their cream canvas tents infested the open grassland on the north-eastern most border of the kingdom.

Weary and in need of a rest after three days scouring the Orville Forest on foot, Arvyn and his companions resigned themselves to visiting the encampment.

Bloodied faces saluted to the royal siblings as they made their way along the lines of tents, towards the large canvas pavilion hiding in the centre of the campsite. The ever familiar sight of the golden cockatrice standing rampant on crimson field greeted them, the expertly embroidered flag fluttering in the gentle afternoon breeze as it brought a relieved sigh to the prince.

"Daryl," Arvyn said, his eyes fixed on the tent ahead of him, "have our men set up a small base on the edge of the camp. Find a woman or two to help Leonie and see to it that she rests."

"Of course, Your Highness."

The princess, her body trembling from the strain of holding her heavy head high for the on looking soldiers, followed her uncle without a complaint.

Arvyn turned to Cliona.

"My brother may need your knowledge on the creatures nearby."

"If he wishes for my help, I will gladly give it. But," she said, lowering her voice as she glanced over the faces surrounding them, "somehow I doubt I will be well received."

The prince nodded, straightening his weary shoulders as he strode towards the command tent.

Silence fell over the tent as he and Cliona entered. The gathered Generals turned their weary eyes onto the newcomers, their looks turned from surprise to hostility when they noticed the woman stood beside him. A few tried to cover up the various maps and reports strewn across the large oak table in the centre of the tent, whilst others turned to the Second Prince cautiously.

Cain narrowed his eyes on Cliona as she entered directly beside his younger brother.

"I will discuss nothing with that woman here."

"Cliona is my aid."

"And Olekeander was alive until she started filling your head with nonsense about magic and mythical creatures!"

Silence fell over the room as a dozen eyes bored into the silver haired woman.

She laid her hand on Arvyn's shoulder, noticing his clenched fists. "I'll wait for you outside."

"All of you leave us," Cain called, sitting himself back into the ornate wooden throne at the head of the long table. "I wish to speak with my brother alone."

The armoured Generals did as they were asked, casting cautious glances to Cliona as she waited until the last man had left.

Jules Orville clapped Arvyn on the shoulder as he went past, offering him an apologetic smile.

Cain narrowed his golden gaze on his younger brother when they were finally alone.

"Where in God's name have you been?"

"Searching for the artefacts, just as father bid me to do."

"Do you have any idea what's been happening to our kingdom since you left? How dare you abandon us in our time of need!"

Arvyn met his brother's scowl steadily as he took a seat at the table.

"Oleksander's dead, Arvyn. Since you left, strange creatures were reported on the eastern border, so he went to investigate with his best men. They were wiped out."

"I know," his younger brother said softly. "You have no idea how much I wish I could have stopped it."

"Then why have we not heard anything from you since you left? Father is threatening war with the east when we no longer have the soldiers. A disease has been killing our people in the south. And you were nowhere to be found. What's worse, Leonie disappeared with just a scrap of a note saying she was following you. Father has taken to his bed with worry."

Arvyn looked away.

Cain sighed, running his hand through his newly thinning hair. "I need you to grow up, Arvyn. Stop chasing fairy tales. Oleksander is gone; I cannot keep Father under control and monitor the Empire's movements on my own. It is time you step up."

"I am almost finished," Arvyn pleaded, reaching his arm over to his older brother. "I just need a few more days to find the ruins."

His brother pulled his hand away, a sigh escaping from his lips as he squeezed his eyes shut.

"In a few days I may not be here any more. We are constantly losing men; Oleksander was the best swordsman in the kingdom, and he is gone. I don't know how much longer I can keep this army together."

"Please, Cain. Give me three days, then I will be here to fight with you, and I will give you the Sword of Nour. I swear."

The Second Prince looked at his little brother. Although it had only been a few months, his golden hair seemed to have dulled slightly, his once soft cheeks bearing the marks of the harsh wind. Even in his armour it was clear that he had lost weight. But, his gaze was just as bright, his tenacious spirit still fighting against the bitter wind of change that swirled around them.

He could only imagine what Arvyn was seeing in him now.

"Here," the older brother said defeatedly, pushing a roughly drawn map towards Arvyn. "My scouts stumbled across some stone pillars and statues in the middle of the forest. I ordered them not to investigate further as we lack the manpower, but it may be of help to you."

Arvyn smiled, taking the parchment gladly from his brother.

Cain lifted his hand to his younger brother's face, brushing against the fresh scar that covered his missing eye.

"If our kingdom is to fall, I want it to do so by your side, Arvyn."

The younger prince nodded, standing abruptly.

Cain watched him leave, his head falling into his hands.

Chapter 32

Cliona sighed, running her hand through her loose white hair as she stepped out of her tent, her skin still warm from her recent bath.

Her eyes drifted over Arvyn's small camp, set up slightly away from that of his brother's thanks to the disdain of the main army for his female companion.

A solemn weariness had been taking hold of Arvyn's men recently, their shoulders slumped and their chatter less frequent than when she first met them.

"Are you hungry?"

She turned to see Kimiro, smiling behind her, two wooden bowls of freshly made steaming stew in his hands.

"I don't see the prince or the duke," she said quietly, taking one of the offered bowls.

The old man inclined his head, unwilling to meet her gaze.

"Kimiro. Where are they?"

He smirked, revealing a pair of long, pale fangs.

Her face paled, the wooden bowl slipping from her grasp. Just as the food was about to hit the floor, Wynne scooped it carefully, his gloved skeletal fingers unable to feel the scalding hot stew splattering over his hand.

Cliona turned her back to them, running towards where Prince Cain's map had denoted the temple's entrance. Nierne and Cuthbert swiftly strapped their swords back around their waists as they chased after her, her long legs covering more of the densely overgrown ground than they expected.

As Wynne moved to follow the chase, Kimiro held up a long, gnarled arm in front of the boy.

"I have to follow," the undead boy snarled.

"Only a chosen few many enter the Temple of Nour," Kimiro replied steadily, blowing gently on his stew. "Should those of us not intended to enter the sacred sanctuary cross the threshold, then our meagre lives would be forfeit and the curse strengthened. There is little for us to do but wait now."

The boy's green bob bounced around his face as he turned abruptly to face the old man.

"So you will send the humans in to deal with it themselves?"

Kimiro sneered.

"Prepare yourself, boy; our skills shall be needed soon enough."

Wynne's brow furrowed once more. But, unable to argue with the veteran, he merely folded his arms and slunk to the floor, angrily eating the remaining stew from the bowl.

* * *

Cliona stood frozen at the entrance to the ancient temple, her limbs refusing to move as the darkness beckoned her forward.

"You wait here," Nierne said, drawing his sword as he reached the top of the steps behind her.

As the youngest of the knights chosen by Arvyn, he prided himself as being the fastest and fittest of their travelling band over the past few months. And yet, he had to force himself to breathe deeply after chasing her through the forest and up the long flight of stairs, the air cold as it raced down his throat as his heart beat frantically.

He gritted his teeth, not wanting for her or Cuthbert to notice.

"Do not take another step," she hissed through gritted teeth, her fists tightly shut beside her as her gaze was fixed on the darkness ahead of her.

He looked at her, his face stern as he went to protest.

"Please, Lady Cliona," Cuthbert mumbled behind him, trying to catch his breath as he appeared at the top of the steps. "Wait at the camp.

"We shall retrieve His Highness," Nierne added. "We are under orders from His Highness to not let you follow."

She turned to the two soldiers, a forlorn smile painted over her pale face as she muttered a few words in a strange, melodic language.

As she did so, her crimson eyes began to glow like clear cut rubies. A strange black smoke seeped out of her body, swirling around her in black tendrils, her silhouette swallowed by the dense cloud.

"What the hell," Cuthbert mumbled, stepping backwards and reaching for his sword.

He felt his foot stumble as he momentarily forgot about the limestone steps behind him.

The smoke closed the gap between them swiftly, a hand grabbing his arm from within before he could fall.

His heart stopped as he met the pair of red jewelled eyes glowing through the smoke.

"The seal will soon be broken," Cliona's voice whispered through the dark cloud. "When that happens, the foul creatures that were sealed as our guardians will be awoken once more. Including the bloodthirsty clan of orcs that the Demon Cult are trying to resurrect." Her grip loosened on his arm. "Your prince will join you as soon as he can, but I suggest you return to the camp and prepare yourselves for combat very soon."

She waited a moment before darting into the entrance without a second glance.

"Do we follow?"

Cuthbert shook his head, his hands trembling.

Chapter 33

The prince crawled along the smooth limestone floor slowly ahead of the duke. The narrow gap in which they had found themselves would have been much better suited to Wynne's small frame, their clothes growing dustier as they crawled deeper into the hidden temple.

Finally, they came upon a large chamber, their eyes struggling to adjust to the bright light as they emerged from the dingy tunnel.

Unlike the rest of the decrepit sandstone temple that the pair had so far explored, this luxurious chamber seemed to be perfectly preserved.

The smooth floor was made of perfectly white marble, tiny silver and gold veins running over the finely polished surface. The walls were of a similar material, although they were carved with the reliefs of countless graphic scenes, of mythical battles and the ensuing celebrations. The faces of twenty baby-faced marble figures looked down from the vaulted ceiling, the ornate flourishes that lined the eaves gilded with gold and encrusted with jewels of various colours.

"I have long been waiting for your arrival, Daryl, son of Theodore and Arvyn, son of Oleksander," a voice echoed across the cool stone.

The duke's eyes flickered over the preserved room around him, desperately trying to adjust to the darkness.

"Show yourself."

Laughter slithered over the cold stone walls, coiling tightly around him.

An icy sensation caused his skin to scream as a chill enveloped his body. His knees hit the cracked white marble floor, pulled down by an unseen force, the prince following suit moments later. As the duke tried to push his body upwards using his sword, the strength of his arms began to fail him. He clenched his fists, his vision beginning to blur and his breathing becoming ragged.

The shadows seemed to pool together, forming a humanoid figure towering before him. Long dark tendrils whipped around their head, swaying in an unseen breeze. A cold hand reached for his chin, the shadows dripping from the slender fingertips, pooling at the being's feet.

Daryl's eyes narrowed, fighting the alluring pull of sleep. He cleared his dry throat, the cold air racking through his lungs.

"I am the gatekeeper to what you seek. I am the barrier holding back the destruction that you wish to unleash. And I shall be your doom."

The duke tightened his fingers around the hilt of his sword, but the weariness had seeped into his bones. His head was forced downwards, as though by an invisible hand.

Arvyn was pushed down, prostrating himself before the shadow as he, too, fought against its strength.

Daryl watched the reflection of the figure as a large two-handed axe began to form from the shadows in their hands.

"I look forward to adding such strong souls to my collection," the figure whispered into his ear, ice rippling unwarranted down his spine.

He closed his eyes as the figure began to chant in a language that he did not recognise. It sluggishly lowered its weapon towards him, his strength draining rapidly into the marble floor below.

He waited for the cold sting of the blade on his neck.

But there was none.

Instead, the shadow was frozen in place, the axe still poised above Daryl's stiff body.

Slowly, he lifted his gaze.

Before him stood a tall figure, her body cloaked in darkness flecked with crimson and gold, her long white hair hanging freely behind her. Her hand had reached for the axe blade, holding the weapon in place as the shadow screamed in silent rage.

Cliona's crimson eyes burned as she stared at the guardian, ignoring the biting pain radiating through her body as her forgotten power fought against the curse for control.

"I dismiss you, wraith. Return to the void whence you came," she snarled in her native tongue.

The shadow cackled as it lurched backwards into a crouch, the axe shifting into the form of a giant sword.

"Such a pitiful creature as you holds no power here."

Cliona held her hand out to the prince, her eyes never once leaving the guardian before her. "Prince Arvyn, lend me your sword."

The prince glared at her, but seeing no alternative he did as he was bid.

Cliona closed her eyes, raising the unfamiliar sword in front of her body.

"In the name of the Emperor, I shall vanquish his foes," the guardian growled, charging forward.

The demonic woman parried the blow perfectly, her feet remaining firmly planted in the ground as the shadow lunged forward time and time again, its precise movements never losing momentum.

The duke knelt beside his prince as they watched the two figures charge at each other, their movements so inhumanly fast that neither the veteran soldier nor the shrewd prince were able to keep up.

"Perhaps we should leave, Your Highness," Daryl whispered, helping his nephew to his feet.

"If she fails then it will fall to us to rid the world of that creature. We stay."

Suddenly, Cliona's stance changed. In a flash, she lunged forward, dodging yet another blow from her opponent as she slashed across the shadow's midriff in a smooth motion.

The shadow, now directly in front of the prince, raised its piercing hazel eyes towards the humans. Black blood spurted from its torso as it crumbled to the floor, its laboured wheezing filling the room.

Cliona stood over the creature's body, using the tip of her borrowed sword to remove their hood to reveal the face of a young woman with pale green skin and hazel eyes that mirrored her own hatred.

"Be at peace on the moonlit hill," Cliona said softly as she pierced the space where the cursed creature's heart should once have been.

She stood over the dissipating shadow silently, her own power dissolving into the gentle breeze that ran through the room.

"I demand an explanation," Arvyn spat, his hand tightly gripping onto her arm. "Now. No more secrets, Cliona."

She sighed and turned to gaze at the single empty seat in the circle, her fingernails digging into the flesh of her palms as she stood steadying her breathing.

"I have run out of patience," Arvyn growled.

"My true name is Cliona Sangaria, Queen and Sword of Nour, leader of the extinct Sangarian Demons and General of the Liberty Army.

The prince's face paled.

"Queen of Nour... So you are the reason that this all happened in the first place."

Cliona inclined her head sadly, resting her hand on the face of her dryad friend.

"I did not cause the war. I merely joined and became a figurehead for the revolution. Granted, I was renowned for my battle prowess before the war began, but I was by no means the instigator."

The prince raised his sword towards her.

"None of this would have happened if I had never listened to you. I should just kill you now."

Cliona met his gaze coldly.

"Even without my interference, the magical barrier on this world was beginning to weaken, and those left to fester here would have broken free from their constraints before long. So tell me, Third Prince of Vyst, descendant of the demon hero Oleksander; will you face their awakening alone? Or will you revive my compatriots and allow us to fight the demonic tyranny alongside you?"

Arvyn paused, clenching his jaw.

"Can you guarantee that they will follow me?"

"No," she replied, her gaze steady. "They will not follow a human prince and I would never ask them to. But, prove your worth and that of your cause and they will gladly fight beside you."

After a moment, he met her gaze once more, his lips set firmly into a line as he inclined his head and returned his sword to its sheathe.

Cliona sighed, a truly gentle smile spreading on her lips for the first time since they had met as she turned her back to him. Her footsteps seemed to echo over the ancient floor as she slowly stepped towards the vacant chair, her slender fingers caressing the back of the black obsidian throne.

"When I take my place in the circle, things will progress swiftly. To break the seal, you must power the artefacts with the blood of Oleksander that flows through your veins and then place them in the owner's hands. When you have finished, return to your brother's encampment as fast as you can. You must prepare for the Demon Cult and the orcs; they will be sure to attack when the magic flows freely through the land once more. I shall join you as soon as I am able."

She sat down carefully, her head held high. Within seconds a black crystalline substance started to encase her body, beginning at her hands and feet and travelling in spiralised circles along her legs and arms. She clenched her jaw against the searing pain coursing through her veins as the curse took hold of her, refusing to release the scream rising inside of her chest.

Ebony tears pooled at the edge of her crimson eyes as she held the prince's gaze.

Satisfied that the black material had fully encased her chiselled face, the prince turned his back to her, reaching for the bag of artefacts that he had left strewn by the doorway of the grand chamber. His hands fumbled as the screams from the Seeker's vision began to ring through his ears once more.

Daryl took the bag from the prince, his face kind as he handed his nephew his small dagger.

"Take your time, Your Highness."

Arvyn nodded, trying to steady his breathing.

He lifted the dagger with his trembling hand, slicing through the flesh of his other hand before smearing his blood over the objects. As he did so, they each began to sizzle and glow, the screams getting louder as he laid them into the statues' hands.

As he lay the book decorated with floral motifs on the last statue, the ground began to quake below their feet, stone crumbling around them.

"Your Highness! We must leave!"

Despite the seasoned duke shouting as loud as he could muster, the prince could only guess at his words as they were drowned out by a roar erupting from somewhere further below the temple.

Arvyn shouted to the duke as they started to run to the exit, sliding through the narrow tunnel as fast as they could.

As debris slammed into the ground to block the chamber from view, the statues cracked.

* * *

Nairne shifted his weight anxiously as he and Cuthbert waited for signs of their comrades, fighting against the intense instinct to flee as the ground shook beneath their weary feet. He almost had when the birds had leapt to the sky, shouting warnings as they raced away from the derelict ruin.

"How much longer do we wait before warning Prince Cain?"

Cuthbert's gaze was trained on the dark entrance before them, his gnarled hand clutching his bow tightly as he tried to ignore the younger man's concerns.

"Just a little longer. I have no doubt that the Second Prince will already be preparing for a fight, considering the sudden earthquake. Our priority is getting Prince Arvyn to safety."

The pair continued to wait in silence as the sun began to descend over the horizon, bathing the world in gold.

At long last, Cuthbert sighed and nodded to Nairne as he turned towards the steps.

Just as he did so, the pair heard the unmistakable sound of boots running towards them, and out from the temple entrance emerged Prince Arvyn and Duke Daryl, both covered in dust from head to toe. As the two soldiers ran forward, the duke fell to his knees, clutching his sides.

"Let me help, Your Grace," Nairne said softly as he lifted Daryl's arm over his shoulder.

Cuthbert gave the prince a worried look over, his brow furrowing as he noticed the fresh blood smeared over the prince's sun-kissed face.

"We need to get to my brother," Arvyn rasped, starting his climb down the steps. "We've woken up monsters and must take responsibility for that. I will not lose another sibling to this damned demon war."

The soldiers quickly followed the determined prince, supporting the duke between them.

Chapter 34

A vast open plain stretched below the crowded hill. Although this would have been perfectly tended farming fields in the summer, now the fields lay bare, thick mud frozen in place over the barren surface. There was no shelter here, no hedges to offer cover for those stranded in the open plain.

Arvyn stroked his mare's neck gently, his golden gaze trained on the assembling soldiers below.

Far in the distance, the enemy gathered. Arvyn had only seen dwarves, orcs and giants in storybooks and the Seeker's vision, and yet here they were gathered, waiting to soak the barren winter soil in human blood.

From what he could tell, their enemy was composed mostly of dwarven soldiers, armed with crude swords and axes, many of them carrying small wooden shields. They wore heavy armour, not dissimilar to that of Arvyn and his comrades, although the legends suggested that they would be thicker and harder to pierce. The orcs on the other hand were fewer, but by no means less of a threat. The shortest that Cain's men had found was at least a foot taller than the average man, each one much more muscular than a human. Both male and females seemed to be prepared to fight with their spears and axes, their mottled dark grey skin protected by simple leather armour and furs.

In all, the Generals had estimated that their enemy was at least twenty thousand strong, more than double their own number.

And that didn't even include the four lilac giants, currently chained at the rear of the enemy's army, chomping at the bit to face human foes.

Arvyn sighed, looking back over his brother's gathered forces, numbering just under ten thousand.

It was true that their father had ordered every trained soldier to join the fight, but many of those were already lost, injured or getting on in years. Even if they had been prime fighters, many were not equipped with decent armour, and a number of the weapons were rusted.

"Should it look like the worst is about to happen," Cain said quietly, glancing at his younger brother, "I want you to take Leonie and run. One of us has to survive to take the throne."

Arvyn clenched his fists tightly around his thin black reins, a scowl lining his forehead.

The mare fidgeted beneath him, her nostrils flaring as she sensed the tension in his legs.

"Help is coming," he said through gritted teeth. "We will not lose today."

Cain sighed, placing his golden helmet carefully on his head, leaning down so that a squire could tighten the chinstrap for him.

"Only the power of God can help us now, brother," the Second Prince said sadly, straightening his back as he nudged his mount slowly forward.

He pushed his mare up and down the line of soldiers, his golden gaze looking out over their dishevelled ranks.

"There is no denying that the odds are against us," he shouted, his deep voice calm as it swirled around the silent soldiers. "But, the grace of God is on our side! On this day, we shall be victorious! We shall vanquish those you dare to threaten our homes and our families!"

Arvyn straightened his shoulders as his brother stopped in front of him, his face firm.

They nodded to each other, as Cain drew his sword, raising the naked blade in the air above his head.

"For victory!"

The soldiers around him cheered, drawing their own blades in anticipation of their orders.

Cain turned away, nudging his mount rapidly down the hill and into the valley below, the cavalry closing in around him as their foot soldiers chased behind them.

The archers loosed their arrows at the waiting enemy. Many fell short, and even those that hit their targets seemed like a minor inconvenience to the muscular brutes before them, their swords and axes still banging hard against their rudimentary wooden shields.

The open plain erupted into a chorus of screams and shouts as the mounted knights crashed into the line of wooden shields.

A number of the horses and riders immediately went down due to the axes and spears of their enemies. Those that didn't slashed at their opponents, soaking the parched winter earth with fresh blood. The foot soldiers arrived not long after, joining in with the deathly ensemble.

It wasn't long until the neat formations of both sides were completely disordered, each soldier surrounded by friend and foe, both alive and dead.

A war horn sounded in the distance, summoning four of the giant lilac creatures that killed Oleksander. If it had not been for the Seeker's vision, Arvyn was certain that he would be frozen in place when he saw their grotesque figures charging over the battlefield with their bulbous spiked clubs.

Arvyn looked out over the sea of bodies, noticing his brother's bright golden armour shining in the late morning sun as he slashed at enemies around him on foot, his horse nowhere in sight.

He gritted his teeth, urging his mare towards his brother quickly, his eye flickering between Cain and the oncoming creature, its club dragging along the ground as it lumbered forward, its pitch black eyes focused on the golden commander.

"Cain!"

His brother turned towards his voice as he pulled his sword from the chest of another fallen enemy.

It was then that he noticed the large humanoid figure lumbering towards him, its bare muscular arms swinging at its enemies and allies alike as it made its way towards him.

"Dear God," Cain muttered, tightening his grip on his sword.

The elder prince frantically cast his gaze over the battle around him, desperately searching for any nearby Generals to call to his aid.

His hesitation gave a nearby orc the chance to stab its spear into the prince's thigh, its sheer strength easily piercing through the gold-plated armour. Cain's face twisted in agony as his hand went to grasp at the hilt, a desperate scream racing from his lips.

Arvyn leapt at the monstrous figure from his horse, his sword cutting through the thick flesh of its shoulder as his body knocked the orc off balance.

He panted as he looked down at his brother, his eye wide as he saw Cain's hands failing to pull the rudimentary spear from his leg, his bloodied hands slipping down the shaft.

"We've lost!"

"It's going to be all right," Arvyn mumbled, his voice uneven as he stood ready over his downed brother, his gaze focused on the giant lilac monstrosity whose shadow now loomed over them.

His gloved hands gripped the hilt of his sword tightly as he prepared for the creature's fury, its wide mouth snarling as it fixed its gaze onto the younger prince, hissing something in an ancient language as it raised its spiked club.

Thunder echoed over the clear sky above them, a single bolt of bright white energy flashing across the battlefield.

Silence filled the air as both sides stopped, their weapons frozen in the air.

A horned figure stood proudly before the two princes, her exposed black hand gripping firmly onto the creatures' spoked club, her fingers effortlessly digging into the knotted wood.

A pair of long silver horns protruded from the top of her head, her long white hair plaited neatly to hang down her neck. Her black cloak fluttered in the breeze against the white breeches that clung closely to her muscular legs. A thick black mist was fading from around her black boots, revealing a fading white magic circle beneath her feet. A large longsword was sheathed at her hip, a red and gold tassel dangling from the black hilt.

"Cliona," Arvyn breathed, his golden eye wide.

She turned slowly to face him.

Her crimson eyes glowed as she met his gaze, a pair of pale canines creeping through her growing smile.

The sound of her laughter filled the air.